CHRYSALIS

CHRYSALIS

A Novel

RICHARD ROMANUS

armida

Copyright © 2011 by Richard Romanus

All rights reserved. Published by Armida Publications Ltd.

No part of this publication may be reproduced, stored in a retrieval system, or transmitted in any form or by any means, electronic, mechanical, photocopying, recording, or otherwise, without permission of the publisher. For information regarding permission, write to Armida Publications Ltd, P.O.Box 27717, 2432 Engomi, Nicosia, Cyprus or email: info@armidapublications.com

Armida Publications is a founding member
of the Association of Cypriot Book Publishers
and a member of the Independent Publishers Guild (UK)

www.armidapublications.com

Summary:
Seventeen-year-old Maria Christina lives in a small mountain village in Greece, where women are judged according to their physical strength. Tall, thin, gangly, and extremely myopic, she lives in the shadow of her older sister, Matoula, who is considered a goddess by all, and who serves as her eyes and ears to the outside world. Less evident is Maria Christina's adoration for Matoula's husband, Yiannis, the handsome and accomplished village doctor. Fate intervenes when Maria Christina's dull life is abruptly interrupted by the onslaught of World War II and the overlapping Greek Civil War.

[1. Historical Romance - Fiction. 2 Contemporary women - Fiction.
3. Literary - Fiction. 4. Action & Adventure - Fiction. 5. War & Military - Fiction]

This novel is a work of fiction. Although this book is based on some true events, it has been fictionalized and all persons appearing in this work are fictitious. Any resemblance to real people, living or dead, is entirely coincidental.

ISBN-13 (paperback): 978-9963-706-09-9

First edition: September 2011

Editors: Katerina Kaisi and Miriam Pirolo

Cover original artwork:
Snow and tree © Le-thuy Do | Dreamstime.com
Bullterfly © Neo Edmund | Fotolia.com

Book and cover design by Haris Ioannides

To the Women of Metsovo

ACKNOWLEDGMENTS

I am especially grateful to Elena Averoff, whose admiration for the women of Metsovo inspired the story and whose encouragement steeled my resolve to write it. I am also indebted to Ioannis Averoff for his guidance and his extensive library. I would also like to thank Kostas "Pappou" Todis, Maria Todi, Apostoles Bissas, Dr. Fanis Bouzalis, Nikolas Mitsos, and Spiros Mavrikis for sharing their memories, and Annabel Davis Goff, Vicky Kyriazi, Flo Conway and Jim Siegelman for their professional advice, and to express my appreciation to my editors, Katerina Kaisi and Miriam Pirolo. Thanks also to Irina Averoff, my brother, Billy, and my son, Robert Christopher for their love and support. Finally, I wish to express my abiding gratitude to my wife, Anthea, who is my muse.

1

There were no women in Metsovo, only men. This had been a source of amusement for countless generations among the neighboring villagers high in the Southern Alps of central Greece. Of course it wasn't true. All the men who lived in this region known as Epirus were forced by the long, cruel winters to drive their flocks down to more mild elevations for most of the year, but it was only the men of Metsovo who left their women and children behind to do the strenuous work necessary for their survival. And it was precisely for survival's sake that strength in the women of Metsovo became the measure of beauty, and it was also the reason Maria Christina Triantafyllou, an aspen among sycamores, was considered the least attractive girl in the village. Moreover in a community where you were considered a near spinster at fifteen, she was already seventeen and not one suitor had appeared, not even a rumor of one. And yet, it was the furthest thing from her mind this morning in October of 1940, as she sat on a small bench in front of a fire in the family's grey stone cottage. In the last few weeks she had found it impossible to concentrate on anything but Mussolini's army amassing on the border not eighteen hours from their village, which was the only route into Greece.

"A cup of my tea, my soul" came a low hoarse voice from the large platform next to the fireplace, breaking the oppressive silence.

"Right away, Pappou."

It was comforting for her to pour warm water from a kettle into a cup filled with his special herbal mixture, then swirl the liquid and carefully add two drops of paregoric. She lit a lamp and set it on the low round table in front of the fireplace. It was always dark in the winter room. The two windows and the door to the room were covered in thick wool weavings to help the room retain as much heat as possible. The only daylight was from a small window beneath the hearth.

Lying in his sickbed, her grandfather spoke with difficulty "How you look like your grandmother just now. So beautiful."

As he took the cup, Maria Christina leaned into the stubble of beard and softly kissed his cheek. Having been aware of her quiet suffering these years, the old man had decided his gift to her would be that of hope. He would teach her to dream. To that end he plied her with stories of his beloved wife, her namesake, who had died from tuberculosis when Maria Christina was only three. And whenever he described his bride, tall and thin, with long chestnut hair and eyes like sapphires, her skin the color of a fresh white peach and her tiny waist, it was as if he was describing Maria Christina herself.

"She was the most beautiful woman in all of Bucharest. And may I be spitting in God's eye if they aren't the most beautiful in the world! And I've been everywhere!"

Of course she stopped hoping and dreaming and believing him years ago, although she continued pretending to him that it must be so. Still, his stories made her feel melancholic, knowing he felt compelled to lie to her because no man would ever find her acceptable as a bride.

His cheek felt warm. As he sipped the tea, he talked about the last day of October 1912. "I was alone in a remote village in the Rodope Mountains in Bulgaria. I don't remember the name now. I was carving an altar screen when I heard from a peddler that the Turkish rule over Metsovo had finally ended. After five hundred years. And I had no one to celebrate."

She had heard all of this before but listened attentively as he then spoke about his three sons, one of whom he had lost in the First Balkan War against the Turks and then his other two in the war that was to end all wars. How tired he was of war. And as he continued, he spoke again about his wife and his voice became softer and slower

"How we used to laugh...so smart, my Maria. Like you. Like..." his voice trailed off.

Maria Christina took his cup and placed it in a niche in the wall, then leaned into him and gently combed his hair with her fingers. Her hand was cool. He stopped frowning and smiled as he looked up at her. Then he closed his eyes, let out a small sigh, and turned his face into his pillow. After a moment he let out another small sigh.

When she thought he had fallen asleep, she took his eyeglasses from his lap and put them in their case and was placing them beside the cup when he stopped her with a sharp gesture and a renewed burst of life:

"You keep them for me, my blood and heart."

The old man smiled at her as he settled back into his pillows. It was her grandfather who first noticed they had the same severe astigmatism when at three years old she was looking at her thumb an inch from her right eye. Her father insisted it be kept a secret if she ever hoped to have a husband. Pappou felt responsible, having passed on this handicap to his favourite granddaughter, and discreetly shared his round tortoise shell glasses with her when they were alone in the house.

As he lay peacefully smiling up at her, Maria Christina

quickly dismissed the thought of life without him. He was old and unwell but surely not near death. It was the anticipation of war that tired him so. She wiped perspiration from his forehead with her apron and softly kissed his nose. Then she rose and returned to the bench, running her hand along a beautifully woven tapestry which wrapped around the curved white chimney just above the fireplace. It was the last of the chimney aprons her mother had woven, and it was becoming dry and brittle from the heat and would soon have to be replaced. She put her cheek to it. Over the years so much of the evidence of her mother's life had disappeared, and the slow deterioration of the fabric only served to deepen the longing for the ghost who died shortly after giving birth to her. Feeling alone and frightened once again, she clutched the glasses to her breast and sat back down on the bench and rocked back and forth a moment. Closing one eye and squinting with the other, she could see huge snow crystals swirling in the wind outside the small window at the base of the hearth, as if they, too, were anxiously awaiting the inevitable sound of war.

2

Matoula always entered like a gust of wind, constantly moving, straightening, dusting, cleaning, teaching, talking, with an easy smile, always heartfelt, revealing perfect teeth. She always knew what the weather was going to be, whose garden was finest, who was fighting with whom, all the latest gossip. Glancing at Pappou deep into his nap, she spoke softly while unloading an armload of packages, two small oak barrels of water, and her two year old daughter, Zoitsa, whom she routinely handed to Maria Christina, who smothered her with kisses as she took off her small shepherd's cloak and unlaced her little boots.

"Costas Stahoulis was dancing outside his *pantopolio*, knee deep in the snow, twirling his draft notice from the Ministry of Defence as if it were a handkerchief."

"It's very comforting to know that clown will be defending us."

"The same battalion my Yiannis will be joining in a few days."

"That's good. Stahoulis will probably be needing a doctor."

Matoula coughed then covered her mouth to stifle a laugh. She loved to laugh, and nobody could make her laugh like Maria Christina. Telling a story, Maria Christina would act out all the parts using different voices, even their cow, Afendoula, and Matoula would hide her face in her hands and laugh until she had to hold her sides.

"No more! I can't breathe!" Then she would walk around all day laughing to herself.

As if nature hadn't been cruel enough, Maria Christina had grown up in the shadow of her stunningly beautiful sister, two years her senior, tall and strong and nimble as a deer, a goddess by any measure, and she was married. For Maria Christina her older sister was the best and worst of her life. Matoula was her eyes and ears to the world. From her earliest memories it was Matoula's loving hand she was holding, always happy Maria Christina was tagging along, describing with exquisite clarity what Maria Christina could see only in blurred images. Especially in the warm summers, in the fields, in the garden, they were inseparable. But Matoula was also everything Maria Christina was not and, as much as she loved her, she envied her. She was aware of it, but she couldn't help it and likened it to a termite infestation that was slowly hollowing out her soul, her ability to love, to care, and in its place leaving nothing but the growing feeling that her life had no purpose.

"You wouldn't believe how many soldiers are on the streets."

"I hope they're more qualified than Stahoulis or we're dead."

"Now sweet?" Zoitsa's little voice whispered in Maria Christina's ear as her aunt took off her second boot. The girl's eyes widened as she waited for her aunt's response.

"After your dinner." Maria Christina kissed her scowling cheek and directed her to play on the floor by the fireplace with the small group of barn animals Pappou had carved for her.

Matoula spoke even more softly so Zoitsa wouldn't hear. "The talk in the village is that the Italians will have to fight for every meter. After five hundred years of Turkish occupation everyone says they're prepared to give their life rather than be occupied again."

"Fearless until the first bomb drops. We're going to be occupied. The only question is will we be eating macaroni or schnitzel."

Just then the door opened and their father, Papa Yiorgos, a village priest, and his older spinster sister, Panorea, entered. They had left before dawn to help their neighbors round up their flocks. The first big snowstorm had arrived early and continued heavily for three days, and many of the villagers' animals had been caught in the blizzard before they could be driven far enough down the mountain. Setting his flat-topped hat on a table, Papa Yiorgos glanced at Pappou then looked to Matoula and whispered "All is well?"

Matoula nodded and he took off his cloak and hung it on a peg as the girls quietly began serving the dinner, a leek and cheese pie.

The priest strode over to Pappou, gave him a closer look and a quick blessing, then stood with his wide back to the fire and spoke to Matoula while stroking his long black beard.

"We drove what we could into the schoolhouse. The rest we corralled in the monastery."

Maria Christina was cutting the pie when she felt her father's eyes.

"You finished your chores?"

"Yes, Patera."

Yiannis came in with a basket of individual cream pies for everyone.

"Fresh from the bakery" he said just above a whisper as he held up the basket. Zoitsa jumped up and ran to her father as he smiled at Papa Yiorgos and acknowledged Panorea and Maria Christina each with a nod. As he scooped up his daughter, he handed his wife the basket.

"What are we celebrating?" she smiled.

"No reason. Just because." He gave her a quick kiss and gently squeezed her hand.

If Matoula was a goddess, Yiannis was a god. Tall and strong with a square jaw, a brush mustache, and a mop of blonde curly hair. A sophisticated Athenian who had travelled extensively, he smoked English tobacco in a splendid pipe made from a rare white mineral found in Turkey and dressed in western clothes and was the idol of all the modern-thirsty young men of the village. While visiting a medical school friend, he saw Matoula dancing during the summer festival of the Prophet Elias and was so taken by her beauty and grace that he arranged to marry her in spite of his family's vehement objections.

Yiannis was also the most beautiful man Maria Christina had ever imagined. From the moment the young doctor from Athens arrived to propose marriage with his friend, the village veterinarian, she found it difficult to keep her eyes from following him. Although she had never actually been close enough to see him other than as a blur, Matoula's description coupled with his soothing voice and mild manner sharpened his image for her, and she constantly fought the urge to stare at him. It was her dark secret that she was in love with him. In her heart she feared she might even sacrifice her sister's happiness if he declared his love for her. She knew it was silly and impossible. He was always painfully polite with her, but he otherwise hardly noticed her. Yet she was incapable of stopping herself. Left alone, her imagination would invariably wander to images of him, standing by the fireplace smoking his pipe, or walking into the room carrying his medical bag, or holding Zoitsa who was tickling her nose in his mustache, and in her reverie Zoitsa's nose would become her own.

Aware these fleeting moments together might be among their last, there was a slow sadness in everyone's gait, a heaviness that was unusual. Yiannis crossed over to Pappou and gently took his hand to feel his pulse. As she stoked the fire, Maria Christina tried not to notice Matoula join him and speak softly in his ear. That morning he and Matoula hid extra sacks of grain and corn and buried the family's few treasures in a room originally designed as a hiding place from the Turks, the 'blind room', which was located under the ground floor.

Talk over dinner was of the impending war. The rag tag army of Greece wasn't prepared.

"Everyone says we have no tanks, no anti-tank guns, not even one good anti-aircraft battery." Yiannis leaned into his father-in-law while filling his pipe.

"From what I see in the village, you don't even have matching uniforms" Papa Yiorgos added, looking up at the ceiling and waving his hands as if churning the air.

"Most of the men are joining with their old hunting rifles."

"Well, at least they're accurate."

"But they aren't modern! Who knows how they'll hold up in a battle? Especially with an army and air force with ten times the fire power."

"Still, we mustn't lose our faith" Papa Yiorgos concluded after a moment's despair.

Following supper the family sat around the fire, Papa Yiorgos and Yiannis drinking *tsipouro* and talking in low dull tones, Panorea embroidering a vest for herself, Matoula at her loom, while Maria Christina and Zoitsa lay on a platform where Maria Christina was quietly teaching her little blonde niece her colors. Before long there was a light knock on the door. It was Saul Chaimaki, a tall, slender Jewish man in his thirties. Speaking barely above a whisper, he explained that he and his brother, Elias, had ended up with two drachmas too many in the till of their small dry goods store, which meant they must have short-changed someone. Since Panorea had purchased some silk from them yesterday, could it possibly be hers? He looked at Panorea, with her grey hair, grey skin, grey eyes, and her grey personality, while she in turn gave him one of her looks.

"I know you always count your change, Kyria Panorea" Chaimaki smiled shyly.

"But I have been to everyone's house who purchased from us. You are last on our list, Kyria, and no one has claimed it." He looked at Papa Yiorgos, "May I keep it?"

"You have every right, Saul" Papa Yiorgos assured him.

"Bless, you, Kyrios." He put his hand over his heart, then backed out of sight with a bow and a small smile.

Thus the few hours of remaining daylight passed, and when the sun finally disappeared behind the barren limestone peaks everyone went to bed. Families in Metsovo customarily slept together in no particular order on two platforms on either side of the fireplace. Maria Christina always made it a point not to lie next to Yiannis directly for fear it would be like sleeping with the devil. This night, on the right platform Panorea lay lightly snoring between Papa Yiorgos and Pappou. On the other, Yiannis and Matoula cuddled like spoons, while Zoitsa curled up next to Maria Christina, who lay awake on the furthest edge, her back against the wall, her mind racing into the future, trying to pray herself to sleep.

After Yiannis believed everyone was asleep, he slipped quietly out of bed, followed by Matoula, who threw a heavy cloak over their shoulders. Maria Christina heard them proceed to the sitting room where they would be lighting a fire. It was where married couples in Metsovo went in the winter to be intimate.

While they were gone, Pappou dreamt he was being visited by his wife, Maria, who was bathed in a bright light and wearing her wedding dress with its gold embroidery shining like stars. And when she lifted her veil she indeed looked almost exactly like Maria Christina, her sweet face looking happy and warm and welcoming, and he missed her so much, and she beckoned him to join her. And he did.

At that moment, Maria Christina finally prayed herself to sleep.

3

It was just before sunrise when Matoula touched Maria Christina's arm, waking her, and softly put her finger to her sister's lips.

"Pappou is gone" she whispered. Her eyes were red and filled with tears.

"Gone?"

"To heaven. Please wake Zoitsa and take her down with the animals."

Maria Christina quickly sat up and turned to see the blurred figures of Yiannis and Papa Yiorgos carrying a body wrapped in a thin blanket out the door. Matoula tenderly kissed the top of her sister's head and pressed it gently to her waist. Then she hurried from the room. Maria Christina remained frozen a moment, then quickly threw a heavy woollen cape over her shoulders and scooped up Zoitsa in a thick blanket and, before Zoitsa was fully awake, was hurrying down the stairs, desperately searching for a way to explain to the two-year-old something she could barely comprehend herself. She showered the child with kisses as the little one fluttered her eyes awake, then set her in the corner on a bundle of hay and turned away to milk Afendoula. Zoitsa was now wide awake and wondering.

"Moumou. Pappou has gone away. He is in heaven with God." She let the thought linger a second before she turned back to the puzzled child, smiling through watery eyes, "And we are happy."

Just then Matoula hurried in from the outside, quickly kissed her daughter, gave Maria Christina a hug with one arm, then ran up the stairs and into the winter room. Within seconds two old women came through the open door, weeping and wailing, and kissed Maria Christina who reached for Zoitsa who had become suddenly frightened. The women continued weeping and wailing and crying out to Pappou as they climbed the stairs, followed by then yet another neighbor arriving wailing and crying. The next few days would be lost to Maria Christina forever, although she would always remember Pappou lying in his coffin facing to the east, clean shaven with his mustache neatly trimmed, wearing his best suit and black curly-lamb cap, a peaceful smile on his lifeless face and a piece of bread in his pocket, so he wouldn't be hungry on his journey, his hands loosely cupped on his chest, and his wedding band on his finger. Now and then someone would put a coin in those hands and ask him to give their regards to a loved one on the other side.

Everyone from the village came to pay their respects, the women wailing and crying as they sat in the sitting room around the coffin, telling Pappou the latest news and who was there and how much they would miss him. After paying their respects, the men would retire to Papa Yiorgos' room to smoke and drink *tsipouro* and talk about Pappou and the coming war.

The funeral was at Papa Yiorgos' church, Agios Demetrius, named after one of the most important Orthodox military saints. It stood under three huge sycamores in the lowest part of the village at the end of a very steep and winding stone path that led to a series of winding stone steps to within sight of the bell tower, then continued down until you stood parallel to the big bells not ten feet away, then down to the entrance of the stately and proud stone church.

Papa Yiorgos led the somber service with tears in his eyes, while the four Triantafyllou women sat next to the coffin with the rest of the family. After the service, the men walked in a procession to the cemetery, while the women returned to the house to lay out the meal they had collectively prepared and await the men.

At the end of the long day, the rituals had done what they were designed to do, exhaust the bereaved by keeping them continually occupied. Maria Christina was thoroughly drained after the last relative had left and the last crumb swept as she crawled into bed next to the spot where Pappou had always slept. Holding his glasses to her breast and laying her other hand on his absent form, she closed her eyes. He had taught her to read and write and created games to make rudimentary mathematics fun. Whenever he sensed she was feeling melancholic, he would remind her that her name, Triantafyllou, meant 'of the rose'.

"There are many kinds of roses" he would kiss her hand, pretending to be a suitor, making her laugh and blush. "Your sister, Matoula Triantafyllou, is a big red rose, like an autumn cabbage. Maria Christina Triantafyllou is a fine, delicate, wild pink rose with brave blue eyes. Each is perfect and beautiful. But remember, even though the wild rose appears to be the more delicate, it is in fact the stronger."

Then he would squeeze her hand to test her strength to which she always squeezed back as hard as she could. Who would tell her now that the world viewed beauty differently than in Metsovo? That her slender wrists and long fingers would be admired everywhere else?

"I'll go drown myself in the well if it's not true!" he would bellow.

The person in the world who knew her best, the man she

would always be closest to was gone. She hadn't even realized just how sick he was. She had been told he was just weak from old age. Then with a long sad sigh, she fell almost immediately asleep.

For the next forty days the Triantafyllou women would not leave the house lest they be spat upon by the villagers, it being considered disrespectful to the departed. In three days a large oak vat filled with water appeared in the courtyard, and Pappou's half-sister, Lena, arrived with a block of black dye and collected all of the tapestries hanging in the house, including the treasured chimney apron, all of the rugs, bed and table covers, curtains, cushions, and the clothes the women would be wearing, including those of Zoitsa. All were to be dyed black and then the weavings returned to their place, tapestries re-hung and the clothes worn for one year.

All the next week Maria Christina didn't really think much about Pappou - only fleetingly and with no sense of loss. Then on the ninth day it began to snow again and, as was the custom, the women of the village came to sit and wail amid the coal black tapestries in the sitting room, while Maria Christina stayed in the winter room in front of the fireplace, holding and rocking a frightened Zoitsa. With one eye closed and the other squinting, Maria Christina looked through the fireplace window and saw a large white snowflake drift onto the glass, stick for a moment, then melt into nothing. That was when she fully grasped that her beloved Pappou was irretrievably gone. A welling in the pit of her stomach wanted to make a sound she had never made before. It frightened her, as it certainly would her little charge, so Maria Christina quickly hid it away in the deepest recess of her being and continued rocking and letting her thoughts wander, until she suddenly remembered a promise he had made he could now never keep. He would take her to see the sea one day. And the welling began again when the door opened and Yiannis and Matoula came to take their daughter downstairs to play in the hay.

After she was alone for a moment, Maria Christina held herself tightly and stared out the little window at the grey light. She knew what it meant to have a wounded heart. But for the first time she would allow the wail in her wounded heart to escape. And when she began, she was astonished at how deep and how great the well of sorrow was, and that nearly no amount of wailing might be enough to drain what now appeared to be a sea of despair. And so she continued wailing for her grandfather, for herself, for every woman in the sitting room who had ever lost someone so important to them. She didn't even stop when Panorea walked in, watched her a moment, then left with a tray of sweets.

The morning of Yiannis' departure, everyone pretended to be cheerful as he stood in the fog at the door of the cottage in his western clothes under a heavy goat-hair cape, with two large heavy woollen sacks strapped to his back, one with medical supplies, the other personal. Holding his walking stick with the handle of white *meerschaum* that Pappou had carved and custom fit to his hand, Yiannis looked tired as he kissed the family one by one inside the door of the cottage. Even Panorea allowed herself to be bussed quickly. When he leaned in to kiss Maria Christina she involuntarily inhaled and, for the first time, smelled his musky odor and blushed. Matoula, who was holding Zoitsa, noticed the moment and thought it sweet. Then she handed the child to Maria Christina and walked with Yiannis to the edge of the courtyard, where they stood a moment her head against his chest. After a moment, they embraced sweetly and kissed, and then Yiannis, too, was gone. Although for Maria Christina, his sweet smell would always remain.

4

By now it was the end of October and the sky had been clear for several days.

The sun had turned the snow in the village to grey-white slush which would freeze later in the day, making the forty-five degree climb up and down the narrow foot-polished stone streets all the more difficult. The autumn harvest had been stored. Children had already gathered the walnuts, men had sorted white and red grapes for the wine making before taking their flocks to the warmer valleys below. Gardens were rich with squashes and pomegranates. Women were stringing garlands of dried beans, peppers, onions, and garlic which they would hang from the rafters. Everyone who remained in the village found time to take a long stroll in the sun, among the butter yellow crocuses and the huge golden sycamores.

With each passing day Matoula reported more and more Greek soldiers from as far away as Crete passing through Metsovo on their way to Ioannina or to the mountains in the east. Overlooking the main square, two older carpenters and a woodcutter, men whose work was seasonal, were sitting drinking *tsipouro* inside Costas Stahoulis' *pantopolio*, and listening intently to his wireless radio as the newscaster assessed the state of Greece's chances in the coming war:

"Poland, Holland and Belgium, all better armed than Greece, were crushed in but a few weeks. France, a nation of forty-five million, collapsed in only seventeen days. The British are suffering great losses."

In the small Triantafyllou garden the air was crisp and clean and refreshing. Even on a clear day the sun would only shine for about an hour on their tiny plot of rich black earth, creeping over the roof of the house behind theirs and lighting the arched gate, then passing over the old hand-turned food grinder and the outdoor shower made of barrels, then quickly lighting the animals' entrance, which was then the first to fall back into shadow as the sun retreated until it disappeared behind the roof of Lena's house below.

Dressed in their black dresses, crocheted wool shawls, and wool aprons, Maria Christina and Matoula were on their knees sweeping slush with their hands, then placing leeks on the earth and covering them with ferns. This would keep them fresh until late spring. Zoitsa was secured inside Matoula's shawl, peeking out, watching, learning, occasionally shouting something into her mother's ear and then laughing, and so the hour was spent with a renewed sense of life.

Yiannis had written from Ioannina. He had reunited with some medical school friends who had also been conscripted, and for them it was as if time had stood still. But he longed for his girls and he missed Metsovo and promised to come home in six weeks for a few days. Matoula carried the letter with her and read it over and over, which vexed Maria Christina, for she longed to read his words, know his thoughts. But Matoula didn't share the contents except that he might be coming home, which so elated Maria Christina that she had to pretend to do some chore so her sister wouldn't notice.

Zoitsa, who spoke before she could walk, was now beginning to speak in full sentences and had become a little chatterbox.

"Why?" was her favorite word. And if she didn't like the answer she would try to change your mind. She had discovered that with a small flirtatious glance, a smile and a kiss, she could have her way with everyone but Panorea, who wasn't so easily cajoled. She missed her Babá and insisted Maria Christina tell the story about the first time he milked Afendoula and squirted himself in the eye, and then she would laugh and hold herself and parrot her mother:

"Stop! I can't breathe!"

And no matter how many times she told the story, Zoitsa would have the same reaction. Several times since the funeral, with no apparent connection to anything they were doing, Zoitsa would stop and look up:

"Pappou is with God. We are happy." Then she would smile and continue as if nothing had changed, as if by knowing death at this early age she now considered it simply another interesting part of life.

Since the road stopped at Metsovo, so did the Greek army vehicles loaded with supplies, which meant that resupplying the equipment centers high in the mountains had to be left to those in the area who were available and who knew the donkey paths which, of course, meant the young village women. Realizing the army would be utterly dependent on these young women for their survival, in early August the Minister of Defence had instructed the mayor of Metsovo to call a meeting of these women in the beech forest above the village. Both Matoula and Maria Christina attended and the speaker gave a rousing speech which invoked the women of Souli, a village three days walk to the south. Now a legend in Greek history, in 1821, twenty-two women, their ammunition exhausted, starving and having gone days without water, realizing they could no longer fight off the Turks, hurled their children over the high cliff at Zalongo and, as the Turks below watched in disbelief, held hands, sang and danced, stepping and bending, until one by one, they stepped off the cliff and fell to the rocks at their enemy's feet, choosing death over slavery.

So it was in early October under the leaves of the beech trees now turned yellow that the women once again met and schedules were given out to everyone except Maria Christina and one other girl, an asthmatic. They would remain "on call". Maria Christina was so deeply humiliated she avoided looking at anyone for the next week, even Matoula. More than ever she was feeling bitter and angry and helpless and hopeless. She bore it silently, of course, and no one but Matoula seemed to notice what had become a permanent frown.

Matoula understood her humiliation, but the resupply was certain to be difficult and extremely dangerous. The women would have to travel on foot high into the mountains in the deep snow by night, packed like human mules with food, woollens, arms and ammunition. The resupply route would be under constant surveillance during the day by the Italian Air Force, so the women would have to go to the depot and return home in the same night. Matoula was part of the first group to make the trek. Throughout that night, although they all pretended, no one in the house but Zoitsa slept. Just before dawn, the door opened and Matoula slipped into bed just when it was time for everyone to rise.

Agios Demetrius' name day came and went. In preparation for the celebration, Papa Yiorgos went about his duties without showing much enthusiasm. It was his job. He knew what was required. During the long winters less was needed since so many of his parishioners were away. In the last few years, his church's name day had become less a celebration for him than a marking of time.

At night, with both Pappou and Yiannis gone, Papa Yiorgos sat up alone in the winter room, slowly sipping *tsipouro* by the fire. He missed having men in the house, the two different generations, older and younger, each with different views of the world. Politics was not a subject for women. He especially missed his father-in-law. The old man's passing was a great loss to him. Over the years he had grown to love the old wood carver. He had come to consider him a model for all men. He admired his courage in the face of his every misfortune, and again as he quietly suffered his long agonizing stomach cancer. More and more he had sought his advice, leaning on it more than on scripture. The priest was supposed to be the wise one in his parish, the one with the direct line to the Almighty. And yet he felt weak and deserted by his God. And knowing the calamity that was approaching, he was beginning to question the very existence of a God.

His mind would also wander to different loved ones spanning four generations with whom he had lived in this room. He would have imaginary conversations with them about how much the world had changed. How so many had passed on and so few brought into the family. Thinking of his father, he decided that it must have been the same for him and his mother and everyone through the ages. You started as the youngest, then watched yourself become the next generation, until finally you were the old man sitting in the chair your grandfather sat in all day or where your dear mother lay in her sick bed, her essentials within her grasp. And everyone knew what was coming and it was all right because they had tried to live according to the laws of God and Christ and the Virgin, and soon they would cross over to their promised reward, thoughts which always seemed to comfort the priest.

Two days after Agios Demetrius' name day, while returning from a visit to a sick cousin, Papa Yiorgos passed a large company of soldiers and army trucks amassing at the main square, usually a sleepy place. At the *pantopolio*, the crowd was much larger than when he had passed it earlier. Everyone was huddled around the wireless listening to the news, so Papa Yiorgos stopped in for a *tsipouro*. According to reports, Greece was being unjustly accused of allowing British warships to enter its territorial waters and of instigating attacks against Albania. For those reasons Mussolini had given the Greek prime minister, Yiannis Metaxas, an ultimatum in the middle of the night, demanding that the Italian troops be allowed to occupy the islands of Crete and Corfu, the country's largest port, Piraeus, and the part of Epirus that bordered the Albanian frontier which, of course, included Metsovo.

The men listening spat on the floor and cursed the Italians. The prime minister had rejected Mussolini's demand and rudely dismissed his ambassador. Even before the three-hour ultimatum had expired, heavily armed divisions of Italian troops, one with tanks, were crossing from Albania into Greece.

Papa Yiorgos never finished his *tsipouro*. Instead he hurried directly to his church to try and calm himself, but he found the door ajar and Aristotle Tritos sweeping the floor. The small square widower, known affectionately by everyone in the village as Tatamare, had also heard the news and had retreated to the one place and activity that quieted him when he was upset. A retired shepherd in his sixties, Tatamare had three married daughters who, having seen so little of him for so many years, waited on him hand and foot. He had become the Candle Lighter, or caretaker, of Agios Demetrius Church as an offering of gratitude for all his good fortune. It was Tatamare who, twenty years ago, first pointed out Pappou's excellent qualities to Papa Yiorgos when the priest had been resentful that he had inherited another dependent.

Papa Yiorgos watched the small, square Candle Lighter disappear behind the altar and listened to the sounds of his sweeping a moment longer, then quietly closed the door and hurried up the wide stone steps towards his house, reporting the news to everyone he encountered along the way, and encouraging them to have faith in God.

5

Maria Christina was in the courtyard, combing Zoitsa's hair for lice, when she first heard the airplanes. Zoitsa was initially excited by the big birds streaming across the sky and the huge snowflakes they were dropping, but became suddenly afraid when Maria Christina reflexively picked her up and prepared to run inside. When there were no explosions, no smoke or fire, but rather a groundswell of voices and cries of surprise, Maria Christina hesitated, then slowly set Zoitsa down and waited as one of the bombers darkened their garden and the giant snowflakes started to land: three in their little patch, and one that slid down the roof.

The snowflakes appeared to be handkerchiefs. When Maria Christina opened one, she was surprised to see it was filled with chocolates and a note which began:

"Roman brothers for freedom..."

Having researched Metsovo, the Italian high command discovered they had a common ancestry. The town had been settled in the 14th century by a group known as Vlachs, a people believed to be descendents of the progeny of Roman soldiers sent to Greece in the 3rd century to guard the high passes, and who had fraternized with local Greek women before they fled in the wake of the barbarian invasion. The village was inhabited almost entirely by these same people who still spoke a language Latin in structure and, to a great extent, used Latin vocabulary, which the high command decided they could exploit.

Zoitsa was naturally pleased when she saw the chocolates, but Maria Christina quickly gathered up the handkerchiefs and, in spite of the child's protestations, scooped her up once again and retreated back into the house.

Before dinner, Papa Yiorgos stood with his back to the fire and reported to Matoula what she had already reported to the others before he arrived.

"Most of these gifts from the sky are now in the pockets of a cavalry unit who just arrived. Given to them by the villagers with instructions exactly where the Italians should stuff them!" He laughed and shook his head "God forgive me!" then laughed again and continued. "Their unit is moving forward to protect the pass. All the available infantry have also been sent. They're moving in small groups with pack artillery, and many guns and firearms. To tell you the truth, Matoula, I'm heartened by their enthusiasm."

His optimism infected the household and there was a temporary burst of cheerfulness as the family went about its day.

Having received the same response to their chocolates and handkerchiefs that their prime minister had given to their ambassador, the Italians started bombing their Roman brothers and sisters. At the sound of the first explosion, the Triantafyllou family retreated to the blind room where they lit candles and Papa Yiorgos led them in prayer. When it first started, Maria Christina felt a strange sense of relief. No more waiting. It was happening and her heart was thumping and her breathing was short and shallow, and all she could think about was Yiannis, who was on the front line covered only by the canvas of a hospital tent. Zoitsa sat tightly sandwiched between her mother and Maria Christina, and became increasingly frightened as the earth shook with each thunderous explosion. And then it was over. The silence that followed was total. It was equally as frightening, as if it was only a pause before the bomb which was destined to be yours. Then, after a minute or two, a sigh of relief, a prayer of thanks, then up the ladder to the ground floor and they would resume their daily chores, while Papa Yiorgos would rush down to the church to assess any damage. It was never touched. But adding to everyone's sorrow and fear, Zoitsa's godmother, Athena Bouba, was killed during the first wave while in her garden storing leeks.

Because Metsovo was critical for their conquest of Greece, the Italian ground invasion was entrusted to the famous Julia Alpine Division of twelve thousand men. Outnumbering the Greeks two to one, and their artillery ten to one, the Italian generals soon became awed by the courage of the Greeks and the accuracy of their artillery. By the time they realized that it was the glare of the sun on their shiny helmets that was signalling the Greeks their exact positions, the fine Julia Division found itself separated on two different mountains, hampered from movement by sudden torrential rains and attacked day and night by small units taking advantage of the element of surprise. In the pass just above Metsovo called Katara, or 'the curse', Italy's proud Alpinists in their smart green-grey uniforms and shiny black plumed helmets were halted for five days by a rag tag army of soldiers wearing mismatched uniforms and shepherd's cloaks. The Italians were evidently weary and, as the blinding torrential rains became sleet and ice during the long nights, thousands became victims of the white death, frostbite, which turned their legs and feet black and swollen like potatoes. They slept in the yellow mud, urinated on themselves, and cracked open the skulls of near dead donkeys to use the steaming brains for warmth.

News of the war travelled quickly from the field to the telegraph lines to the wireless radios and, after returning home from the village every day, Matoula would deliver the news to Panorea and Maria Christina, who always expected to hear the worst. Yet in only a few days five thousand Italians, surrounded and exhausted, surrendered, and a panicked Rome ordered the few thousand still remaining to retreat with all possible speed.

Neither Maria Christina nor Panorea could believe their ears. Or their eyes the next day, when the bombs stopped dropping and houses in Metsovo suddenly were housing Italian prisoners of war and the women were treating them as recalcitrant adolescents.

"After all, a mother birthed them as well."

Matoula reported that, throughout the village, heads were held high and chests were puffed. Talk was that they were the first to defeat the Axis, fighting with the same valor and wile as their ancestors who had defeated the Trojans, the Persians, and the Turks, and that this was simply another glorious page in their three thousand year history. Everyone was mad with pride and patriotism, flags were flying everywhere. With each victory the people would emerge from their houses and cheer and dance and sing in the streets. Church bells would ring madly and the village would remain alive late into the night.

"If you want to visit Italy, join the Italian army" Maria Christina said dryly to Matoula one night during a victory celebration, a joke Matoula spread until it was on the lips of everyone in the village by morning.

Papa Yiorgos held special prayer services both at home and at Agios Demetrius to thank the legendary warrior for his help. His faith had been restored. There was indeed a God. And he was a wise and just God, and simply because the weaver didn't see the pattern of the tapestry until it was completed and he finally turned it over didn't mean there was no pattern, or that life was random and there was no power in prayer. And he now went about his duties with a renewed vigor and a special place in his heart for the saint whose stately church he pastored.

Another letter arrived from Yiannis. He was still in Ioannina and was up to his elbows in blood, trying to stitch together wounded Greeks. His leave was, of course, cancelled and he would be moving east with the army to set up a field hospital. God knows when and from where he would be able to write again. But he loved his girls and missed them, and wanted to be remembered by the family and the boys at Stahoulis'.

So life continued normally in Metsovo for the little family with one small exception.

While everyone seemed happier, Matoula seemed to grow dispirited and appeared unusually tired. After much prodding, she confided to her sister that she had missed two periods in a row and her breasts had begun to swell. Maria Christina's mind immediately raced to the fact that in a few days Matoula was again scheduled to resupply the troops. And because the army was pushing the remaining Italians towards the Albanian border, the equipment center had been moved further away and the women were no longer able to reach it in one night. They needed to lay in the snow without moving during the day, so they had been instructed to wear dark earth colors that would appear like rocks to the Italian Air Force, who were constantly patrolling. Trekking back down from the resupply center to Metsovo in one night was not a problem, since it took half the time.

Maria Christina was relentless in her appeals to Matoula to be her substitute. She argued passionately, first for the safety of the baby.

"The baby will be fine" Matoula shrugged her off.

Then for the health of the mother.

"I'm pregnant. I'm not sick. I feel fine."

Finally, Maria Christina begged her to give her the chance to finally be respected by the community. She was stronger than anyone imagined. She could do it, she was certain of it. It would mean so much to her. So much. When she finally, tearfully exhausted her arguments, Matoula cleverly told her that she would leave it to someone with the wisdom of Solomon to decide. Matoula was certain Maria Christina could never survive the resupply. It was dangerous even for her. So Matoula agreed if Maria Christina could get their father's permission, which she knew was impossible, she could take her place. But she wouldn't allow her sister to use the pregnancy in her argument.

"The first to know should be Yiannis. So for now it has to remain a secret."

"Of course. I understand" Maria Christina bit her lip, deeply resenting her sister's utter lack of sympathy and support.

Even though it had begun to snow, the church was filled to overflowing on Sunday morning and Papa Yiorgos, known to have the best singing voice of any priest in the village, had been in excellent form and was now in an exceptionally good mood as the three women served him wine and feta cheese pie, which he ate hungrily. When he had finished, he bowed his head and clasped his hands, after which everyone stopped and did the same. A thank you for the blessed meal, and the priest stood up and stepped to the fireplace. Maria Christina moved close to him and quietly asked him if she could speak to him in his room.

Though there were only four rooms in most houses in Metsovo, the master of every household had one room which was exclusively his, where he would conduct business or just be alone. Papa Yiorgos' room contained books and mementos which included a photograph of himself with the Archbishop of Epirus, and valued icons handed down from unknown generations. In winter a fire was lit every morning, so the room was still warm when the father and daughter entered. Maria

Christina was sorely tempted to tell her father the truth. But she understood that it was not her secret to tell.

Trembling slightly, she held her hands behind her back as she stepped to the fireplace. Papa Yiorgos waited patiently. It was quite unusual to have his younger daughter request a private conversation. Maria Christina started by saying how she felt as though she had been unjustly undervalued by the mayor's wife.

"It would extinguish any chance of ever finding a husband, Patera. On the other hand, by joining I could prove I was worthy."

The more she talked the faster the words came, until Papa Yiorgos backed away and with a hand in the air he ordered her to stop.

"You are much too delicate."

"But Patera..."

She had been dismissed. And before she could blurt out the truth, her father had turned and left the room.

The night before Matoula was scheduled to leave, the two sisters slept together and held and cradled each other as they sometimes had as children, mother and daughter, taking turns, each closer to the other than anyone else in the world. Just before she drifted off to sleep, Matoula thought she heard her sister whisper in her ear.

"I'm going with you."

6

Matoula slept later than usual, her feet close to the fire, with a sweet smile on her face. Zoitsa finally nudged her on the arm, startling her. One look from Panorea and Zoitsa retreated, ever the innocent. As Matoula yawned and held out her arms to her daughter, she was already wondering if she had actually heard Maria Christina whisper in her ear or if she had only dreamt it. She didn't know how to confront her sister without humiliating her but, before she could give it another thought, Zoitsa was in her arms and her day had begun even before she was ready. As she climbed out of bed, she was feeling slightly nauseous and was on her way to find a piece of bread, when Lena stepped in with some sugar candies she had just made.

Lena waddled around the room with a kiss for everyone. Nearly as wide as she was tall, she was always cheerful, especially after her husband died. A miscarriage during her first pregnancy eliminated the possibility of ever having another child, and her husband never forgave her and became a most disagreeable and abusive man during the few months of the year he was at home.

Panorea and Lena had been next-door neighbors and the very best of friends since they could remember, and whenever the two were together they would gossip and laugh, which

Maria Christina thought provided Panorea her only form of amusement. It was rare and always sweet to see Panorea smile and hear her laugh. It was a deep laugh, usually the same three sounds, ha ha ha, followed by an exclamation like, "Christ and the Virgin Mary!" or "Well" followed by maxims like "The drowning man grabs his own hair!" or "Well, ha ha ha, one hand can't clap alone!" Maria Christina could imitate her perfectly.

Lena was especially cheerful this morning as Matoula tore off a piece of bread and ate it while pouring herself a mug of hot water. Her nausea was already subsiding and she was beginning to feel ready to face the day.

Maria Christina had been awake most of the night and had slipped out of bed and down the stairs to have all of her chores done before dinner. She was feeling especially strong today. Besides proving to the world that she was worthy of a husband, she desperately wanted to help the men in the mountains. Greek men. It was her fight, too, and she was determined to do her part.

It wasn't until just before dinner that the two sisters found themselves together. Matoula sat on the little bench in front of the fireplace next to Maria Christina and watched her stir the coals for a long moment, waiting for a sign. Maria Christina was extremely annoyed with her sister and didn't acknowledge her presence at first, something highly unusual. When Maria Christina finally did look at her, it was barely an icy glance, then she turned quickly away. Matoula knew then that she hadn't been dreaming, and that look was her agitation at having to wait so long for a response. Matoula had all but dismissed it as a possibility, and was taken by surprise. After taking a mental breath to process the news, Matoula leaned into her sister and proceeded guardedly, hoping she might still be wrong:

"Will you walk with me to the depot?"

Maria Christina smiled and spoke very softly, "And beyond."

Matoula's face withdrew into a frown, seldom seen, as she looked back at Panorea, who was snapping beans by the counter, bending her ear in their direction. Matoula put her arm on her sister's shoulder to block her aunt's prying eyes:

"You can't. You mustn't. Have you told Patera?"

Maria Christina smiled smugly and leaned into her sister's ear, "This will be *my* little secret."

"Patera will never forgive you."

"Patera would never forgive you if he knew tonight you might be carrying his grandson. Besides, he will be happy when I find a husband."

Just then Papa Yiorgos entered from his private room, and the girls immediately went about cutting and serving today's pie of feta cheese and wild greens and pouring water. Both felt relieved, although Maria Christina felt more like screaming "Yes, I can!"

Upon reflection Matoula couldn't deny that being part of the resupply could dramatically change Maria Christina's life. A simple solution to a very complex problem. Of course their father would be angry but, as Maria Christina noted, he would be very happy if she found a husband. Besides, she would be there to look after her. Also, her sister never exaggerated but was always precise in her language and she insisted she was stronger than anyone imagined, and she was certain she could do it. So Matoula didn't object further. After dinner, the sisters napped together with Zoitsa between them and, before anyone awoke, the two slipped out of bed, threw on their cloaks and left the room. Papa Yiorgos heard them but never moved, assuming Maria Christina was simply escorting her sister to the end of the courtyard.

At the depot, there were ten other women in the resupply group standing in a cold fog, including one of Tatamare's granddaughters, Irini, tall and wide with rusty red hair. 'The quiet one' Tatamare called her. Old men and children were unloading army trucks filled with supplies. No one questioned Maria Christina when she walked to the loading area with Matoula. A young officer just took her measure and dictated the cargo, then a group of younger girls loaded and strapped their loads to their backs with woven chords and wished them well. Six of the women, the strongest, carried guns and ammunition, four carried foodstuffs, one carried foodstuffs and medical supplies, and Maria Christina carried the mail. Matoula's cargo consisted of four heavy bags of corn flour and beans. It was growing dark very quickly and so the team started up the mountain.

When Maria Christina didn't return after a few minutes, Papa Yiorgos decided she must have walked Matoula to the edge of the village. When twenty minutes passed, he guessed she must have walked her all the way to the depot and he rose out of bed, went to the window, and threw back the weaving to watch for her return. When an hour passed and it had already grown dark, Papa Yiorgos flashed angrily at the thought she might have disobeyed him, and grabbed his great black coat and flat-topped hat and went to look for her. At the depot, he spoke to the young girls unloading trucks who told him Maria Christina had gone with the others. Turning to the officer in charge, he exchanged some angry words then stormed away. Walking down the icy street to his house, he slipped and fell and landed on his elbow, which enraged him even further.

Now, in the winter room, he was pacing and fuming, while Panorea was tending the fire and Zoitsa was playing with her marbles on the black rug.

"She's been a curse since she was born!" he barked at no one in particular.

"Now, brother…"

"It's a blessing her mother is not alive to suffer this!"

"You'll make yourself sick."

"I'll take a stick to her!"

"You're frightening the child."

And so the evening continued until Papa Yiorgos had a stomach ache and Panorea's head was throbbing and Zoitsa was especially whiny and incapable of either sleeping or being amused. No one slept that night or even pretended. Papa Yiorgos was too agitated, and when Panorea insisted he retire to his own room, he left, only to return a few minutes later needing to have an audience for his ranting and raving.

The path up to the equipment center was on average a forty-five degree angle through a landscape shaped over many thousands of years by the erosion of water, resulting in unusual surfaces and sub surfaces, sinkholes, vertical shafts, disappearing streams, springs, and caves. Through this rugged range of the Southern Alps there was a path that had been established centuries ago, the result of allowing the donkeys, who always found the easiest, laziest route, to lead. But now there were snowdrifts across the trail which made it more difficult, and there was a full moon so, although they could easily see where they were going, the Italian Air Force would be out looking for them even at night.

The temperature continued to drop through the night and the wind was against them as they struggled their way up and down the winding mountain paths, sometimes through spider-like leafless oak and pine forests and other times over bare terrain that looked like glaciers, the biggest, strongest first, making a path for the rest, and finally Maria Christina. Matoula glanced back at her sister, two steps behind, lugging the bag of mail, smiling with steam coming from her mouth. Matoula felt pleased. It had been the right decision. Maria Christina, if anything, felt even stronger. The more they trekked, the more powerful and determined she became. As she marched along imagining herself a soldier, she began to hum the Greek folk song, *Dance of Zalongo*, based on the incident of the women of Souli. After a chorus, she began to sing the words:

"The fish cannot live on the land
Nor the flower on the sand
And the women of Souli
Cannot live without freedom"

Matoula smiled as her sister continued, and joined in the second verse:

"So, goodbye springs,
Valleys, mountains and hills
Goodbye springs
And you, women of Souli"

By now the whole group was singing and laughing.

"The women of Souli
Have not only learnt how to survive
They also know how to die
Not to tolerate slavery"

The group sang the chorus again and then started at the beginning, substituting Metsovo for Souli, and when they were finished they sang another song and another, patriotic songs from the revolution of 1821 learned in childhood, and then they sang the national anthem, and the songs so lifted their spirits that the night passed quickly as a kind of patriotic celebration. Twice they had to hold still while three Italian planes raced overhead, but being able to outwit the Roman fliers inspired them even more, and when the sky was clear they continued marching and singing louder than ever.

As the sun began peeking over snow-capped Katara, the sound of Italian planes greeted the women who were midway through a small piece of open table land, so they decided to stop for the day, just where they were, because even the Italians might notice a group of rocks that continually changed locations. Matoula and Maria Christina lay next to each other. Bearing the cold while climbing up a mountain was one thing, but having to lie motionless in the snow for hours was entirely another. And it wasn't long before the sun was covered by a dark grey sky and large snowflakes began falling and Maria Christina, exhausted from such a difficult climb, was chilled. Her teeth began to chatter, and her whole body trembled. Matoula saw her distress and crouched over her to give her added protection from the wind and snow. After a few minutes Maria Christina stopped shaking.

"Thank you, Mata" she looked up at Matoula and kissed her cheek which was hidden inside an ice-crusted hood. Then Maria Christina sank into the snow, closed her eyes, and began to daydream: she was at the equipment center and a tall handsome officer from Crete with blonde hair and a brush mustache was helping her unload. When their eyes met, he smiled:

"Thank you for your bravery, Kyria. Well done."

He was slightly taller and looked stronger than Yiannis and she could see in his eyes that he thought she was very beautiful, so she smiled back with the confidence of a warrior and the seductive voice Pappou always used when he kissed her hand and told her she was a wild rose.

"May Greece live in freedom" she said, knowing it was the perfect response.

"May I show you to some refreshment?" he gestured to a mess wagon and offering his arm, escorted her to it.

Then her mind emptied with the beginnings of sleep, so she began the daydream again, from the moment their eyes first met.

"Thank you for your bravery, Kyria."

His face inside the blonde hair and brush mustache was the last clear thought she had as she drifted off again, this time thinking of Pappou and how she wished she could tell him she was on the resupply, and how proud he would be of his wild rose.

The snow continued through the day but only dusted the figure in slate grey crouched over her younger sister. The wind swept it off the goat-hair shepherd's cloak before it had a chance to set. It wasn't the cold so much as the wind, thought Matoula. She was becoming very concerned for Maria Christina and, in spite of the fact that she was weary and sleepy from the trek, she knew she had to stay awake to ensure her sister made it through the day. What was keeping her awake was the thought of the look on her father's face if she brought him Maria Christina's frost-bitten body. But her mind kept wandering to gentler, sweeter things. Yiannis. How she ached for him. To see his strong face. She couldn't wait for him to read the letter she had written, telling him they were having another child. She dreamt of touching him. Holding him. Making him laugh. She was composing a letter to him in her head. What she missed most was not being able to whisper in his ear over and over, "I love you. I love you." It was so simple, yet it was her favorite thing to do. And how much she missed him. Even surprising herself. And how happy he would be when he came home. She would see to it. And as Matoula sailed off to sleep on dreams of happily ever after, after the war, she became unaware of the icy wind, and in its place a feeling of warmth and comfort enveloped her weary body.

At precisely that moment Yiannis, somewhere in the mountains near the Albanian border, was sitting, leaning against the tent of the field hospital writing a letter.

"Dearest", he began. Then he rested his hands on his lap and looked up at the ceiling. After a moment he smiled, sighed, then fell fast asleep.

Maria Christina was awakened by one of the women trying to stir Matoula. Maria Christina opened her eyes to the sound, then turned to see she was still being covered by Matoula like a shell.

"Mata." Maria Christina poked her, "Matoula?"

Two women picked Matoula up under her arms and laid her on her back in the snow, her face hidden under her hood. Another pulled back Matoula's hood. In the light her face appeared pale purple and there were ice crystals on her eyelashes and the tip of her nose. Matoula hadn't moved. She was frozen in position. The woman put her ear to Matoula's mouth and felt her neck for a pulse.

After a moment she sighed, "May the Holy Virgin protect her."

One of the women offered her hand to Maria Christina, "I'm sorry, Maria Christina."

Maria Christina's mouth was open but no sound came, only air.

"She just wasn't strong enough."

Maria Christina fell to her knees beside Matoula and held her tenderly, kissing her frozen face. The pain was unbearable. She couldn't breathe. When she finally exhaled, it was a silent scream.

How sad for the girl. How sad for both of them, their lives only beginning. How cruel the fates. How some have to suffer so, while others don't know the meaning. The young spinster's heart was irretrievably broken and bleeding pain.

No amount of suffering would ever be enough. Every breath became a silent wail, too powerful for a voice. Every thought had to be censored for fear that it would become too difficult to bear.

"We must continue" another woman took Maria Christina by the sleeve and pulled her up. "Irini has also left us. We must be strong, Maria Christina."

Maria Christina leaned down into Matoula's hood and kissed her frozen lips, wishing the moment would never end and that she wouldn't have to continue beyond this kiss. Then she covered her sister's head and, as if a curtain had been drawn and the actor, who a moment before was weeping real tears, now seemed not at all affected, Maria Christina picked up Matoula's burden with a strength that amazed everyone, then added the mail bag and joined the line on their way to the equipment center. After a few steps, the strongest of the women waited for Maria Christina to pass and tried to slip the mail bag from her shoulder and add it to her own, but Maria Christina gestured her away.

There was no more singing that night. Nor would there be for Maria Christina for the rest of her life, she was certain of that. She could hardly open her mouth or open her eyes to the snow. She hated the sound of the wind and feared she would die before she had sufficiently paid for her terrible sin.

7

It was rage that carried Maria Christina's heavy sacks up that frigid mountain, a rage that could have carried them half way around the world. Always sweet, gentle, light as a song, even if sometimes melancholic, Maria Christina now knew what it felt like to want to kill. Italians. Men. God. Herself.

At the equipment center, a tall and slender, sandy-haired officer, startling in his good looks, lifted two of the sacks to lighten her load as Maria Christina backed into the loading area.

"You are amazing, Kyria."

She never noticed him. And when he offered to escort her to some hot soup, she said she wasn't hungry and started back down the mountain, leaving him staring after her in disbelief as she disappeared into the night. She needed Matoula. And so she quickened her step down the mountain watching for the pole which marked the spot where her sister lay.

There were indeed two poles. One was for Irini. Maria Christina hadn't even noticed her before now. She was lying in a fetal position, like a child who had been dusted with snow. Irini, the quiet one. Poor, sweet Tatamare! How Maria Christina ached for him as well. Maria Christina stood over the frozen young woman and prayed silently for a moment. Then she stepped over to Matoula, who was as they had left her. Maria Christina could feel her heart breaking all over again, as she knelt down and brushed the snow from Matoula's face and kissed her cheek. She remained kneeling for an hour or more, until she heard the sound of the other women returning. Three women lifted Matoula onto Maria Christina's back and secured her. Then Maria Christina proceeded down the mountain to face her father and Panorea, and finally Yiannis, and most difficult of all, little Zoitsa. A part of her never wanted the mountain to end, and yet the greater part ached to be punished. As she continued her descent three Italian planes roared overhead. Maria Christina didn't notice. Nor did they.

From the edge of the village to Agios Demetrius Church, women had already begun wailing as word spread before Maria Christina had even reached the main square. Several offered to take Matoula from her, but Maria Christina carried her as if she were the Holy Cross. As villagers lined the street down to the Triantafyllou cottage, Zoitsa was whisked from the winter room to Lena's house which was now crowded with her cousins.

Papa Yiorgos sat in his chair in his study, staring at the fire. She had killed his wife and now his favorite. It was biblical in its challenge as a priest and as a man, and he was overwhelmed with the fear of failure. How could he not be judged according to the way he dealt with this outrage? It was odd. He wasn't breathing heavily and his blood pressure seemed normal. He was relaxed. In truth he wasn't feeling anything. It seemed dangerous. As if the Devil was about. He had always dreamed of having a son who would also become a priest. Someone to walk to the church with, to assist him in the services, someone to whom he could pass the cup when he was too old to work. That dream was dashed, of course, shortly after Maria Christina's birth. And although one might wonder if in some way he held her responsible for not being able to have a son, the priest himself had examined and dismissed the thought. He simply preferred Matoula. She was his ideal woman. She would have made an excellent son. And if one day she had given him a grandson, his dream might still have come true. Yet, given the choice between which daughter should undertake such a difficult mission, it would have been unconscionable of him not to choose Matoula. He had prayed that he would never be in the situation where he'd have to choose which one to save if he could only rescue one. Oh, Matoula! Oh, blessed Thimi, his wife long gone! Each person you love is given a piece of your heart. And when they're gone that piece is buried with them. How little heart can you still have and live, he was wondering when he heard the outer door open. In a moment Panorea stepped in, followed by several weeping women. After a moment, Maria Christina entered, her face covered in ice, Matoula on her back. Three of the women untied the frozen cords and lifted Matoula from her sister and set her gently on the floor.

Papa Yiorgos looked at the frozen figure at his feet, which was hidden beneath the goat hair cloak. Then he calmly blessed it.

"Bring her to the winter room and lay her by the fire."

The women lifted Matoula and carried her out of the room.

Maria Christina never needed a mother more, and never would she find one less agreeable than Panorea, her arms folded, head bowed, waiting for instructions from her brother. Papa Yiorgos couldn't set his eyes on his daughter.

"Panorea, leave us."

Panorea obeyed and the two stood by the hearth for a long moment.

"Oh Patera…!"

"Don't speak."

The two stood there for the better part of an hour, she, ordered not to speak, shaking, the ice slowly melting from her face and cloak, hoping her father would beat her, and he, unable to even look at her or to make a sound, afraid he would explode and snap her neck like the head of a chicken. At the end of an hour, Papa Yiorgos turned away and sat at his desk.

"Leave me."

And she did.

8

Maria Christina went directly to the winter room and washed and dressed her sister and put a piece of bread in her pocket, then went about her other duties the rest of the day with a great deal of care, but without any feeling whatsoever. It was Panorea who told Zoitsa her mother was with God and Pappou. Zoitsa did not embrace the idea as she had with Pappou and wanted to know "Why?" It was a simple question that no one seemed to be able to answer to her satisfaction.

The next day at Agios Demetrius, Matoula's coffin stood alongside Irini's. For Papa Yiorgos it was the most difficult service of his life, and when he faltered or simply stopped in the middle of reading the text, one of the other priests would continue, but not until they waited a moment for the pastor to recover.

Tatamare spent the entire service with tears streaming down his face. What was especially sad for him was the feeling of never having really known his granddaughter. In fact, no one seemed to know her very well. She had lived to serve and tried so hard to please without asking for anything in return, even of anyone's ear to share her troubles.

Maria Christina, her face hidden inside her long black scarf, sat lifelessly near the coffin, oblivious to Zoitsa, who could not be controlled. Zoitsa wanted to go home and would not sit still and would not be silent and screamed when Panorea pinched her. All Maria Christina could think about was the frozen face of her sister lying in the snow.

Knowing that her father could not bear the sight of her, Maria Christina made a bed downstairs in the stable with blankets from her dowry chest. She took her meager meals there as well. Feeling undeserving even of food, she allowed herself only bread and cold water. As days passed, she occasionally would eat a raw leek or a potato while silently going about her own as well as Matoula's duties, which included becoming Zoitsa's primary caregiver. Becoming thinner by the week, she had been growing stronger by the day until she was little more than muscle and bone.

Other than Lena, no one outside the house knew Maria Christina was living with the animals, and when she confronted Papa Yiorgos and cautioned him that, if the villagers knew, they would stone him, he reacted without a hint of embarrassment and dismissed her in a sentence.

"It was her choice, not mine."

Having lost her mother and frustrated by her inability to get answers, Zoitsa cried herself to sleep every night for weeks. She couldn't understand why she couldn't go with her mother and Pappou, or why her mother couldn't come back and where was heaven anyway? And where was her father and what was war, and why couldn't she sleep with Maria Christina and the animals? She didn't want to sleep with Panorea. She snored.

Seeing the hell that Maria Christina had created for herself, the hardened heart began to slowly melt and breathe once again. First there was a look of pity that Panorea made certain Maria Christina would notice. Then later a small smile. Still later, Panorea began extending herself, in small ways at first, to lighten her niece's load. In that way Panorea felt she was being magnanimous and forgiving. Once, the old spinster wished she had run away to Athens while she was still of marriageable age, but she didn't have the courage to defy her own father and had been too afraid the reward wasn't worth the risk of shame, or worse. Over the years she had come to realize that everyone had a cross to bear, and if you tried to throw it off, it would only become heavier. Maria Christina's misfortune gave her additional comfort that she had made the right decision.

However much Panorea sympathized with Maria Christina, her primary concern was for the man who had replaced her father. Lately the priest had been keeping more and more to himself. And he had become even more religious.

"The Good Lord never closes one door without opening another" he had become fond of saying. It was one of Pappou's sayings and now it seemed to him the answer to so many questions, large and small.

"Good morning, Papa Yiorgos. It looks like snow again."

"Yes, well, the Good Lord never closes one door without opening another."

The phrase gave him hope that there was yet something awaiting him which, though it might never equal his loss, might at least offer some benefit. At home, he now almost never spoke except to ask for something. Once he would have commented on everything, now he was silent, as if he were preoccupied thinking deep thoughts, dark thoughts, ones he couldn't share. Panorea thought it unhealthy, but the more she tried to engage him, the less he would allow himself to be engaged, waving her away with a "Stop!"

Panorea began to rely on old Tatamare for advice. He reassured the spinster that she was right to feel sympathy for Maria Christina and she should not be timid about showing it. So when her brother dismissed Lena's objections to Maria Christina living with the animals, Panorea looked at him for a moment as if he were a snake. In retrospect she realized that was the moment when she felt a new distance between them, and he began refraining from speaking with her altogether, unless it pertained to some immediate necessity. Even though she was ten years older than her brother, she had trailed behind him constantly, anticipating his every want since he was a little boy. And still she had no idea what he was thinking or feeling, other than when he occasionally looked at her as if she was Judas Iscariot himself. Tatamare always tried to relieve her of any concern, saying her brother was simply still in mourning and it would soon pass. But he knew better than anyone that the priest would never be free. His anger would get dissected and buried in pieces, but it would always live just beneath his veneer of pious optimism.

Although publicly Papa Yiorgos seemed his usual self, privately he was busy trying to navigate a river of confusion and anger, with wide emotional swings from soaring hope to utter hopelessness. And he couldn't understand how someone like Panorea or Tatamare could simply go about their day as if nothing had happened. It wasn't human. Tatamare had said his granddaughter's death made him sad, but he was happy for her. He firmly believed Irini was an innocent angel who was with God, and there was no doubt that God existed and, in His infinite wisdom, decided all things, and it was good, and he was grateful for His intercession. His innocence was both touching and annoying to the priest. In his mind Tatamare was another unquestioning sheep and, even though he was supposed to be the shepherd, Papa Yiorgos wished his flock was a little more curious, more literate, more thoughtful.

"Whosoever knows for certain is the most easily fooled" he would say to himself, unsure if he had read it somewhere or if it was one of his original thoughts. He loved nothing more than engaging in philosophical discussions with Yiannis and Pappou. During these discussions Papa Yiorgos felt closest to God and His infinite wisdom and he considered these moments a high form of prayer. That kind of dialogue was not possible with anyone in the parish of Agios Demetrius, which was inhabited by the poorest, least educated families.

But Papa Yiorgos was still grateful to be the pastor of his church at this time, giving comfort and hope to the many with sons and daughters in the war. For himself, he could find no comfort or hope in anything but the giving of it. Other than to his daughter. His rage towards Maria Christina had unnerved him, and he now spent hours alone in front of the fire, pouring over passages in the Bible and the pages of Yiannis' and Pappou's books, looking for the key to forgiveness. Now and then he would set a book down and ponder his daughter's childhood, looking for any clue of her lack of character but, upon reflection, Matoula had been the headstrong one. Maria Christina was always delicate, careful not to offend, someone who might easily disappear into the landscape and go unnoticed if left alone. He hadn't realized until now how little he had known his youngest daughter and for that he was angry, especially with himself.

Yet he didn't know where or how to begin to forgive her. Prayer? Finally they were just words if they weren't heartfelt. He was convinced his daughter's betrayal even undermined his credibility as a priest. Who could respect a pastor who couldn't even control his own child! And as he sat alone and drank *tsipouro* night after night, he would go around and around trying to find an answer, until he crawled into bed half asleep and remained in that state for the rest of the night.

Whenever she thought about her sister, it was only for a second and it was still Matoula's frozen face that stared at her. Yet Maria Christina gave all appearances of being beyond grief, as if it had happened a generation ago and she had gone on with her life. She still hadn't shed one tear. Not one. She didn't wail on the ninth day with the other women. Instead, she held Zoitsa by the fire in the winter room and told her stories of ancient Greek gods, while the others were howling and weeping in the sitting room.

As the household was once again in mourning, Lena would bring provisions every day, always taking time to visit with Maria Christina, cheerfully telling her the gossip, who had the best garden, who was fighting with whom, just like she knew Matoula used to do. Afterwards, she always insisted on holding Maria Christina tightly for a moment before kissing her and saying:

"Somebody loves you."

Lena was convinced she was the only one able to grasp the whole picture. She loved Maria Christina like a daughter and had spent many hours with Pappou speaking of her and her situation. She saw the envy. She could almost hear it in her voice whenever she spoke about her sister. She also was aware of the fascination with her sister's husband. She understood why Maria Christina needed to go on the resupply. It was as much for Papa Yiorgos' approval as to prove to everyone else, including her sister that she was a worthy bride. She also knew that Matoula would have been incautious with regard to herself in order to protect her younger sister. There was no one to blame. Maria Christina's mother died because she just wasn't strong enough. Matoula died for the same reason. Yet no matter how hard she tried to persuade her niece she was not responsible for either of their deaths, she knew Maria Christina silently carried the guilt in her soul and the weight of it was slowly drowning her. And at the moment there seemed to be no lifeline in sight.

9

After the deaths of Matoula and Irini, there were no more jokes about Italians in Metsovo. Young Greek soldiers were returning home from Ioannina in coffins. Others never returned at all, having been declared missing in action. The war was going to be painful and everyone was holding on to each other even tighter, as Yiannis' battalion helped push the retreating and exhausted Italian force over the Albanian border. Thousands in the Greek army were now suffering frostbite, many of whom would be disabled for life, and Yiannis had been given the painful job of severing frostbitten limbs before the soldiers were taken to the hospital at Ioannina. It was the perfect assignment for him. Having received two letters from home at the same time, one from Papa Yiorgos and one from Matoula, the war disappeared for him, if only for a moment. He, of course, opened the one from Matoula first, and read it as he walked back to his tent and wept over the sweet words written by his dearest.

"A child! How glorious!"

After reading it again he carefully folded it and replaced it inside its envelope.

As he entered his tent and sat on his cot, he opened the letter from his father-in-law.

'My dearest son-in-law,
It is with great sorrow that I...'

Yiannis saw the name, Matoula, then quickly scanned the letter, noticing words like "resupply" and "frozen". His hands began shaking so violently that he was afraid he might tear the paper, so he laid it on the cot and read and reread it carefully, disbelieving the words, as his mind slowly, numbly received the information,

'...a moment ago so alive! Now gone!!'

"Matoula! My God! A child!" The letter from Matoula, now nearly forgotten, was crushed in his fist. As he opened his hand, it clung to his perspiration for a second, then fell onto the bed. Holding his hands over his eyes, he slowly laid back on his thin pillow. Even before a moment had passed, a young orderly in a bloody surgical coat stepped in. He was needed. A new group had just arrived from the front. Yiannis nodded mechanically, then sat up and followed him out, grateful for the diversion. He would deal with all this in pieces, between the lives and deaths and limbs of others.

10

By now, almost everyone in the village had lost someone in their family and it seemed they were all wearing black and everyone's house was dressed in mourning. And yet life continued. Thomas, the veterinarian, was still making his rounds, Tatamare was keeping Agios Demetrius spotless, babies were being born, the same men were sitting drinking *tsipouro* and listening to the news on Stahoulis' wireless radio, only Costas was now with the army in Albania and his painfully shy older brother, Spiros, ordinarily a cobbler, was running the store. Holidays were celebrated: Christmas, New Years, The Epiphany. In the Triantafyllou house, which was still in mourning for Matoula, no holidays were celebrated including Zoitsa's third birthday.

As the winter wore on, Maria Christina began thinking about the Palm Sunday holiday in April. It was the holiday when prospective brides paraded themselves past the bachelors. They would meet in the village and walk to the Monastery of Agios Nicolaos, which was even lower down the mountain than Agios Demetrius. The monastery was accessible only by a long, steep path from below. The men would congregate at the bottom and wait for the girls to pass, most of whom were wearing two dresses, pleated and ballooned to make them look larger, hence stronger. After the girls passed, the boys would run up the long steep hill to the monastery and wait for the girls. The first girl to arrive with the least effort was the most beautiful. And so on.

For Maria Christina, the holiday this year and the promise it brought to so many, together with the years of her own unrequited hope, all had been looming in the back of her mind. From the age of eleven she had been one of those young women, and for the past few years it had become more and more painful and humiliating, being rejected like a three-legged donkey.

While sitting in her nest with Zoitsa, under her horsehair blanket, reading one of Pappou's children's books to her niece, Maria Christina's mind kept returning to that event. After a moment, the weary Zoitsa closed her eyes and fell asleep. Outside of the house Zoitsa had become her helpmate, leading her by the hand as her mother had, though without Matoula, they never ventured far from the house. Maria Christina set the book down with a sigh, then took off her grandfather's glasses and picked up their case. For a moment she stared blankly into space. Other than Zoitsa, she was alone. Now that Matoula and Pappou were gone, she had no friends. The closest was her cousin, Sophia, three years younger, but she hardly ever visited, and when she did, it was only to admire Matoula.

Maria Christina looked at the glass case. Instead of opening it, she set it back in its place. Then she put the glasses carefully back on her nose and slipped the bows over her ears. Never again would she be walking to Agios Nicolaos Monastery with the other unmarried girls. There was no more need to pretend. Or to hope. Maria Christina hung her head for a long moment in order to fully accept the sad fact, then she slipped out from under the blanket, stood up, and looked around. Until that moment she only dared use the glasses for reading. Walking around the stable touching things, sizing the animals, viewing them from different perspectives, it was a new world. She could reach out and touch something without guessing. Seeing everything clearly and in focus was like a miracle. She was free.

Trembling with excitement, she opened the door to the terrace. She saw the garden. The oak barrel shower. Lena's stone house. The top of a huge sycamore tree over their tiled roof. Each tile was distinct. It was overwhelming. She lowered her head, almost afraid to look up, there was too much to see. She stepped back inside, wrapped the sleeping Zoitsa in a blanket and, using the blanket as a shawl, created a seat for the child as well as a cover. Zoitsa awoke from her nap and peered out over her aunt's shoulder as they spent the better part of the day looking at things, large and small, that Maria Christina had only seen through Matoula's eyes. Fine shapes, subtle colors, the different grains in stones. A black beetle. Maria Christina stared at this creature she had never seen before nor knew existed, as it crawled along a stone wall.

"*Korios!*" Zoitsa laughed as she crawled her fingertips quickly over her aunt's head, trying to scare her. Matoula must not have told her about such creatures, knowing they would be frightening to her myopic sister. Separate branches of trees that were once just a blur of green. Pine needles. Cones. The separation in the cobblestones. It became a game. Maria Christina would point at something she was seeing clearly for the first time, like a small cluster of narcissus sticking out of the snow, and Zoitsa would shout in her ear.

"*Loulouthia!*"

Late that night Maria Christina slipped out of her bed and stepped outside to look at the sky. It was overwhelming. The amount of stars - so many more than she had imagined. It took her breath away for a moment and she stood staring at the universe until dawn.

There are some doors which, once opened, can never be closed. From that moment Maria Christina would wear Pappou's glasses everywhere, except while sleeping or taking her sister's place on the resupply line. Metsovo was still the end of the road and the supply route became increasingly longer. Almost every resupply group lost one or two women, and yet the human train continued even when it snowed or the fighting paused. The interval between Maria Christina's assigned treks had become shorter because so many women had been lost. She also had volunteered to take the place of anyone unable to make their scheduled trip, and would always carry one of the dead back to the village. There was no more singing. But hiking through the snow with a heavy load as part of the resupply was the one thing that made Maria Christina feel that her life mattered. Although, at the end of each journey, the blur of red roofs huddled together in the snow in the village below, the agony of an unwelcome child returning home, overwhelmed the sense of purpose.

The men watched with pity as the skinny young woman with glasses walked through the market place, her long hair in two plaits, her kerchief no longer tied fastidiously on the top of her head at a rakish angle like all eligible girls in Metsovo, but at the base of her neck like all women who were unavailable. The women who washed their clothes at the stream would watch the ugly duckling, so strong yet so flimsy, scrub and beat her clothes as if she were settling scores. She had made her mark among all of the women of the village, who now admired her for her strong will. They viewed her as an example of what was possible. But Maria Christina was too blinded by her shame and too intent on doing what she was doing to notice either the pity or the admiration. Wherever she went, whatever she did, her eyes hardly left the ground and most certainly never looked into someone else's eyes to see her own reflection.

And so the winter continued in this fashion while the war stood still, and the injured were being tended in overcrowded hospitals in Ioannina, while Yiannis and the troops at the front continued living on scant rations supplied by selfless young women like Maria Christina, who thought they were doing nothing exceptional, nothing women hadn't been doing in Metsovo for centuries.

11

Lena was in tears as she entered the house on the first day of March, with the news that Bulgaria had granted Hitler use of its territory. Neither Maria Christina nor Panorea could speak for a moment. Disaster was once again quickly approaching, and all they could do was wait. And pray. Maria Christina picked up Zoitsa and led Panorea to Agios Demetrius to tell Papa Yiorgos and join him in prayer.

Eight days later, the BBC announced that the Italians opened an offensive on the entire Albanian front, using all their divisions supported by several hundred fighters and bombers, and every other resource they could provide. Mussolini had assumed command of the campaign himself and was watching from an observation post at the front. No one spoke at Stahoulis', even when ordering an ouzo or buying a kilo of sugar as they waited for news. People pointed, nodded, paid, and retreated soundlessly. Everyone was thinking of a loved one. For thirteen days the place was packed as the battle continued. Both sides were reporting heavy casualties. Yiannis hospital was overflowing, men were waiting on stretchers in carts and in the fields. Finally, the Greeks prevailed. But even though Mussolini's assault was generally deemed a humiliating failure and thousands of Italians were returning home badly mutilated, thousands were left buried in Greece's frozen ground, thousands more were missing in action, and they calculated that forty thousand were now prisoners of war held by the Greek army, no one in Metsovo was celebrating. At Stahoulis', their heads were mostly downcast but for a few moments of great pride while listening as the wireless transmitted Winston Churchill's words.

"Today we say that Greeks fight like heroes, from now on we will say that heroes fight like Greeks."

But there were dark clouds everywhere. Although everyone went about their business in the usual manner, there was a renewed caution. No plans were being made. Increasingly scarce foodstuffs were being hoarded. Belts were being tightened, tempers were shortened and many usual pleasantries ignored as the villagers were preparing themselves for the inevitable German invasion.

12

In early April of 1941 there was still snow on the ground when Greek soldiers began streaming through Metsovo on their way home. Many of them had even thrown off their arms, too weak to carry them. They were hungry and tired. Many had died along the way. Papa Yiorgos and the other priests collected and stored the discarded arms in the ceilings of some of the smaller churches in the village. There was no hope of resistance. The Greek army was weakened and exhausted from the campaign to push the Italians further into Albania and was certainly no match for the Nazis, who had just invaded from Bulgaria. In two weeks the Greek air force had been completely destroyed. On April 26, the group at Stahoulis' learned from the wireless that the last British tank had pulled out of Athens, the Prime Minister had shot himself and the King and his closest advisors had fled to Crete with the nation's gold.

Again there was an overflow into the street as the men huddled around the crystal set and listened and spread the news to the ever growing crowd. The Greek army was encircled and cut off and several generals had surrendered. The Germans were marching into Athens. Men wept and women hugged their children.

Word quickly spread that the Italians had been given Epirus to govern and would be sending only a few *carabinieri* to oversee Metsovo. Of course the penalty for all forms of resistance would be death. Using a radio, breaking curfew, knitting socks or supplying food or shelter to the resistance were all capital offences. Before the occupiers arrived to disarm them, all the Greek soldiers had left Metsovo and Stahoulis' wireless was hidden in his blind room, under the floor of the kitchen. Every night at 8:00, a group would gather there, shoulder to shoulder, straining to hear the BBC in Greek:

"This is London, good evening…"

This broadcast was the principal source of news of the war in Metsovo. The news would then be spread to the others who were eagerly awaiting, yet another capital offence. Metsovo was once again under occupation.

For Maria Christina the longer days brought a promise of their own. Wearing her grandfather's glasses, she spent more time out of doors with Zoitsa, planting leeks and potatoes, the early beans, and corn, picking crayfish out of the grass, or dealing with shopkeepers. She not only counted her change before leaving a shop but she counted everything twice and twice measured every yard of fabric or kilo of grain. She was unconcerned about the Italians, who seemed more interested in being loved by the villagers than feared, although they were not above a rape or two. But they didn't seem to be attracted to skinny women with glasses and a bun. Maria Christina had become a younger Panorea. She hardly spoke to anyone about anything that could be mistaken for a pleasantry. Zoitsa was the sole exception. Her niece was now more precious to her than ever and for her she had endless time and patience.

With the change of season, the child, who had never been ill, developed a fever which no amount of mountain tea or wrapping in wet sheets seemed to cure. Her healthy appetite diminished until she was no longer interested in eating or drinking anything. Alarm bells were ringing in the minds of everyone in the house, and so the old doctor was summoned. Having gone into retirement when Yiannis had settled in Metsovo, Pandelis resumed his practice when Yiannis had gone off to war.

"Keep her as cool as possible and try to make her eat, and send for me if there's any change and I'll come by tomorrow" was all he could say.

Having tried every remedy known in Metsovo, each member of the Triantafyllou family searched for an explanation. Maria Christina was beginning to imagine herself an angel of death. Papa Yiorgos was convinced it was a biblical test for him: if after his wife and his favorite daughter, his only granddaughter was taken as well, would he still believe in His Goodness? And if he couldn't, would he remain a priest? Panorea thought they had been given the evil eye. Everyone was pouring their own anxieties onto the little girl who couldn't seem to get warm, yet was burning up and, other than pray for her, there was nothing they could do but watch the life in her grow dimmer.

On the fifth night of the fever, Maria Christina had a dream in which a beautiful woman in white, bathed in light, smiled at her and spoke in Vlach.

"I have heard your prayers."

The next day, Maria Christina learned from Lena that Yiannis would soon be coming home. Papa Yiorgos had received a letter from him. He was now in Ioannina and would be home in about two weeks. It was the answer to her prayers. Maria Christina knew it would strengthen the spirit of the three-year-old and immediately began pretending with the child that her Babá was walking through the door with his arms filled with firewood. Or that she was sitting on her Babá's shoulders as she picked almonds from the tree and dropped them into the sack he was holding out for her. Maria Christina filled her niece with these images and overnight her spirit was strengthened and the fever finally broke.

The first thing Zoitsa wanted to do was to go down to her father's vineyard and walk through their house, which was still just a shell with no roof, doors, or windows. Outside the entrance there was a table under which, on warm sunny days, Zoitsa would sit playing with her marbles, while her mother and father sat and had tea and olives. Zoitsa wanted to sit there and have tea and olives and, on the first warm sunny day, they did. Maria Christina pretended to be Yiannis and did quite a convincing impression, and so Zoitsa's appetite slowly improved and her complexion brightened. She couldn't wait to see her Babá. Couldn't wait. Maria Christina was excited to see Zoitsa with him. And her father. His presence would restore them. And yet, having been responsible for destroying his happiness, Maria Christina felt her very presence could only be torturous for him, as it was for her father, so she planned to remain out of sight as much as possible. And yet she couldn't help imagining him coming through the door or greeting her father or sitting by the fire. Each night before she went to sleep, her mind invariably wandered to thoughts of him, wondering what he was doing at that moment, and with whom. And she knew it was wrong and she couldn't help herself.

It was the custom for men in Metsovo, who had lost a wife, to wear a black vest and arm band, and not to shave for one year, which made Yiannis' face hidden inside his six month blonde beard look even more pale and drawn. For the new widower the path to Metsovo was long and sad, as each step brought him closer to his great loss. But the walk served its purpose. It was one of those moments in life when major adjustments had to be made, life reorganized, options considered. Perhaps he should take Zoitsa and go back to Athens. On the other hand, why not stay in the house with Papa Yiorgos until his own house was finished? Who in Athens would see to Zoitsa better than Papa Yiorgos and Panorea? There was Brooklyn, New York, his brother, who owned a business supplying butter and eggs and other specialty items to big hotels and restaurants. He had often written that he would welcome him as a partner. Yiannis had seen enough blood to last ten lifetimes, maybe butter and eggs and a whole new life. Maybe find a wife. Maybe. So many choices yet so few, and nothing that equalled a fraction of what he had lost.

Outside of Metsovo, he took a detour down to his vineyard. It was an oddity to have a house outside of the village, let alone in the middle of a vineyard, but it had been Yiannis' dream ever since he and his brother had travelled the Chateau regions of France. The vineyard lay in a valley below Agios Demetrius. Just to see it moved him deeply. To touch the vines. Walk through them. They represented life to him. Renewal. As he stopped and looked up at Agios Demetrius, he took a deep breath of the sweet air, then stopped mid breath as he heard voices. They seemed to be coming from the shell of his house. A girl's voice.

"Zoitsa!" he whispered. "And a man!"

The old work table was now inside the house and Maria Christina and Zoitsa were sitting having tea, when Yiannis quietly peeked around the door frame and saw Maria Christina pretend to twist her mustache like he was in the habit of doing, and raise her glass and speak with his same tone and cadence:

"May you have male children and female goats."

"May all Nazis go to the devil!" Zoitsa giggled as she twisted her fake mustache.

"May the Holy Virgin protect us!"

"Long live Greece!!" Zoitsa screamed.

And as the two clinked glasses and sipped their tea they heard the sound of laughter from outside the doorway as Yiannis stepped in, grinning, with tears in his eyes and his arms wide open. Zoitsa was frightened at first, not recognizing this bearded stranger.

"Moumou!"

"It's Babá!" Maria Christina quickly explained as Yiannis took the startled child in his strong hands and lifted her high in the air, face to face, until she could stare into his eyes and see past the beard. She screamed as she showered him with kisses. Was there ever anyone so happy to see another? She might never let go for fear he would leave her again. Yiannis held her tight and spun around on his heels and rocked her from side to side and held on as tightly as did his little girl. Maria Christina was embarrassed to be a witness to such an intimate reunion, so she turned away and started back to her house, disappearing from view before Yiannis even realized she had left.

Yiannis opened his pack and retrieved a small package wrapped in brown paper, which he gave to his wide-eyed daughter.

"For me?" she said, with a heart-breaking innocence.

Yiannis nodded, "I'm sorry I missed your birthday, my soul."

"Me, too, Babá."

As Zoitsa carefully opened the package, Yiannis sang the traditional birthday song.

"May you live Moumou for many years
Growing old with white hair
And spread your wisdom everywhere,

And wherever you go people will say,
'There walks a wise woman'."

Out of the wrapping came a small box with a painted pastoral scene. Zoitsa looked at it.

"Oh, Babá!"

"Open it."

She looked at him, could there be more? Her little fingers discovered the lid and, when she raised it, the box rang with chimes, playing a melody neither recognized, except to say that they both thought it was very beautiful.

On his way to the Triantafyllou house, Yiannis set his pack down at Agios Demetrius and gently disengaged from Zoitsa and set her on the stone bench outside to play with her music box, while he went inside to say a prayer. His heart was aching for his wife, though he dared not show it in front of Zoitsa. After kissing the icons, Yiannis stood, head bowed, and uttered a prayer of thanksgiving and asked for the strength to endure. When he stepped out of the church, Zoitsa jumped into his arms. Outside, his pack was gone and he caught a glimpse of Maria Christina carrying it on her back before she disappeared past the bell tower, hurrying home.

Perhaps no one other than Zoitsa was as happy to see Yiannis as Papa Yiorgos, who grabbed his walking stick and flat top hat and went down the street to meet him. He had so much to say to him. There was so much to talk about, but mostly it was going to be so nice to be able to sit by the fire and have a stimulating conversation. Yiannis looked thinner, smaller, paler than when he had left and his father-in-law could not help but wonder.

"Have you been eating well enough? Have you been working too hard? It all must have been so very difficult! What would you like? Shall we kill a lamb? Would you like to see where Matoula is buried now or later?"

"Later, Patera. When everyone is napping. And alone. Maybe with Moumou. Maybe first on my own."

When they arrived at the house, Panorea was warming a cheese pie on the fire, which she immediately abandoned to greet Yiannis with a surprisingly warm hug and an offer of her cheek to be kissed. It was so good to be home. It was so good to have him home. The energy suddenly changed. There was a light in the room. Papa Yiorgos had to guard against smothering the poor returning soldier with questions and offerings and pinches and gentle slaps. He was suddenly laughing easily at almost every little thing, while Yiannis wore a continual smile and ate Panorea's perfect cheese pie and drank the thin red wine. Papa Yiorgos talked about Hitler's strategy in the coming days, and how he had been so impressed with the Greek army's bravery and their knowledge of classic history that he had declared Greek soldiers should not be taken prisoner, and officers could keep their side arms.

"You kept your sidearm, didn't you?"

Yiannis nodded his head wearily as Papa Yiorgos continued.

"He's convinced we're the true descendents of Pericles and Leonidas."

"Then he should realize he'll not have an easy time in Greece."

When the meal was finished and it was time for the usual nap, Yiannis excused himself and took Zoitsa to pick narcissus. One might have thought it would have been a hard day when you had a three-year-old child holding onto your hand and chattering, and all you wanted to do was drink yourself to sleep. And yet, with a self-control he never realized he possessed, Yiannis walked the whole way holding the tender little hand as they talked, delighted to hear such full sentences, complete thoughts, coming from this small child.

At the cemetery, Yiannis and Zoitsa arranged the flowers on the grave. Then Yiannis took a breath and blessed himself three times, which Zoitsa immediately imitated. Yiannis started the prayer children say before going to bed, and was soon joined by his daughter:

"I kneel and cross myself
Arms for battle at my side
God's servant they call me
And I fear nothing
Arms for battle at my side."

Then Yiannis picked up Zoitsa and kissed her, "We'll come visit every day. But now I am very tired, my angel. I need to sleep."

With Zoitsa at his side, Yiannis slept deeply, drowned in the sweet smell of the innocence of his child and home. When he awoke, Papa Yiorgos was already sitting by the fire, anxious to share more of his views. And as the afternoon continued, Zoitsa finally separated from her father and sat on the carpet, playing the music from her box over and over again. When the daylight suddenly dimmed, it occurred to Yiannis that he hadn't seen Maria Christina since she disappeared behind the bell tower.

"And what has become of Maria Christina? Is she not happy to see me? I had only a glimpse of her today."

"Maria Christina has imposed a punishment on herself for disobeying me and causing us all such anguish."

"Why, what do you mean?"

Papa Yiorgos paused for a moment to stir the fire, "Maria Christina has committed the sin of hubris."

"Hubris? What are you saying? What punishment? Where is she?"

"She stays with the animals."

Yiannis' mouth opened in disbelief. Then he stood and looked down at his father-in-law, "Patera, may I speak with you in your room?" Without waiting for a reply he left.

When Papa Yiorgos entered, Yiannis was standing facing the fireplace, holding his pipe.

"I am so happy to have you home."

"With the animals! Maria Christina! And you allow this? You allow this?"

Papa Yiorgos stiffened, preparing to defend himself: "It was entirely her decision. I said nothing."

"How could you allow your daughter to live with animals? Is she an animal? Are you an animal?"

"I expressly forbade Maria Christina to be part of the resupply and she disobeyed me and--"

"And for this she lives with animals?"

"It was her decision."

"What she did, every woman in Greece was duty bound to do. You had no right to forbid her! Hubris? It wasn't hubris. You are not God. It was her duty. And she did it."

"I must say, I--..."

"Patera." Yiannis put his hands on the priest's shoulders and spoke quietly, "You think she was responsible for Matoula's death?"

It took Papa Yiorgos a long moment before he was able to utter his response.

"It seems obvious."

"Patera. Matoula was pregnant. In her last letter she told me she was not feeling well."

He had to pause a moment to choke back a sob. "She should not have gone. She was the one who committed the sin of hubris." Yiannis moved to the door then paused and turned. "If Maria Christina continues to live with the animals, I will have to take Zoitsa and leave this shame and return to Athens or go to America. I will not stay here."

Panorea had been listening from the doorway, Zoitsa from the carpet, both frozen, straining to decipher the words coming from Yiannis. Papa Yiorgos, unable to speak, just gave a nod.

As he left the room Yiannis turned to him: "Patera. In the end we do what we have to do, not what we want to do."

Papa Yiorgos needed to hear this. More than anyone he needed a shepherd. After Yiannis left, the old priest sat on the little bench in front of the fireplace, his head bowed, staring at the wool slippers on his feet.

13

The night Yiannis returned, Maria Christina had a dream that greatly troubled her. She saw Matoula lying in her coffin on the dining table in the winter room, Yiannis standing over her weeping. After a moment, he turned to Maria Christina, who was standing near him, and he put his arms around her and pressed her to him. In his anguish he showered her with hungry kisses. Closing her eyes she completely surrendered to him as he swooped her up and carried her to his bed. She had never imagined such bliss. When she opened her eyes to see him clearly for the first time, she could only see an infinite number of pinpoints of light against a backdrop of the darkest eggplant. And then the pinpoints of light disappeared and there was only black. She was blind. And for a long moment, as Yiannis continued showering her with his lust, she realized that what she had gained, even if only in her imagination, was so much less significant than what she had lost. Matoula had been her eyes.

Maria Christina awoke trembling with tears in her eyes. It took her a moment to orient herself. She was no longer sleeping with the animals but with Panorea on one of the platforms, while Yiannis slept with Papa Yiorgos on the other. Zoitsa had spent the night going from Yiannis to her and back again, then back again, then yet again. For the first time since her mother's death, she wasn't crying herself to sleep.

Maria Christina quickly and quietly climbed out of bed and put on her cloak and left the house in the dark and raced down to the cemetery, not knowing why or exactly what she was feeling other than a tremendous need to see her sister. Be near her. Even in the starless night Maria Christina could find Matoula's grave. Staring down at the marker a moment, she let out a cry. Small at first, and then another, louder, longer. And another, greater, until finally the gates opened and the sea of sorrow once again overflowed and poured through her eyes and heart and mouth and soul. How could she have coveted her husband? Her happiness! How could she so greedily have devoured her sister's love and given so little in return? She knelt before her sister's grave, aching for her forgiveness, and remained there weeping until the sun began to show itself over the eastern peaks. It was good and necessary for the young spinster. It would allow her to breathe once again. At least for a while. She might even be able to join the world. Perhaps even look another directly in the eye.

Once the villagers realized he had returned, the young doctor was immediately back at work. A great deal of his time was spent tracking down medical supplies, which were now extremely scarce. He was forced to use folk remedies to treat patients, donkey milk as an antibiotic, tying onions around the throat to ease swollen glands or garlic in heated olive oil for earaches. By post and telegraph he organized a network of trade between old medical school friends and army doctors. Any spare time was spent trying to find building materials to finish his house. It was now more pressing than ever. Without Matoula's influence, he began to see Papa Yiorgos differently and was feeling more and more uncomfortable in his presence and was especially concerned about his influence on Zoitsa.

Continuing to ponder his choices, he decided against uprooting his daughter from friends and family after having so recently lost her mother. Zoitsa was most comfortable with Maria Christina who, for now, was the best possible substitute for Matoula. He would simply not allow his father-in-law to care for her in any meaningful way. As for himself, he had made several good friends. And there was 'Matoula's Vineyard'. Soon he and his little girl would have their own home and in a year or so, he reluctantly would look for a wife. But for now he could see no one in the room but Zoitsa. He was looking for signs of Matoula, the way she smiled and cocked her head, the way she raised her nose when she said no. Even while engaged in conversation with Papa Yiorgos or Panorea, his gaze would wander to Zoitsa, and each time he recognized his wife in his daughter, it gave him a fleeting pleasure which was immediately followed by a deep dull pain. Yet the trade was worth it. Father and daughter were inseparable, except when Zoitsa left her father to sleep with her aunt, or when Yiannis had to see a patient, at which time he would leave her with Maria Christina.

Regardless of the demands on his time, Yiannis always found an hour or two each day to take Zoitsa to visit her mother. They would put fresh flowers on her grave and say the child's prayer, then linger on the ground and he would tell her stories about her mother, how she was the most beautiful woman in the village, stories when they first met, sometimes looking at the grave and speaking to her.

"Remember that, Mata?" or "Did you hear what your Moumou just said?"

In between the stories, Yiannis began teaching her English. First nouns. Stone. Flower. Then numbers. Then simple verbs. It became fun for them. Zoitsa in turn would teach Maria Christina the games and thereby the language.

Panorea was relieved to have Yiannis with them again, a captain in a sea of troubles and, finally, a conscience in the house. She couldn't do enough for him, constantly pestering the poor man, who was only interested in putting distance between them.

"Do you want some tea? Are you warm enough? Would you like a *tsipouro*? Shall I get you a blanket? Another pillow? Some pistachios? What if I shell them? I have some leek pie still warm. Would you like some with some wine? We still have some wine."

Maria Christina sensed his need to be left alone and finally came to his rescue by asking Panorea to teach her to weave. She wanted to finish the tapestry her sister had started. It had always been Maria Christina's responsibility to make the cheese, milk the cow and the goats, and collect the eggs. She had never been taught to weave or sew or do fine embroidery. She was never able to see well enough.

Quietly delighted, Panorea proceeded teaching her from the beginning, as if she were a child. The old spinster marvelled at how quickly Maria Christina learned the craft, even though she was slightly clumsy at first, having never developed her hand to eye coordination. Although Panorea had been her primary caregiver, Maria Christina's teacher had always been Matoula, so she and her aunt had never been so intimate. Thus, the tutorial every evening served to deepen their relationship. Panorea began to see Maria Christina as herself at age eighteen, in her loneliness and solitude, too old to hope and too young to stop dreaming. Maria Christina was also feeling closer to Panorea, welcoming each pitying smile as maternal.

Papa Yiorgos had aged a decade in one month. His beard was suddenly completely grey. A certain amount of life seemed to have drained away, leaving a weathered, shepherd's face worn out by circumstance, every line reflecting an old trouble. There was a slight stoop in his walk and a diminished nimbleness in negotiating the steps and cobblestones. As many times as Yiannis tried to explain to him, reason with him, argue with him, Papa Yiorgos still couldn't release his anger towards Maria Christina. He was no longer even sure why. But then, he wasn't aware his anger was slowly giving way to grief, something far more difficult to endure, and which was indeed affecting his health.

After a particularly troubling night, when Papa Yiorgos dreamed he was drowning Maria Christina while she was still an infant, he went to see Archimandrite Petsalis, known in the community for his wisdom and his excellent education. His was the main church, Agia Paraskevi, a handsome stone monument twice the size of Agios Demetrius. Located in the center of the village, it was frequented by the wealthy, the large sheep owners and other privileged families of Metsovo. Its much admired pastor had started his career as Papa Yiorgos' deacon, but now his rank in the ecclesiastic hierarchy was above the old priest. The Archimandrite, an intense, celibate priest, was delighted to see him and especially to be asked by Papa Yiorgos for his counsel. After retiring to the rectory, the tall, elegant Archimandrite served coffee while they discussed the status of the occupation. Then the younger priest clasped his hands on his lap, cocked his head and smiled with bright blue eyes.

"Now, tell me, Papa Yiorgi. What is troubling you?"

"Archimandrite, I have been wrestling with the notion of 'forgiveness' and I must confess I am puzzled. A parishioner has come to me with a story about betrayal which I must say, makes one shudder to hear, and yet the dear man seeks to forgive his transgressor. He says he understands why he was betrayed, but it doesn't seem to change the way he feels about it. The best he could say was that he was trying. I didn't know what to say to him. Do you have an answer?"

Papa Yiorgos bit the lower end of his lip, a habit of his when he was about to listen intently. The Archimandrite stared at the older man for a long moment, then breathed in deeply and stood and walked to the fireplace, where he thought for another moment while he stirred the fire with a poker. Then, setting the poker down, he leaned thoughtfully against the mantle then looked back and blinked several times.

"Forgiveness. Why our whole religion is based on the notion. It is most inspiring. Yet I believe only God can forgive completely. I think the best the rest of us can do is strive to approach His ideal. Through prayer and fasting, through understanding and analysis, slowly step by step, opening our hearts. The effort itself is an act of forgiveness."

Papa Yiorgos looked up at him. The Archimandrite smiled reassuringly. Papa Yiorgos nodded numbly, then politely thanked the Archimandrite. How could he have hoped this arrogant young goat might help him! Rank was certainly no substitute for wisdom! Pappou always said the Archimandrite was brilliant! Based on what? He was always an ass! He left the rectory at Agia Paraskevi filled with anger and disgust.

"Prayer and fasting! I'm fasting constantly! Everyone is! We're practically starving to death! He's not living in this world!" he blurted out loud as he stomped home in the fog back down to his little house. In the best of times, food in Metsovo was always scarce. Other than a breakfast of cracked wheat soup or hot water with bread and yogurt or feta cheese, for most people the mid day meal had to last through the rest of the day and night. Hungry children were told that it was unlucky to eat after dark. Someone might die. Meat was reserved for Christmas and Easter and only after fasts of forty days. Everyone also fasted every Wednesday and Friday. Thus, even though most of their time was spent husbanding animals, gathering food and water and wood, the inhabitants of this small mountain village lived a hard life that the Archimandrite evidently was spared.

Passing the small village cemetery, Papa Yiorgos paused at the entrance, gave an exasperated grunt, then crossed himself three times and stepped in. Lying side by side in the first row were Pappou and Matoula. Below the gravesite was a small building, the village ossuary, which housed his wife's bones as well as those of his father and mother and other relatives, including his grandmother, who had been especially dear to him. In fact all that was the joy in his life was now just remains within these cemetery walls.

No one was about, so the priest went inside and walked by its rows of wooden boxes, finally stopping at one that was at eye level. Beautifully carved, it held an old photograph of the deceased, a woman who greatly resembled Matoula, with her name and dates carved underneath:

Thimi Triantafyllou
1904-1923

The sight cut through the crust of an old wound. More than anyone, his wife Thimi was the greatest loss of his life. He almost never visited her. Seeing her picture and name always flooded him with memories of younger, better times filled with the hope and the resilience of youth, which now only reminded him of what was never to be. It had been eighteen years and still he could barely utter her name without choking. But now, this morning, he was drawn to her. The greatest loss leaves the greatest need. He took off his flat-topped hat and leaned his forehead against her picture and closed his eyes. He had been without her for so many years, he had long ago stopped missing their daily life together. What he missed now was that he hadn't been able to continue his life. Have more children. He missed the love of a woman and all that a good wife would have brought to him. Why had he even become a priest? To please his mother? She always told him it was a good job: it paid well, you had the respect of the community, you could have a family, you could have it all. And he did, until he lost Thimi and, according to the canons of the church, a priest could only marry *before* he was ordained. He could have left the priesthood and taken another wife, but how would he have earned a living? It was a silly law, but it was inviolate. He was trapped.

Outside the ossuary he paused in the thick wet air, suddenly having to catch his breath, when he heard Zoitsa's voice approaching the gate. As Zoitsa and Yiannis entered the cemetery, Papa Yiorgos stepped back inside. He didn't know why. Perhaps he didn't want to interrupt their time with Matoula, or maybe he was in such anguish he simply wasn't ready to be in anyone's company. He stood in the shadows just inside the door as father and daughter set fresh flowers in the vase by the grave and solemnly said the child's prayer.

The old priest remained hidden during the prayer and afterwards, when Zoitsa asked her father to tell her about the time he brought home a chicken and her mother asked him to kill and clean it. And Yiannis continued the story.

"I couldn't kill the chicken. I couldn't even take it out of the bag it was flapping around in!" Then he flapped his arms like a chicken "bach bach bach!"

Zoitsa threw her head back and laughed as her father continued.

"I was hoping your mother or your great aunt Panorea would come home and take over! I've never killed anything! Ever! I'm a doctor! I'm supposed to make everyone better!"

And on and on until Zoitsa was holding herself "No more! I can't breathe!"

It so reminded Yiannis of Matoula that he hugged his daughter so hard that it scared her a moment.

After they had left, the priest remained inside the ossuary another moment then he crossed himself three times and left, quickly blessing the graves of Pappou and Matoula as he hurried out of the cemetery and disappeared into the fog. One might have hoped he had just taken a small step on the road to forgiveness, but unfortunately the tears were bitter, not sweet.

And in fact, if it is true that anger feeds on itself, the priest left the cemetery angrier than when he arrived.

Maybe Pappou was right that the Lord never closed one door without opening another. New relationships were being formed around the hearth while old ones were unravelling. For the aging priest, however, the doors were only closing. He could feel the growing distance between himself and Yiannis and it made him ache. It had started the day Yiannis had come home, and it seemed as though there was nothing he could say or do to change it, even though he understood why. He understood many things. It just never seemed to help.

Later that evening, as Papa Yiorgos sat by the fireplace with Yiannis in silence and Zoitsa slept on her father's lap holding her music box, Panorea helped Maria Christina with the tapestry Matoula had been working on before she died. Having faithfully followed her sister's drawing, she was now tying the last of what looked like a random series of knots. Once tied, Panorea cut it away from the loom and turned it over to reveal a young woman with dark hair in a field of green, holding out a small blond baby to a tall blonde man with a mustache, a cow looking on in the background. It almost brought tears to Panorea's eyes. Maria Christina pressed her aunt for answers.

"Do you think it's good?"

"Mostly. And very often it's the mistakes that give the piece its uniqueness. Its charm."

She was referring to the fact that the man's mustache was not exactly under his nose but four threads to the left, and that the cow had only three legs.

"Why don't weavers get to see the right side as they work, the one without the threads and knots. Why do we only see the wrong side?"

"Because that is how we understand life" Panorea had a trace of a smile, as if she had been waiting her whole life for someone to ask her the question.

"During out lifetimes we do a lot of things and a lot of things happen to us. Often we don't know why. But when the Archangel Michael comes to take us from this earth, he turns the fabric of our life over, revealing the complete design, clear for the first time. It is only then that we understand."

Maria Christina's first thought was that it had been more words at one time coming from her aunt's lips than she had ever heard. Upon quick reflection she was touched by the thought. It made her wonder about her own life, and how much of the design was still unfinished. Matoula's frozen image still haunted her. As had occurred with her mother's works, some day there would be no chimney aprons or blankets, nothing done by Matoula's hand would remain. And wherever and whenever it occurred to her, sometimes while shopping, or seeing a weaving left to dry on a balcony, or even while washing clothes down at the river, it made her wish she could throw her head back and wail again. But she didn't. Some small voice always told her that this time she might never be able to stop.

When Yiannis was around, she could feel him reaching out to her but she would not allow his kindness to tempt her.

"We have to talk sometime" he said to her one day, on that rare occasion when they were alone.

"Yes, of course, we will talk, sometime" she replied as she scooped up a small barrel and backed out the door to the public fountain. Whenever they did speak, she used as few words as possible. Helpless in his presence, the only place she had ever felt comfortable with him was in her imagination. But since her erotic dream, she was determined to at least try and banish him, even from her mind. It was a promise she had made to her sister to gain her forgiveness.

Yiannis was certain she felt responsible for his wife's death, but thought it would serve no purpose to try and convince her she was wrong. He believed she was too filled with grief and guilt for reason to penetrate. The more kindly he treated her, the further she would retreat. As the weeks went by, the two continued to be intimate strangers, each thinking often about the other. Yiannis' thoughts were in no way romantic but filled with a sense of compassionate concern. The two were linked together by the untimely death of one they both loved very dearly and yet, underlying it all, felt but denied and therefore undetected, was a bond that was continuing to deepen between them.

14

Even though she was too afraid to look Yiannis in the eye, Maria Christina watched him compulsively when she could, becoming increasingly aware that he was even more worthy than she had ever imagined. She was also concerned about his health. He had been working himself tirelessly and had begun losing weight. Zoitsa told her that he was throwing up a lot.

"Not because he's sick. Babá told me he was just remembering the war."

Even before spring melted into summer, Yiannis and Zoitsa were spending more and more days and even nights in their shell of a house in the vineyard. When they slept away, it seemed an eternity until Maria Christina saw them again, and she now dreaded the day when their house was completed and Yiannis, with Zoitsa at his side, loaded a donkey with Matoula's and Zoitsa's dowry chests and led it down the mountain. It would leave the Triantafyllou home forever hollow. No child's voice. No men's voices against a crackling fire. No conversation at all. Silence. She would be knitting, embroidering, or weaving with Panorea's guidance. A low fire. Papa Yiorgos sitting, staring into the fire, waiting for those promised doors to open.

For Yiannis, the first night he slept with Zoitsa in their unfinished house was unbearable. Sitting by the empty fireplace drinking wine, the young widower was aching for a companion, but was still unable to see beyond the past.

In Yiannis' life, Maria Christina was barely more than a shadow, never around until he looked for her, then suddenly she was there. He became dependent on her to care for Zoitsa at a moment's notice, which made Maria Christina feel needed, wanted. It made the time she spent with Zoitsa playing "English" with her young tutor or telling her niece, whose memory was already beginning to fade, stories about her mother and Pappou, the most precious.

Within several weeks of Yiannis' return, an epidemic number of eligible young ladies in Metsovo had suddenly become ill and in desperate need of his services. Knowing in a few months Yiannis would be free to marry again, hearts were lifted in hope. He had proved himself very important to the community and was considered by all an ideal husband. Papa Yiorgos had already been subtly approached about possible matches for Yiannis, and each time he was stunned by the broker's insensitivity. As if he hadn't heard them, he redirected the conversation into the great losses they were all suffering. Losing Yiannis to another family through marriage was a possibility Papa Yiorgos wasn't yet prepared to consider.

Waiting for the opportunity to capture an equal in natural gifts was the unusually large Olimbi, the daughter of a wealthy sheep owner who lived in a mansion above the village square. A huge round woman of sixteen, Olimbi was certain that besides being rich she was uncommonly beautiful and, as a result, she was always cheerful and happy to a degree commensurate with her size. Not only did she never see the glass half empty, she never even saw it as half full. For her it was always brimming.

"Olimbi, did you hear about the two Italian soldiers who followed some of the girls into Agios Nicolaos Monastery? Katsio, the nun, was screaming while they were taking my young cousin

Katerina away, but she managed to hook herself around the leg of a loom and wouldn't let go in spite of the severe beating she was receiving. They broke her arm but she still wouldn't let go."

"Imagine that! Ha-ha he-he ha-ha! Good for her!"

Her two-octave-laugh could be heard everywhere. As a neighbor, it was one of those sounds to which you become so accustomed you have to concentrate on listening for it in order to hear it. But six months after Matoula's death, it was heard for the first time all the way down the mountain and into the Triantafyllou house, where it pierced the three-foot thick stone walls and sounded to the family like a flock of geese had nested in the eaves.

Unlike the eligible girls who were fainting and dying of fevers, Olimbi's battle plan was to orchestrate a web of joy and beauty. She began slowly. One light extended laugh as she passed the house on her way to light a candle at Agios Demetrius in the morning and another the next afternoon. Song like. Bird like. To create a yearning. There were also the chance meetings, the comings and goings, always elegantly dressed and carrying something enticing, flowers, scented candles, candies. In Yiannis' life she seemed to be turning up more and more, and there was a naughtiness in her eye that didn't escape him. But Yiannis, ever the gentlemen, completely ignored her and indeed went out of his way to avoid her, even to looking over his shoulder and around corners and peeking out of windows to see if it was safe to approach or leave a house.

Frustrated by her failure to attract even a fleeting glance from the good doctor, Olimbi suddenly set upon him on the wet stone steps of Agios Demetrius, and purposely slipped and fell into his unwilling arms, then bounced off and fell down a step or two and remained a sprawling laughing mass, waiting for him to help her up and then to examine her for any possible bruises. Yiannis yanked her to her feet. She was surprisingly light, he thought. Then he looked squarely at her.

"You look fine, Olimbi. You'll excuse me but I have an emergency."

With that he ran up the steps and didn't stop until he was in the forest above the village, where he sat under a beech tree and wept. He knew every eligible girl in Metsovo and there wasn't one who even vaguely interested him. And he didn't know how, at this point in his life, without uprooting his young daughter and moving back to Athens, he would ever find a woman with whom he would want to share his life and his child. Should he sacrifice the rest of his life for Zoitsa, for the sake of one child? And as he sat and looked down at the village, at its smallness, it's isolation between huge snowcapped mountains, he was filled with anxiety. He knew there was no certainty in life. The world was in such disorder one could only concentrate on the day. On the hour. The larger picture was too terrifying to contemplate, and for all he knew this very moment might be better than any he would ever know again, and so within the hour he was sitting with Zoitsa next to Matoula's grave teaching his daughter the word 'smile'.

A woman with less self confidence would have been deterred by the lack of success of her attempted seduction, but for Olimbi it somehow seemed to further obscure reality. Concluding that she had overwhelmed Yiannis with her charms, she decided to make herself less visible, less available. And so all but Olimbi's musical laugh retreated into the background of Yiannis' life, as he continued looking for materials for his practice and his house. The *carabinieri* were now calling on him with different physical complaints. He would treat them as he would any patient, which endeared him to them, which in turn helped him acquire building and medical supplies, but ever so slowly and in very small amounts.

For many, life in Metsovo in the summer of 1941 began to promise a breath of normalcy, but for those who had lost someone or something, the more things came to life and burst into flower the more they were reminded of their loss.

Costas Stahoulis, unhappily, was one of those unlucky enough to return with less than when he led the dance gracefully in the square at his going-to-war party. It had happened in Albania in the middle of the day. Yiannis had just finished amputating the arm of a boy who wasn't old enough to shave when they brought in three men. One of them was Stahoulis, who was feverish, standing with the aid of two crutches. Stahoulis was so happy to see Yiannis he burst into tears. Yiannis would give him the best of care. It didn't take Yiannis more than a glance to know what lay ahead. The black skin, the lesions. Frostbite. Even before Yiannis had given him a hug and kissed his cheek, he tried to imagine Stahoulis without his right leg. The one he led with and twisted and stamped when he danced. The one that booted some undesirable out of his *pantopolio*. The one he took for granted would always be there. To see his friend so ill and frightened was almost too much for Yiannis to bear, so he leaned into Stahoulis' ear and spoke softly.

"You are going to have to give up that leg, probably up to the knee, do you know that?"

Stahoulis dropped his head and nodded.

"I will make all the arrangements for the surgery and afterwards I will be here and I will make certain you get the best of care. But I am going to ask my colleague to do the procedure. I'm sorry. It would pain me too much to be able to give you my best work. Do you understand, Costi? Do you understand?"

Stahoulis gripped his hand around Yiannis' neck and brought him close to his face and kissed him on the cheek. Neither ever mentioned it again. Having left dancing with a handkerchief in one hand and a *tsipouro* in the other, Stahoulis was once again behind the counter in his *pantopolio*, walking back and forth without a crutch, trying to get accustomed to his new wooden leg.

As the summer ended in Greece, a frightening reality was becoming apparent: because of the fighting none of the commercial growers had been able to plant the basic crops. Even in the best of times Greece only grew forty per cent of its food. Now, between a total sea blockade by the British and the Italians having no surplus, the scarcity of food and goods became so acute that common thievery was becoming rampant.

As the days shortened into fall an early winter followed, thousand of Greeks starved to death. In the early mornings, in Athens, trucks would pick up the bodies of those who died during the night, while skeletal children stepped over them on their way to school. Epidemics of cholera, diphtheria, and typhus broke out, spread by lice. Mass graves were dug in the gardens of the royal palace.

Unlike people in the cities, who had no gardens but had large contingents of soldiers to feed, inhabitants of rural villages in the mountains, like Metsovo, had only a few *carabinieri*, and small gardens which served them well. Due to Yiannis' foresight, the Triantafyllous were also still able to draw from the sacks of corn, rice, and wheat he had hidden in the blind room. But for most of the village, there was no wheat, no bread, no rice, no oil or salt to be bought. But at least they were assured of eating, even if the fare was meager, so when the threat of famine in the cities had first surfaced, Yiannis wired his parents in Athens, begging them to come to Metsovo if they were in any distress. But it seemed they would rather starve than forgive, because the next day there was a return telegram from them with the message that they had no son.

In the village, commerce had simply stopped. Tinkers couldn't get copper, Costas Stahoulis' brother, Spiros, couldn't get shoe leather, Saul and Elias Chaimaki had no dry goods, Papa Yiorgos couldn't even get candles or incense or oil for the church lamps and was now using butter. Parishioners had stopped dropping coins in the candle collection box and were depositing buttons instead. All the coffee houses in the village were filled with men with nothing to do and nothing to drink but mountain tea. And although credit was still available, there were no goods to buy or sell. Occasionally, Yiannis would bring home a few eggs or some potatoes given as payment by a grateful patient.

On the anniversary of Matoula's death in December, all of the black rugs and wall hangings, blankets and pillows were replaced with new fabrics in the traditional deep natural colors which helped lift the aura of gloom from the rooms. The memorial service at Agios Demetrius was very well attended, unlike that of Pappou. As he read the prayers, it made Papa Yiorgos sad that the man who had so influenced him was so easily forgotten, that all of the old people were so quickly erased, and now that he was one of the old people he, too, would soon cease to exist even in anyone's memory. Yiannis kept his head bowed and spent the whole time wiping tears from his cheeks. Maria Christina sat among the family with her arm around a nervous Zoitsa, absently patting her niece's arm trying to quiet her. She hardly heard the words her father was intoning. Her thoughts wandered instead to what some of the women had been talking about recently on the resupply treks. 'Equality' was the word most often repeated. Equal rights for women, who were presently second-class citizens and were treated in fact as if they were forever children. It was patently unfair and it was an argument that was becoming increasingly popular among the women in many of the surrounding villages. What was needed was a revolution.

"After the revolution women will work side by side with men."

"Women will drive cars, fly airplanes, be lawyers, they would even have their own money."

These were arguments Maria Christina found appealing. She couldn't understand why women were treated as inferiors. There had been great world leaders throughout history who had been women. Why should the Greeks discount half their population because of their gender? She also thought it outrageous the rich could continue to accumulate more wealth while the poor were so neglected.

After the service, she discussed the idea with Lena as they walked arm in arm in the procession back to the house. She was not surprised to discover that Lena agreed and that most of the people in their neighborhood sympathized with the Communists.

"Pappou thought women were in fact superior" Lena reminded her.

"How could Yiannis be so against the Communists?" Maria Christina paused at the gate to their house, "He even thought a dowry was unfair to women."

"It's all so confusing" Lena agreed. "No wonder your grandfather chose this time to leave."

Later at the house, after Yiannis lowered Zoitsa from his shoulders and everyone assembled greeted him with "Eternal be her memory", he hiked to the highest peak of Katara where he sat for the rest of the day. As the sun began to set, he climbed back down. When he arrived home, he showered and shaved his face clean and trimmed his mustache. His whole being felt lighter. Refreshed. Renewed. He would start a new life in the morning. Then he went to sleep and didn't open his eyes until dawn the next day. He lay a half hour or more, torn between the two worlds, old and new. He knew that once he buried Matoula away in his mind, she would remain locked away forever. But he had loved his wife so deeply, he didn't want to let her go. Perhaps he should never remarry. Perhaps. As the thought lingered in his head, it gave him the peace of mind he needed to climb out of bed and begin another day.

15

The smell of wild hyacinth filled the air before the winter of 1942 had completely vanished. For Maria Christina it couldn't have come too quickly. It meant that she could take the tapestries off the windows and doors and convert the winter room for the summer. But more importantly she could now plant every inch of black dirt they owned and watch as the spinach, pumpkin, and zucchini gradually grew as well as the carrots and scallions she planted in the pots usually reserved for flowers. The Triantafyllou household had managed to weather the bitter season the way custom had wisely dictated, a string of religious celebrations to keep the spirit strong, Christmas, St. Basil's Day, The Epiphany. Then the personal celebrations, Yiannis' name day, Zoitsa's fourth birthday.

In Athens, carts were still collecting the dead bodies in the morning as the shortage of food continued to be critical. A puppet government had been formed, but most of the Greeks looked more favourably on roaming bands of former soldiers who were raiding government warehouses, distributing food, destroying tax and debt rolls, interrupting supply lines and attacking German troops. In heavy reprisals, the Germans burned down entire villages and brutally tortured and massacred the inhabitants. Their tactic worked. The raids quickly dissipated.

But the resistance continued to grow. Armed groups were secretly forming in the mountains, and a national underground intelligence organization of women was passing on more and more information to the armed groups and to the Allies. It was formed in Athens shortly after the occupation by a mother of seven children, Lela Karayianni, and named 'Bouboulina', in honor of the great heroine of the Greek war of Independence from the Turks. The group began by helping allied soldiers, separated from their units with needed refuge and support. Ultimately, it became so effective at intelligence it had moles in all of the German and Italian high commands.

Although there were only one hundred and fifty members, the national intelligence organization's web covered the entire nation, even reaching as far as Metsovo, where one member had interviewed and recruited Maria Christina over a year ago. She would never learn how or why she had been chosen, and even wondered if it had been Matoula they intended to recruit. But at the close of the forty-day memorial service commemorating her sister's death at Agios Demetrius, Maria Christina was seated in the front row with the family accepting sympathy from friends and neighbors, when a woman, whose face was obscured by a veil, took her hand and slipped a note into it, then touched her cheek and whispered.

"Life to us."

On the way home, Maria Christina discreetly opened the note:

"If you love your country meet me tomorrow at sunset in the church courtyard."

Maria Christina could neither sleep nor nap in anxious anticipation of the meeting, and the next day, as the sun began to move towards the peaks of Katara, she slipped out of bed and out the door and hurried to her father's church. The woman was already waiting, sitting on a bench under a huge sycamore. Wearing a shepherd's cloak with the hood raised over her head, the woman spoke just above a whisper with a delicacy and refinement Maria Christina had never encountered before. As they sat and talked, Maria Christina realized that the woman spoke Greek like Yiannis, which meant she was probably Athenian. Her cloak had opened slightly, and Maria Christina could see she was wearing fine European clothes and she was rather slim. As she spoke about the importance of secrecy, it occurred to Maria Christina once again how little of the world she had seen and how much more she longed to know. Later the woman's face would fade, but for Maria Christina the image of a slim, self-assured, gentle woman would remain forever as a model for herself.

It would be Maria Christina's only face to face encounter with her recruiter. They communicated through written messages left in a small brown envelope glued to the back of the icon of Agios Demetrius in the upstairs gallery of the church. Maria Christina didn't know if she was in contact with anyone else in Metsovo or if, indeed, it was even the same woman with whom she exchanged notes.

Although everyone in the village knew secret organizations existed, no one at the time had heard of Bouboulina, so there were no bows to be taken, no special privileges for risking her life for men she didn't know, foreigners. Her first charge had been a pilot from New Zealand on his way to Igoumenitsa, where he would be smuggled by boat to Egypt. After insisting on leaving before Maria Christina thought he was ready, she walked with him and, when he became too weak to continue, she carried him on her back through the snow and delivered him to the port and onto a deserted fishing boat named *En Plo*. She now had an English flier living in a shepherd's summer cabin in the mountains. Each night she would bring him cornbread, cheese, water, two prunes and either a walnut or a piece of dried apple together with news of the war in the little English she knew. He was still too ill to be moved, and all of her home remedies had failed to improve his deteriorating condition, so Maria Christina finally had no choice but to finally ask Yiannis to attend to him. When the flier started to recover, he began calling her "My Angel" and told Yiannis how beautiful he thought she was. Maria Christina laughed and blushed and told Yiannis he would no longer be needed.

Later, as she lay in bed, she wondered if the Englishman wasn't delirious. Would he think that the mysterious woman was attractive? Would Pappou? Her grandfather had never lied to her about anything else. Could he have been telling the truth?

The healthier the flier became, the more he behaved like Pappou, kissing her hand and telling her how her lips reminded him of one of England's finest pink roses, "The Scarborough Fair". His manner reminded her so much of her grandfather that she allowed herself that moment's enjoyment, knowing that it also gave the poor flier pleasure to be able to flatter a young spinster. When the flier was well enough to travel, Maria Christina borrowed a donkey and a cart and took him to Igoumenitsa under a load of hay. As she watched him board the *En Plo* and blow her a kiss goodbye, she felt a little sad. She would miss his courtliness.

By now she had fully accepted her lot and decided that in order to help repay her great debt and to make her life worth continuing, she would devote herself to the service of others. Women from the village were now including Maria Christina in all community efforts they previously had denied her. Besides her astonishing ability to endure physical hardship, the other women were struck by how intelligent she was. The many hours spent reading with her grandfather had broadened her view of the world and sharpened both her wit and her judgement, and when questions were asked in any group, almost to a woman, everyone would look to Maria Christina to hear what her response might be.

Twice a week Maria Christina would hike with different groups of young women to the village of Koutsoufliani, three hours by foot. It was the nearest village in Albania after the Katara pass. There they would trade dowry weavings, clothes, silver, anything of value with the inhabitants for wheat, corn, rice and other necessities. Having given up all hope of marriage, Maria Christina traded her own dowry, twenty of the most excellent blankets, twenty-four cushion covers, five thin blankets, and ten rugs of various sizes, two even woven by her mother before she was born. She also took things for neighbors and relatives, hardly ever carrying anything back for herself, and only occasionally something for the house. Their sacks in the secret room were still one-quarter full, and there were so many in Metsovo who were in dire need. Her original intent had been to do penance, but she soon realized the pleasure she received far outweighed the labor. To walk in the fields among the yellow broom and rose trees and to look down for the first time and see for herself that every few days a new variety of flower presented itself, followed the next by dozens more, some so tiny, yellow, purple, orange, white, flowers she had never been able to see before, and the wild pansies yellow, white, aubergine, and here an acre of blue forget-me-nots and there a sea of yellow and white narcissus swaying with the wind. It was like witnessing the unfolding of a most divine delicate weaving, all of which inspired in Maria Christina a growing sense that she was part of a larger landscape, and in some way she, too, was beginning to unfold, and her purpose was only beginning to reveal itself. In the midst of the rubble that was her damaged soul, a seed of hope had somehow survived and taken hold and, like a vine reaching for the sun, it was growing slowly yet determined, winding its way out of the darkness.

After several months of eating with the family and several more without the strain of having to resupply the army, Maria Christina had begun to gain weight and, together with the new muscle formed by her labor, her body now resembled that of a long distance runner. Her face had also changed, her cheekbones weren't as hollow, and Yiannis thought to himself that she had grown an inch or so taller.

For Yiannis, the sudden intrigue surrounding Maria Christina was a most welcome diversion in his life. He was not only delighted to help but, even more, he was becoming increasingly curious about his sister-in-law. Although she swore she wasn't a member of any secret organization, according to the Englishman, she obviously seemed to be a member in good standing of some kind of underground group. Yiannis was now keeping a closer eye on her, sleeping with one eye open, watching for the nights she would wait for Zoitsa to leave her side, then slip out of bed and out the door, leaving Papa Yiorgos snoring, Panorea dreaming, and him wondering what this unlikely freedom fighter was up to. And now, when walking to his land or examining a patient, Yiannis would sometimes suddenly think of Maria Christina and smile.

One morning, after having been out all night attending a sick child, Yiannis opened the door to the house and was startled to hear a laugh from inside that sounded exactly like Matoula. It was Maria Christina reacting to Zoitsa tickling her, and it so startled him that he couldn't speak for a moment. Echoes of his wife were everywhere, reminding Yiannis of his loss: in his daughter, in Maria Christina, and Papa Yiorgos, the author of many of the family mannerisms, even in Panorea. Later that morning he would realize that, by being bound to this family, he would never be healed. But by early afternoon he realized that this was as it should be and once again he thought of Maria Christina and it made him smile.

16

The first time Maria Christina saw the Italian soldier, she had just returned from Koutsoufliani with two large sacks on her back and was distributing the grains to those whose goods she had traded. The soldier was a mid-sized, swarthy looking, ruggedly handsome man leaning against the wall outside the telegraph office. He was smoking when he saw Maria Christina. Looking her up and down, he flicked his cigarette and stepped in front of her.

"Want to fuck-fuck?" he tried in Greek as he smiled and rubbed his crotch.

Maria Christina looked at him with narrowed eyes and a curled lip and pushed her way past him. The soldier laughed and watched her continue at a hurried pace until she disappeared, then went back inside.

Later that week, as she approached the telegraph office on her way to the central market, he stepped outside and once again stood in her way and began calling after her, as if she was a chicken:

"Fuck-fuck-fuck-fuck-fuck! Fuck-fuck-fuck-fuck-fuck!"

Maria Christina turned on her heels and walked back down the mountain with him following a short distance behind, continuing his call until she stepped inside the gate to her courtyard and slammed it shut, locked it, and ran into the house and slammed the door and went directly to the kitchen and took hold of a chopping knife. She did not put the knife down until the door opened a half hour later and Papa Yiorgos entered and poured himself some tea.

The next time she had to go to the central market she wore Panorea's old clothes and took a different route, walking with a stoop resembling her father's, and covered her face so you could only see a piece of her glasses. She also took the knife. She didn't meet the soldier this time. After two more outings without incident, she decided perhaps he had left Metsovo and she probably didn't need the knife any longer. Yet she preferred to err on the side of caution and tied it to her apron under her cloak.

Holding a basket containing a piece of leek pie, a small keg of water, a tin of tea, and two prunes in one hand, Maria Christina had the other free to hold Zoitsa's hand as they walked down the mountain to Yiannis' land, where he was building a corral for a horse he intended to buy. When they arrived, Yiannis was sitting under the oak beside the house. He grinned when he heard his daughter's voice then watched as Zoitsa clung to Maria Christina's cloak and wouldn't let go as she set the basket on the table. She was begging Maria Christina to stay this once and share their mid morning snack. Upon hearing his daughter's plea, Yiannis insisted Maria Christina remain, and they could all walk back together.

"Just for a moment. To quiet Zoitsa." She sat at the table on the edge of the chair and unloaded the basket. "I still have much to do."

Yiannis smiled "I can imagine."

"We all do what we can. Your grapes seem to be growing nicely."

"Thanks to your care while I was away."

"Thanks to your friend, Stahoulis, who came home just in

time to supervise." She never looked directly at him but mostly watched Zoitsa playing under the table with her marbles "I knew nothing about tending vines."

Neither Yiannis nor Maria Christina, who had never been alone like this, found the moment of silence that followed uncomfortable but, rather, each took the opportunity to sense the other's simple presence.

Zoitsa loved being with the two of them. It was like having a mother and a father again. She felt safe. Happy. The world made sense again. She listened attentively to the conversation as it resumed. The talk remained simple and cordial. The child understood almost everything they were saying and was afraid to interrupt for fear of giving Maria Christina an excuse to leave. She especially loved how Maria Christina could make her father laugh. She hadn't heard him laugh in a long time. She also loved hearing them talk about her strong will and curious mind. And when Maria Christina joked that she demanded almost constant attention "Like tending to a fire in the wool closet" her father laughed especially hard and the two heard a titter from beneath the table, which made them both laugh even harder. It was during the short silence that followed, when Yiannis looked at her and smiled, that she felt rapturous and then suddenly became overwhelmed by a sense of shame. Her cheeks reddened then the color drained from her face as she quickly rose from the table, excused herself, bid Zoitsa goodbye and hurriedly left. Zoitsa thought it was naughty of her aunt to leave so abruptly, and without even kissing her good-bye.

The soldier was sitting on a low limb of a huge sycamore at the edge of the vineyard when Maria Christina passed underneath, muttering to herself. He jumped down and covered the startled girl's mouth before she had a chance to cry out.

"I want to fuck you" he said calmly in her ear as he put his other hand between her legs, rubbing her coarsely while backing her up against the huge trunk of the tree.

"Fuck yourself in hell!" Maria Christina whispered in the soldier's face, whose whole being swelled with surprise when she plunged her knife through her cloak and into his stomach, then sliced upwards with all the rage she had locked away, thrusting so hard that his toes were no longer touching the ground. She stood holding him there, staring into his frozen eyes, before she stepped back and he fell to his knees. She spat on the ground.

"Achriste." Trash.

Then she dropped the knife, turned and ran without looking back until she closed the gate to her house. After standing in the courtyard for a few moments, shaking and listening for footsteps, she took two large buckets and raced to the public fountain nearby. Grateful that no one was around to notice her blood stained cloak, she filled the buckets, then carried them back to the house where she poured the water into the barrel shower. Still shaking, she stepped inside the shower in her clothes, pulled the release, and let the icy cold water pour down on her until all the blood had washed away, all the while fighting the urge to vomit. Then she rinsed out her hair, peeled off her wet clothes and covered herself with a thin towel before stepping out of the shower.

Yiannis would always remember the moment he opened the gate to the Triantafyllou's house and saw Maria Christina as if for the first time: her long shapely legs, the towel clinging to her small waist, wringing out her long chestnut hair. Zoitsa screamed when she saw her and before Maria Christina could wipe her eyes enough to see, Yiannis was already on his way back towards his vineyard. On their way home, he had spotted the dead soldier and had blocked Zoitsa's eyes so she wouldn't see, pretending it was a game. When he arrived back at the soldier's body, he knelt down and checked for any vital signs.

"This man hasn't been dead one hour" he said out loud.

The bloody chopping knife was nearby. He picked it up and examined it.

When Yiannis delivered the dead soldier to the *carabinieri*, his comrades were angry but not surprised. He had been lewd and insulting to many of the village women. Probably an honor killing. Someone's outraged brother or husband. Yiannis told them there was no weapon by the body. Two *carabinieri* walked back with Yiannis to the scene and found nothing but a pool of blood where the soldier had stood and then fallen. The *carabinieri* brought in dozens of men for questioning. Evidently they had never heard that there were no women in Metsovo.

Being an Athenian, Yiannis was not one to regard heft as beauty and, having enjoyed a glimpse of such a fine female form who was, after all, his sister-in-law, he not only felt embarrassed for her, but a sharp sense of guilt in what he at first regarded as a betrayal of his wife. And yet the image of Maria Christina, which only lasted a second, would stay with him, creeping into his consciousness at the oddest times, like when he was with a patient or praying in church.

The next day at dinner, Maria Christina was stunned to see the same knife in Panorea's hand when it was time to cut the cheese pie. No one else seemed to think it was unusual, but they did think it odd when Yiannis burst out laughing for no apparent reason.

17

At the beginning of June, the hard-drinking retired colonel of the Republican Army, Napoleon Zervas, returned to Epirus where he was born. Word spread quickly throughout the region that the well-loved Zervas was forming a guerrilla force. Fearless but not flawless, the card playing *bon vivant* had the ability to create the spark that could ignite an armed resistance movement. Of course one of the first he approached in Metsovo was Yiannis, the seasoned front line surgeon. The meeting had taken place in a temporary camp Zervas had set up at Katara, where he was combing the neighboring villages for recruits. Yiannis told the swarthy, stocky colonel he would think about it. And he did, although he didn't discuss it with anyone. He would have appreciated Maria Christina's thoughts on the resistance, but after their tea she had become like a shadow again and he hardly ever saw her, and never alone.

In July, the Germans ordered the Jewish men of Thessalonica, each identified by the Star of David sewn onto their garment, to assemble in Freedom Square where they were beaten and humiliated. The next afternoon, Yiannis stopped by Stahoulis' *pantopolio* and, after a *tsipouro* or two, Costas talked non-stop about the incident, insisting that, after the Jews, the Vlachs would be next.

"You're being unreasonable" Yiannis told him. "The Nazis consider the Vlachs their friends."

As if he hadn't heard a word, Stahoulis continued "The only chance we have is with Zervas. He's independent. Nobody's puppet. Not beholden to any foreign influence like the Communists." Tears formed in his eyes "I just wish I could join him myself and punish the bastards. Not just the Nazis, Yiannis. We also need to beat these Communist bastards." Costas slapped the table "Or we'll just be trading one bastard for another."

Costas' passion resonated with Yiannis, who had already decided that joining the resistance was his duty and inevitable. It was a question of when and perhaps Costas influenced the timing. Even though Yiannis had been home for over a year, it felt like only a few months to him. There was so much to do, and there was Zoitsa who was growing so quickly, and there might even be a new beginning to his life. Couldn't he stay just a little while longer?

But the Communists already had a number of guerrilla bands in the mountains and a underground apparatus in place. By the end of August, Zervas' guerrilla force numbered almost two hundred and fifty men, and they desperately needed doctors. Maria Christina was already part of a group that was walking from Koutsoufliani to Zervas' main camp twice a week with supplies. And as each day passed, Yiannis was feeling more and more guilty that, while Maria Christina was risking her life, he was going about his days uninvolved in the struggle. He also feared she would regard him as a self-involved coward at the very time her esteem was becoming increasingly important. So, with a heavy heart, he decided that after the grape harvest he would join Zervas.

"How sad" he often said to Costas, "to waste life on war."

Yiannis kept his decision to himself and tried to make the harvest as much of a celebration as possible. One huge wooden tub was filled with grapes and every friend and family member stepped and danced in the tub for four days. The wine, which they would all share next year, was stored in six large oak barrels in the cellar of Yiannis' house.

Zoitsa was crushed when her father told her he was leaving again. She asked the questions children have been asking for millennia, although she already knew the answers: "Why." "Is there no other way?" "Do you have to?" "Can I come with you?" Each answer led to another question, to another answer, to a tantrum, until the night in the courtyard when Maria Christina, with tears in her eyes and her hand over her mouth to keep from crying out, was standing in front of Papa Yiorgos and Panorea, watching Yiannis, on one knee, wipe away the child's bitter tears with his handkerchief, trying to explain one last time.

"It is for you that I do this, Moumou. One day you will understand."

Then Yiannis kissed his trembling daughter on the forehead, and gently pushed her into Maria Christina's arms. After a sigh, with his walking stick in one hand and his pipe in the other, Yiannis waved goodbye to the others.

After everyone started back inside, Maria Christina stayed behind a moment to savour the last trace of him, the click of his stick against the stones as he proceeded up the dark street. Maybe now, she hoped, she would stop being preoccupied with him.

18

The day after Yiannis left to join Zervas, everyone in the Triantafyllou household was listless and quiet. Even Afendoula gave little milk that morning and almost none in the afternoon. No enticement by her cousin Sophia to go out and play could distract Zoitsa from lying on the platform with her thumb in her mouth, staring out the window, listening to her music box.

"Don't regret what has befallen you, think of what hasn't" Papa Yiorgos told no one in particular as he sat looking out the same window into the street. It was a maxim he had learned from the old candle lighter, Tatamare. Lately, he had been spending more and more time with the retired shepherd, who now appeared to the priest to have a saintly aura. He had decided Tatamare was a living example of a man who had completely surrendered to God's Divine Plan, and he was now convinced that it was the shortest path to earthly happiness and the surest way to heaven. And so the priest was, on the one hand, desperately seeking to surrender himself and, on the other, so tightly strung that everyone in the family was afraid any little upset might break the thread, so they tiptoed around him, fearful they might be the catalyst.

The old shepherd always treated the pastor with reverence,

believing that a priest was a calling from on high and not merely a job. In spite of the fact that Papa Yiorgos always thought he had become a priest for practical reasons, Tatamare convinced him one morning that it could not have been his decision. It was the first of the month and, as was customary twelve times a year, the priest would go to each house in his parish to bless it and, in return, receive a small donation.

As they walked up past the bell tower of Agios Demetrius to start their rounds, the old shepherd made an argument so simple it was decisive:

"No shepherd would let the sheep decide for themselves who to put a bell on. Nor would he let a sheep put a bell on himself. Only the shepherd decides which of his sheep he can trust to lead his flock down the correct path. So it is with the Good Shepherd. It is He who decides which of His sheep should wear the bell."

Papa Yiorgos looked at him with wide-eyed fascination for a long moment as he revisited the logic of the argument over and over in his mind, until he suddenly burst into tears. Tatamare immediately understood how profound the moment was for the old priest. He had given him an insight, one he had never grasped before. He had been ordained by the Lord Himself.

From that day Papa Yiorgos began to think of himself as the sheep with the bell, singled out by God to lead His flock on the path of righteousness. More and more he identified his voice with the bell and adjusted his tone to what was appropriate to the moment, speaking to the world sometimes in deep full bell sounds, and other times in soft light tinkle tones. His services became more thoughtful and heartfelt. He was even moved to tears when reciting passages dealing with Christ's passion and death. His rich baritone voice, always the best of the village priests, had now become even more full-throated and soulful. People started coming simply to hear the age-old Byzantine melodies sung to perfection. Soldiers home from the war, shepherds who had lost their flocks, men who never went to church were now attending his services, praying for the safety of their families. And so the day after Yiannis' departure, which he now viewed in a positive light as simply another part of the Divine Plan, the priest's mind was filled with uplifting thoughts.

Agios Demetrius' name day, October 26th, was the following Saturday, and Papa Yiorgos went about the preparations with a renewed vigor. His parishioners were equally energized by their pastor's soaring spirit as he enlisted every woman he came across to help decorate the church or prepare the spoon sweets of rose petals and nuts, and every man to volunteer to play his instrument, or otherwise participate in the celebration and dance in the courtyard after the mass. It was a rousing success. Maria Christina and Zoitsa attended with Panorea, but neither spinster danced, while Zoitsa sat on Maria Christina's lap the whole time, her head against her aunt's breast, sucking her thumb, indifferent to the festivities.

The elation from the celebration lingered for days among the villagers. There was a renewed optimism. 'Resistance' was on the tip of every tongue, and the Metsovites became less pleasant to the *carabinieri*, who were not insensitive to the looks and sneers and rude behavior. The murder of the Italian soldier and other incidents of resistance caused the *carabinieri* to begin arresting villagers. Spiros Stahoulis was falsely accused of spitting at an Italian soldier, and scheduled to be transported to a prison camp in Italy. If they had known that Spiros had been the lookout behind the counter of his brother's *pantopolio* when the group gathered in the blind room to hear the BBC broadcast, they would have summarily executed him in the village square.

When she wasn't doing her chores or working for the resistance, Maria Christina was knitting undershirts for Zervas' fighters. But whatever she was doing, she would occasionally pause and stare into the distance for a moment and think about Matoula, nothing in particular, maybe just her smile. She never thought about the dead Italian soldier again.

Now, when Zoitsa would ask her to imitate her father, Maria Christina would resist. Even before Yiannis had left, she had ached for him. He was in her thoughts constantly. The more she tried not to think about him, the more she would think of him and the harder she would pray to be free of him, until she realized that even by praying to be rid of him she was thinking about him. She didn't know what to do. There was no one in the world with whom she felt comfortable enough to talk about it, so she silently endured fighting the nearly uncontrollable desire.

In the mountains, Yiannis' hospital was now one small tent with an even smaller one for supplies. He wrote to Papa Yiorgos:

'I do whatever I can with whatever I have.'

Zervas had designated him his personal physician, and the guerrilla group was attacking Italian supply lines along the pass then quickly retreating back to the forbidding mountains. Yiannis went where Zervas went, and the group was constantly moving.

'It seems we're in three places at once. I'm always waiting for something to arrive from the last camp or waiting the return of some item prematurely delivered to the next.'

A major portion of the supplies for the German forces in North Africa was carried by a railway line linking Germany with Greece. The most vulnerable point on the route was in central Greece, where a series of three long bridges crossed steep precipices at Mount Parnassus. The Allies had decided to try and blow up the longest, the one over Gorgopotamos, the 'Rapid River'. Late in the fall, a small group of British and New Zealand officers parachuted near the foot of the mountain, where they tried to enlist the Communists in their effort, but their local leader, the short, black-bearded Aris Velouchiotis, refused to even have a meeting. A small Allied delegation then walked ninety miles in the snow over narrow mountain paths to meet and recruit the services of Zervas, who immediately agreed and led a contingent of his best men, including his personal physician, towards Parnassus. Not to be outshone by his guerrilla rival, Velouchiotis sent an even larger contingent to aid the Allied endeavour.

The guerrillas were meant to engage the Italian garrison guarding the three bridges long enough for the Allied officers to set their explosives. The fighting was intense. Almost immediately Yiannis was overwhelmed with casualties in his small field hospital. Earlier he had tried but failed to coordinate both supplies and manpower with the Communist medical team and so, doing the best he could with what he had, he and two aides worked feverishly into the night, digging metal out of the wounded with no anaesthetic, having to use woollen undershirts for bandages.

Just before dawn on November 25, the foundations of the bridge crumbled and the supply line to Africa was broken. All through Greece, in large cities and small villages like Metsovo, spontaneous celebrations quietly erupted with people gathering in the street as word leaked from secret wireless radios. They were convinced that the guerrilla forces, now a unified resistance, together with the aid of the British, would soon drive the Germans out of Greece.

The moment Yiannis was finally able to lie down on his

cot and close his eyes, the image of Maria Christina passed through his mind. The first time he had gone to Ioannina for medical supplies, he made a point of noticing the women, and even engaged one or two in conversation, but he quickly realized he wasn't even a little interested in them. Each time he returned, he even imagined this or that one on his arm, but the more he imagined, the more his thoughts returned to Maria Christina and how perfect she seemed, and the more perfect she seemed, the more he thought about her until he stopped imagining any woman other than Maria Christina. In every situation. Alone together. With Zoitsa, the three of them. He remembered her sapphire eyes before she covered them with Pappou's glasses. Her body wrapped only in a thin towel, her fine chestnut hair. The longer he was away from her, the more she became idealized: a graceful and beautiful animal, unusually intelligent, excellent company, loyal to a fault, moral, in short, everything he could pray for in a wife, and a few gifts for which he would be considered too greedy to ask.

In Vlach society it was not unusual for a widower to marry his sister-in-law, and certainly Papa Yiorgos would be thrilled beyond measure should Yiannis ask him for her hand. But Yiannis wanted a willing bride. He wanted romance. He wanted love. And the question which loomed over each image of Maria Christina was, 'What did *she* want?'

19

With the destruction of the bridge at Gorgopotamos, Zervas' reputation reached a new height. His numbers swelled. The British began to drop more weapons, clothing, and gold sovereigns by parachute. Everyone in his band now received two gold sovereigns monthly, one for himself and one for the needs of his family. Papa Yiorgos was stunned when Maria Christina handed him an envelope she had carried in the mail from Zervas' camp, which contained a gold sovereign and a note from Yiannis. Papa Yiorgos read the letter out loud. Yiannis would be sending one a month. He missed everyone – he underlined 'everyone' – and would try to come home, even if only for a few days, for Zoitsa's fifth birthday in January. He also advised at the end of every letter that, once having read it, they should immediately burn it, which Papa Yiorgos did. Maria Christina leaned into the fireplace as the paper was burning to get a last glimpse of Yiannis' handwriting. It was only a second, but long enough to see it was still forward looking. 'Optimistic', Pappou would have concluded. Maria Christina smiled, then pushed away an image of Yiannis looking dashing, standing in front of the fireplace smoking his pipe, and abruptly went about her day.

When January came, it felt as though another month and a

half had passed before the morning of the 7th when Yiannis, deep in snow to his knees, struggled with three fellow fighters on their way home to Metsovo. For one of his companions it was a sad trip. His younger sister had frozen to death during a resupply and he had missed the funeral and wanted to visit her grave. Her name was Katerina and Yiannis knew her as a tall square young woman of sixteen with an angelic face that always seemed to be beaming. She was engaged to marry in the spring. As the four men tramped through the snow, each volunteered they had lost one of their family's women and then were suddenly struck by the fact that it seemed more of the women of Metsovo had given their lives for the resistance than had the men.

As Yiannis approached the village, he bid his fellows goodbye and took a different path down the mountain to his field, where the tips of his grape vines peeked out from a smooth blanket of white. As he looked over at his house, still without a roof, he imagined it finished and furnished. It was a typical Metsovoan house, slightly larger than average. How deeply grateful he would be to simply sit in front of a fire with Maria Christina and Zoitsa, maybe another child or even ten if she'd like. Then, God willing, someday, grandchildren. He would continue to add to the house. Matoula would forever remain alive for him in Zoitsa, Maria Christina, the vineyard, and in his memory. He could have it all, and it would be so simple, if only the rest of the world would cooperate.

As he continued towards the village, he was approaching Agios Demetrius when he heard a scream and Zoitsa suddenly appeared above a snow bank grinning and waving.

For days Maria Christina had found reasons to be around the church where she could see the vineyard. She knew he would stop there first and she was aching to see him. To know that he was whole. Finally, late in the afternoon, while sweeping the snow from the stones with Zoitsa in front of the church, on the one day when she had all but given up hope of his ever appearing, out of the corner of her eye she saw a figure in the vineyard. For a long second her whole world stopped. Then her heart leaped. He was swinging his walking stick.

His shout was thrilling to her. As he waved wildly to Zoitsa, shaking his stick, Maria Christina lowered the giggling child from her shoulder and watched her dash off to meet her father. She wanted to shout, too, but instead, amid short bursts of laughter, she hurried home to alert the others.

When Yiannis opened the gate, Papa Yiorgos could immediately feel a warmth towards him that he was certain had been lost forever. It made him glow and he considered it a sign he was forgiven and all would be as it once was. And it was true. Having thought about his father-in-law these past few months, Yiannis had decided that two such exquisite women as Matoula and Maria Christina could only have come from worthy parents and he had vowed to be more understanding and patient with the priest.

Panorea went into such a frenzy of fussing over Yiannis that Papa Yiorgos had to sit her down and calm her while Maria Christina, with her proud new assistant, Zoitsa, cut a leek pie and poured wine and water. The talk was of the resistance and Zervas.

"He's a whiskey barrel of noise" Yiannis was saying. "And it's that noise that keeps him afloat during his great bouts of doubt, especially after having drunk himself silly. But he's smart. And he can rouse the men to fight like the ancients."

As he spoke, Maria Christina and Panorea exchanged smiles, as did Papa Yiorgos and Panorea. Everyone was so happy he was home, a bright light in the darkest time of year. At Stahoulis' *pantopolio*, Yiannis couldn't put his hand in his pocket. Costas took out a bottle of *tsipouro* from his private stock and poured freely while Yiannis regaled all assembled with stories of Zervas and the bravery of the group, including some of the boys from Metsovo. Whenever a stranger entered the grocery, he would stop in mid-sentence and the group would remain silent until the stranger realized there was nothing on the shelves and left.

The week passed with a renewed sense of promise as the Triantafyllou family and Yiannis spent joyful hours together. Everyone was free and pleasant with each other. It was as if Matoula was just out of sight. Maria Christina and Yiannis first realized that they understood each other without having to speak. They used the signals they had each independently developed with Matoula, which seemed to cover most occasions, so that a certain nod of the head meant 'thank you', another meant 'please', while a particular gesture was a call for help, and so on.

Several times Yiannis tried to engage Maria Christina privately, but she was quick to anticipate him and would feign some chore or sit beside Panorea or Zoitsa. He had so much to say to her, but he didn't want to appear presumptuous and ask for a private conversation in front of the others. Unable to discuss his dilemma with anyone, from time to time he visited Lena, who always served him a spoon sweet in a glass of water. At first she would casually steer the conversation from the occupation to the Triantafyllous, how Papa Yiorgos tended his anger like Yiannis tended his vines. Then to Panorea, how she tended to Papa Yiorgos and, finally, to the real target, Maria Christina. Lena was much wiser than Yiannis suspected. As much as he tried to disguise it, Lena quickly sensed his interest in her grand-niece might be more than that of a brother-in-law, and she always spoke of Maria Christina in the most glowing terms, while all the while trying to fathom just how interested he really was in her.

Towards the end of the week, Yiannis realized his sister-in-law would never give him the chance to say the things she was obviously not ready to hear, and it made him sad. The afternoon before he was leaving to rejoin Zervas, he stopped by

Lena's house to say good-bye, looking tired and downcast. After he sat and she served him a walnut spoon sweet, she waited for Yiannis to determine the course of the conversation. A moment of silence passed, then Yiannis looked at her then looked away and pretended to examine her chimney apron.

"Lena, do you suppose if a man was interested in marrying Maria Christina, do you think she would be so inclined?"

"Well", Lena smiled, "I suspect it would depend on the man."

"A decent, respectable man."

"Like a doctor?" she smiled knowingly. He snorted at the insinuation, as if the idea was preposterous and continued seriously.

"Her father still can't look her in the eye when speaking to her. As long as he encourages her guilt, she'll never be a willing bride. A pity for her and her father. But doesn't Zoitsa look more and more like her mother?"

All afternoon there was thunder and lightening, a sign that a heavy snow would follow. When it grew dark and it was time for Yiannis to leave, everyone assembled in the courtyard to kiss him goodbye. Yiannis was especially delighted by the smell of roses as he leaned in to kiss the delicate cheek of Maria Christina, a moment he would remember in the long months ahead. For her part, Maria Christina stood still while he kissed her cheek, careful not to inhale. She couldn't help but notice, however, how soft his lips were and that his brush mustache tickled.

Zoitsa was standing straight and tall, trying to be a big girl, when her father knelt down to kiss her. Tears poured out of her eyes in a flood and she began trembling as he kissed her forehead. For a moment it was impossible for him to leave. Finally looking over at Maria Christina who understood, Yiannis stood slowly as Maria Christina scooped her up and the two had one more embrace and then Yiannis smiled at everyone and waved with his pipe and walking stick and once again was gone. There was no echo of his stick on the stones. They were covered in snow.

Maria Christina thought she might have imagined it – that his last glance, before he turned and left, was to her. But more importantly, for the first time she saw fear in his eyes. It had suddenly started snowing. The moon was full but was slowly being obscured by a low dark cloud moving across it. She and Zoitsa remained looking up at the moon a moment. After Panorea went into the house, Papa Yiorgos lingered at the door and watched Maria Christina distract Zoitsa from her sadness by coaxing her to catch snowflakes with her tongue.

"Don't stay out too long. The child will catch her death" he said, and then he went inside. Maria Christina kissed Zoitsa and immediately followed, already worrying whether she would ever see Yiannis alive again.

20

The winter of 1943 was even more bitter than the previous ones. In the countryside, Germans were terrorizing the villages and stripping them of food and tools. In the cities, carts were still picking up dead bodies on the streets every morning. Yiannis continued to reach out to his parents in Athens but every communication was remained unanswered.

Events in the wider war, however, were improving for the Allies, so the Congress of the Greek Communist party met in Athens and decided to try and monopolize the resistance so they would be in control of Greece when liberation occurred, which now seemed imminent. The Party had no intention of allowing its military wing to concentrate on the liberation of Greece to the detriment of its ultimate political aims. Thus, the Congress declared that anyone who wasn't with them was against them and would be considered a traitor. Their guerrilla forces then began a series of attacks on a number of resistance groups including some of Zervas' smaller camps. Many of the independent groups were slaughtered when they wouldn't agree to swear allegiance to the Communist cause. Zervas had foreseen this and had always kept a suspicious eye on Velouchiotis, and his forces were prepared for them. He had even spoken to

Yiannis about its inevitability. In one of his letters to the family, Yiannis wrote:

'Zervas has convinced me these
are the first battles of a civil war
that is irreversible and will be long
and bloody.'

In Metsovo the villagers suddenly seemed tired, like animals weary from overwork, marching numbly forward. Three years of war and occupation were also weakening the ties of the family. Some members were Communist, some Royalist, some Republican, and the distinctions were becoming sharper and the words exchanged more heated even as hope grew that the occupation would soon end. Having clung to centuries old traditions which defined each woman's place in society, traditions that had maintained them as a people for over a millennium, the idea of an entirely new way of life, coupled with the every day struggle of living under a brutal occupation while still fighting to survive the elements in this small mountain village, was numbing for everyone but Papa Yiorgos. He was energized. More and more he would speak his mind, assuming that the Good Shepherd was guiding his thoughts and his words.

Having not slept well due to a shoulder still sore from a fall on the church steps, the priest was passing Chaimakis' Dry Goods Store massaging his aching bones when he noticed that an Italian soldier had cornered a young boy with the point of his rifle. As the soldier wrenched a small woven bag from the child, Papa Yiorgos stopped and watched him take a wheel of cheese from the bag, then throw the bag away.

"Leave the boy alone!" the priest angrily shouted as he approached the soldier shaking his walking stick.

At that moment, the Chaimaki brothers, having heard the priest's booming voice, both turned to look out their store window and saw the soldier turn and aim his rifle at Papa Yiorgos' face. The priest wasn't cowed and continued towards the soldier and, looking him in the eye, grabbed the wheel of cheese from his hand and picked up the discarded bag in one motion, then handed both back to the boy, who dashed off. The priest turned back to the soldier and spoke in Vlach, hoping the soldier might understand the Latin.

"May a black bullet find you!"

Whether the soldier understood was unclear to the Chaimaki brothers, but the Italian glared at the priest for a few seconds then took his rifle butt and slammed it into Papa Yiorgos' face, breaking his nose and sending blood flowing down his mouth and onto his black cloak.

In Zervas camp in Katara it was the middle of the night and Yiannis had just fallen asleep when his orderly, Haralambos, a short square jovial man of forty with a red face and red beard nudged him.

"Sorry Doc, but a Kyria Triantafyllou wishes to speak to you."

Yiannis' eyes widened as he sat up and brushed his hair with his fingers. He hadn't been in the camp for two days and he had been hoping to see Maria Christina and indeed had just been dreaming about her. He became flustered and couldn't remember anything about the dream as he followed Haralambos out of his tent and saw her looking so beautiful in her kerchief and shepherd's cloak. She began speaking very fast, and he could hardly hear her over the pounding of his heart, but he heard that she was sorry to interrupt his well-deserved rest, and Zoitsa was fine, but Papa Yiorgos was in trouble and needed his help. As she relayed the sequence of events as told to her by the Chaimaki brothers, Yiannis heart finally stopped pounding long enough for him to recover his wits.

"Please come inside. It's more private."

"Thank you" she whispered. "But I have to leave with the rest of the supply group in a few minutes."

"I love you" he almost said out loud.

"I need you to write a letter to Patera pleading with him to hold his tongue and control his temper so as to not endanger himself. That he would be worth nothing to his flock if he were dead. It would mean a great deal to him to hear that from you. And to the rest of us who depend on him."

"Why, of course. Certainly."

Yiannis ushered her into his tent, then followed and went to a small portable writing desk which was open with pen and paper waiting and a note to the family, leaning against the ink bottle, written a few hours before. With a trembling hand he carefully began writing the same words Maria Christina had just spoken.

Just when she thought she could watch him write forever, she turned and forced herself to step out of his tent where she inhaled the crisp air with a gasp and looked up at the stars. It was only then that she was able to breathe a sigh of relief. After a moment, she began to think:

"How tired he looks. And anxious. He's lost weight. Yet he seems strong."

In another moment Yiannis appeared and handed her the two letters. She glanced at the handwriting: still optimistic.

"Maria Christina" he whispered, hardly knowing where to begin.

She could tell by the tender way he said her name that she didn't want to hear what followed.

"I have been wanting to speak to you" he continued softly.

Maria Christina was about to beg him to stop when Haralambos appeared out of the dark.

"Sorry, Doc, but there's a woman, one of the supply group. Sprained ankle. I don't know if she can make it back down the mountain. She's unusually, er, large, if you know what I mean."

"Olimbi!" Maria Christina laughed, amused and relieved, quickly covering her mouth.

"Olimbi! For God's sake! Olimbi!"

"Don't worry" she said between titters, "I'll tell her you were in surgery. And I'll help her back down." Then she leaned into him and kissed his cheek and was gone before he could recover. He thought he heard her laugh as she trailed off in the darkness, although he wasn't certain. As he returned to his tent, he smiled and touched the cheek she had kissed.

After Haralambos left, Yiannis was too excited to go back to sleep and he lay on his cot until just before dawn when he was scheduled to make his rounds. The night's events had given him hope. He had almost forgotten the sound of her laugh, and as he tossed and turned, he laughed softly to himself, several times even speaking out loud the thought that was keeping him awake:

"I know the key that will unlock her heart."

Maria Christina left Zervas' camp with a deeply disappointed Olimbi, her fleshy arm around Maria Christina's shoulder and her massive body leaning lightly against her for support.

"Your brother-in-law, he seemed well? Was he happy? Did he look tired? He's such an inspiration. Did he happen to mention my name?"

"I heard him say it twice."

"Twice!"

As the resupply group continued its tramp down the mountain in the dark, there was hardly time for Maria Christina to reflect on the fact that she had just kissed her sister's husband. It was almost involuntary. 'Sisterly' she tried to convince herself. But her heart knew better. It was about to burst. And she couldn't quiet the nagging voice inside her, usually like water dripping on a stone, but now raging. Why couldn't she control herself? What was wrong with her? Was it the devil's work? Thus, while Olimbi relentlessly steered the conversation back to Doctor Yiannis, Maria Christina silently prayed for God's strength to fight the lust lingering from the taste of his sweet cheek.

21

As the spring of 1943 unfolded in the Southern Alps, Yiannis went with Zervas from camp to camp which were scattered all through the mountains, and which billeted their five thousand fighters. Sometimes, he would stay for a day or two to help if an extra surgeon was needed. The Republican soldiers were fighting both the Germans and the Communists, whose compliment was now approaching eighteen thousand. As spring ushered in a hot summer, life didn't change much in Metsovo. The women continued resupplying the resistance, the men at Stahoulis' *pantopolio* continued receiving war news from the BBC's nightly report. It was during one of those broadcasts that Costas learned that the boat taking his brother Spiros to Italy was sunk by an English submarine with only a few survivors. Costas collapsed and had to be revived by Pandelis, the old doctor, who luckily was in the blind room at the time.

In August, Yiannis remained in the main camp in Katara. He wrote to Maria Christina that he had a very serious matter to discuss with her. He couldn't leave the camp, but would she stop by to see him during her next resupply? The two had been corresponding since their last meeting in Katara. Yiannis had initiated it. Once every other week he would write one letter for the family, which included war and other news about Metsovites, especially if they were parishioners of Agios Demetrius, and then he would write a separate letter to Maria Christina, ostensibly for Zoitsa, but which was actually intended to open the heart of his intended bride. His first letters opened with "My Dear Sister-in-law and Darling daughter", then he would inquire about Maria Christina's health and Zoitsa's progress. He would always express how grateful he was to have his daughter in her perfect care, and would never fail to include a new English word for her to teach Zoitsa. They were usually funny words like 'nincompoop' or 'tumble' but sometimes he would also send a serious word like 'love' or 'happy'. After the first few letters, he began telling stories of Haralambos. His new orderly was a childhood friend of Zervas, a man full of fun who couldn't stand the sight of blood and so spent most of the day with his eyes closed or turned away. Yiannis wrote wonderful anecdotes describing Haralambos latest antic, which made them both laugh. As the weeks went on, the letters became longer and more frequent: once a week, then twice, and were now addressed 'My Dears Maria Christina and Zoitsa'.

Thrilled as she was to receive these letters, Maria Christina remained formal in her replies, always referring to him as 'My Dear Brother-in-law', never writing about herself except as it pertained to Zoitsa; how well his daughter was developing physically, and what new skills she was learning, and how she was becoming a fine young lady. The letters always concluded with a note from Zoitsa in English in which she would describe some newsworthy event to her father. 'Yiayia Panorea burned her finger.' 'Mister Chaimaki gave her candy.' She would always ask about Haralambos, and included a painting or drawing for him. Yiannis' favorite was a picture painted on a small piece of board: Zoitsa holding hands with him and Maria Christina, standing in front of his house, which she had imagined finished. The colors, the details, Yiannis' mustache, his pipe,

Maria Christina's glasses, her favorite kerchief, the vineyard, moved Yiannis to tears.

Maria Christina had taught Zoitsa to read, write, add, subtract, draw and paint. She had almost forgotten her mother completely. Her only vivid memory of her was of the morning she was sleeping late and she wanted to go to her but was stopped by Panorea's scolding look. She tried and tried to remember her, but her face kept changing. Sometimes she looked like her aunt and at others like Panorea and even Lena and, once, her grandfather. People were always telling her how much she looked like a blonde miniature of her mother and it would send her flying to the nearest mirror to see her mother's face in the reflection, but all she ever saw was her own.

Zoitsa was tall for her age, with thick hair in two plaits and large round eyes of the darkest brown. Fetchingly shy around strangers, she would never tilt her head to look up at grown ups but would look up only with her eyes. She was athletic and elegant, smart, and loved to laugh like her mother but, unlike her mother, Zoitsa had an air of melancholy. She never complained to anyone in the family, but Maria Christina could see a sadness lurking just behind her eyes. Even as an infant she had possessed that quality. And unlike her mother, who was always on the move, Zoitsa, even as a baby always preferred to sit quietly, thinking and watching.

One day when she was still three and her mother wasn't dead six months, she looked up from her drawing and watched Maria Christina tie a cloth containing a cheese ball to a hook on the ceiling in order to strain the remaining milk.

"You should marry Babá."

Maria Christina dropped the cheese ball,

"Po po! Christ and the Virgin Mary!"

Months later, while watching her aunt weaving on her mother's loom, she raised the subject again.

"You should marry Babá."

"Po po! May the Holy Virgin protect us!"

Now at five, Zoitsa was capable of demanding a rational, reasonable response.

"I don't understand why you don't marry Babá?"

"Stop talking nonsense about things you know nothing about."

"But why?"

"Because it's nonsense."

"Why nonsense?"

"Because it is. Now leave me, child. Holy Mother of God!"

It was then that Zoitsa painted the picture of the three of them that her father so treasured. Perhaps he would get the message. And he did. Which is why he valued it so. And yet, he didn't dare act for fear it was still too soon for Maria Christina to consider. Zoitsa finally dismissed the idea as impossible and never raised it again.

For the first time Zoitsa had a separate life. Maria Christina was away more often and Panorea was burdened with too many household tasks. More and more alone she was left only with her favorite friend, Thimi. She was the daughter of Lena's nephew, and was named after Papa Yiorgos' late wife. Thimi was short and chubby and smart. She also wanted to learn English, so the two could speak without being understood when they were with other children. 'Nincompoop' was one of their favorite words.

Thimi was a happy girl. The two spent long hours in the yard, jumping rope or sneaking out of the yard and running the twenty meters to the public fountain for a cup of fresh water. They weren't afraid. The Italians never bothered children. On the contrary, once a soldier even gave them each a piece of candy. Of course, the two scamps had chores to do, and it seemed with every season there were more, but they didn't mind. They still had plenty of time to play, and sometimes Maria Christina would walk with them down to the vineyard where they would play in the house at being grown ups and drink tea and speak in English.

Zoitsa was discovering the world was not always simple or nice. So many children she knew had lost someone during the war. She had lost her mother and now she was terrified that one day it might be her father who would be gone. Thimi herself had lost one of her aunts and a cousin who was a soldier. They would stop whatever they were doing when groups of planes would fly overhead. The children had heard the Germans were burning villages and looting their food and tools, and were killing people everywhere and, as they did their chores and played, there always loomed in their child-sized minds the unspoken possibility that their village would be next, and the two would sometimes sit in a corner of the yard and cry together. It felt better afterwards. The grown up world seemed so mean and crazy. Why couldn't they all just go home and leave them alone?

It was the middle of the night when Maria Christina arrived in Zervas' camp above Katara, and Haralambos stepped inside Yiannis' tent and, in his booming voice, announced Kyria Triantafyllou, whom he had been expecting. After he stepped out, Maria Christina entered shyly and Yiannis rose from his portable writing desk with a letter addressed to Papa Yiorgos in his hand.

"Thank you so much for coming" his voice sounded more tired than he had wished. "Before I forget" he handed her the envelope, then smiled as she took it, carefully put it inside her cloak, and pulled out two small jars of rose petal and honeyed walnut spoon sweets, and a half filled pouch of his favorite English tobacco, which made his eyes open like saucers.

"Where?? How did you?!"

Incapable of looking at him, Maria Christina only nodded and smiled and twisted her head a certain way which meant "Don't ask". Through contacts she had made as a part of Bouboulina, Maria Christina had become extraordinarily resourceful, from furnishing olive oil for the lamps in Agios Demetrius to providing rare medical supplies, a mystery to everyone.

Yiannis could see Maria Christina was uncomfortable, "Would you prefer we spoke outside?"

"I would, yes."

He followed her out of the tent. They stood in front of the entrance for a moment, while he tried to recollect the first two lines of the speech he had rehearsed a thousand times and was now having trouble remembering. Maria Christina stood motionless, staring at his feet, concentrating on maintaining her balance which was faltering. Finally, he spoke and her vertigo disappeared, making way for the force of the words that were streaming over her.

"I loved your sister very much, you know that."

His voice was choked and his eyes were filled with tears and for the first time Maria Christina saw Yiannis as a young boy who needed to be held. She could hardly contain herself, but she stood motionless as her own tears suddenly streamed down her cheeks.

"I know you somehow feel responsible for her death and I hoped that time would allow you to gain some perspective. Especially in the light of so many other women having given their lives for the resistance."

As Yiannis continued, Maria Christina turned and slowly walked away with Yiannis following close behind.

"Matoula always pretended to be stronger than she was, because that is what people expected of her. Wanted from her. I know. I was her doctor as well as her husband."

As the two strolled around the camp under a half moon, Yiannis explained as he had done in his letters how grateful he was that Maria Christina was in his and Zoitsa's life and how much he needed her and admired her. Maria Christina was so beguiled by his sweet words and gentle manner that she almost didn't hear:

"...and I want to marry you, Maria Christina."

She took another four steps before stopping suddenly and turning to him.

"I want to marry you." he repeated more slowly, "Desperately. But only if you will open your heart to me." Maria Christina covered her mouth with her hand to keep from crying out loud. Her one and only thought was that he must be ill.

"I want to have children with you" he whispered.

Maria Christina stared at him a moment. It was difficult to see him in the dark. She now wished they had remained in the tent with its lamplight. She took his hand.

"My dear brother-in-law, I hardly know what to say. I know you're under a great deal of strain--"

"I know this is sudden for you" he gently took her other hand, "but you have been on my mind and in my heart for a long time now."

"And I am certainly honored--" she could hardly breathe.

"Of course I wouldn't ask you for your answer now."

"But this is--not--yes! I will--you will have my answer soon!" she gasped. "I will write to you."

"Please, try to imagine the wonderful life we could have together."

"Yes, of course. I will. I will write" she said over her shoulder as she turned and quickly disappeared into the night.

22

It was just before dawn when Maria Christina knocked lightly on Lena's window and only two minutes later when she was holding a cup of cracked wheat soup and sobbing by the hearth.

"I'm a wicked, wicked woman!"

Lena was certain she was finally confessing to killing the Italian soldier - something Yiannis had shared with her - and she had even begun defending Maria Christina for gutting the beast, when she realized she was confessing to something else entirely: Yiannis had asked her to marry him which meant he must be out of his mind and she must be to blame for always having desired him.

Lena leaned back and burst into a gale of laughter, then she jumped up and hugged Maria Christina from behind and kissed her cheeks and did a little dance around the room "He loves you, you fool! Say yes!"

Maria Christina stopped mid sob and looked at her great aunt as though she had gone insane. Lena danced her way back to her grand niece and gently put her arms around her and held her tenderly like a child.

"I knew he wanted to marry you" Lena spoke softly in her ear. "He as much as told me so. He loves you, my soul."

Maria Christina tried to push away from her great aunt's arms.

"Me? How could he possibly love me?"

Lena held tight "How could he not?" Then she rocked Maria Christina slowly with a mother's tenderness she had never known. It was overwhelming. She, the bride of Yiannis, the most desired man in Metsovo. It was absurd.

"It must be the war that is speaking" Maria Christina remained rocking in her great aunt's arms. "Perhaps it's out of gratitude for being Zoitsa's guardian. Or simply out of pity for me. He must be very lonely."

Lena shook her head and laughed softly. A child being told that they are stupid or ugly often enough will continue to believe it, no matter how celebrated they become for their intellect or their beauty. She released her hold on Maria Christina and walked to the window and pretended to look out while deeply engaged in thought. She might have wept both tears of joy and of sadness for her poor grand niece. A well-deserved happiness was within her grasp which could easily slip away. Lena finally turned to her.

"Perhaps you are right, my child - although I am certain you are not - but let us say that it is the war speaking. Then you must say to him 'If after you've returned home from the war and one full season has passed, if you still want to marry me, ask me again.'"

Maria Christina stood and put her arms around her great aunt's waist and held her tenderly.

"Thank you, Aunt Lena" Maria Christina spoke softly in her ear, "I will do as you say. But no one must know, so that when he decides not to marry me, no one will be disappointed."

Yiannis was surprised when Haralambos interrupted his sleep to announce the arrival of Kyria Triantafyllou, only this time he wiggled his eyebrows to tease his exhausted superior. As Haralambos stepped out, Maria Christina entered and stood in front of a startled Yiannis who froze as he rested on his elbows.

"Forgive me for interrupting your rest, but regarding a proposal of such importance, I thought it only proper that I give you my answer in person" she recited, looking at the foot of the cot. "If after you've returned home from the war and one full season has passed, if you still want to marry me" she looked up into his wide eyes, "I would be deeply honored to be your bride."

Appalled at herself, she turned red, then backed out of the tent and disappeared, leaving Yiannis blinking and wondering for a moment if he had just been dreaming. Then grabbing his pipe, he sat up and filled it with a pinch of the English tobacco. He started to laugh. There would be a happy ending to his life after all, and he couldn't wait for it to begin.

As the months of 1943 slowly passed, the two quietly ached for each other. Their correspondence continued, although interrupted from time to time as the war intensified. When the letters did come, those to Papa Yiorgos and the family were filled with warnings, while those to Maria Christina and Zoitsa were still light and disguised the despair he was beginning to feel. He didn't mention his intention to marry to anyone other than Haralambos, from whom nothing could be hidden.

The spring of 1943 had brought the worst bombardments of the war to Metsovo. In order to survive, most of the villagers had left the town and hid in the forests once again, building *kalivis*, small cabins, to protect themselves from the cold and rain. The Germans periodically sent dogs to track them, and when they found their prey they would often execute them. Papa Yiorgos and his family remained in the village, praying in the blind room during the bombardments. Word was spreading that the attacks on Axis personnel now involved thousands of guerrilla fighters and the Nazis controlled only parts of the North East, the Centre, and the South West of Greece, and only precariously. They had withdrawn entirely from some towns. The Triantafyllous were beginning to feel as though their prayers were being answered.

At Stahoulis', Costas was in the secret room railing to several men that the Communists had become so powerful they now exerted effective control of most of the capital.

"And whoever controls the capital controls Greece!"

With three taps of a cane from above, Costas suddenly stopped. It was the signal to come upstairs. Costas climbed the ladder as an old white haired man raised the door from above and pointed to the front window, which was covered by a dark curtain. As Stahoulis peered out from behind the curtain, he saw two dozen people of various ages from nearby villages, all with the Star of David sewn on their sleeves, being marched down the street in leg chains, led by a squad of German soldiers. For over a year all of the Jewish newspapers throughout Greece had been closed and all Jews were forced to wear the star. Jewish families were also routinely expelled from their homes to make room for Germans and by early fall, the Jewish inhabitants of Thessalonica were being packed into box cars like sardines and being sent to the Auschwitz death camp. As Saul and Elias Chaimaki shuffled past, their heads bowed, their necks all but invisible, and their eyes darting back and forth, seeing the horror of their fate in other people's eyes, Stahoulis cursed himself for being so helpless, and returned to the blind room with the news.

And still they were hopeful. The Soviets were making gains on the Germans in the East while, closer to home, Italy decided to surrender to the Allies. In September, the eighteen thousand man Italian Pinerolo Division surrendered to the Communists. Stahoulis understood the significance right away. Their surrender brought a windfall of arms, including mountain artillery, mortars and machine guns to the Communists, which would give them the confidence to attack any group that posed a threat to their supremacy anywhere in Greece. At the same time, the

Germans commenced an aggressive attack against the Republican Army. For ten days Zervas' forces drove back the Nazis and inflicted heavy casualties. In a letter to Papa Yiorgos, Yiannis wrote: 'It was our first real battle and the men were stunning in their ferocity.'

But before the letter reached the family ten days later, the Nazis were reinforced by five battalions from the Edelweiss Alpine Division and Zervas, realizing they wanted to destroy his forces completely, ordered a retreat to the east only to find his troops face to face with a large concentration of Communist units armed with the surrendered Italian weapons and headed by Aris Veloukhiotis, who had been crossing the mountain range to crush his rival. Fighting fiercely on high rocky ridges on two fronts, the battle lasted four days until the Republicans fought what they thought would be their final hopeless battle.

In Metsovo, the news came over the wireless that Zervas had been caught between his two enemies and had been defeated. For the people of Metsovo the bulletin was shattering. Maria Christina immediately started out on a resupply to the main camp, but when she arrived it was a deserted smouldering ruin. Deeply shaken she remained in a constant state of high anxiety while waiting for more information, fearing and expecting the worst like everyone in the Triantafyllou household, but also hoping and praying.

It was during that time that a squadron of Veloukhiotis' guerrillas arrived in Metsovo, led by a small mean looking man of fifty, Zaralis, one of Veloukhiotis' captains. He gathered the women in the town square intending to punish those that had fraternized with the Italians. While a number of the men watched, the women were all assembled, and Zaralis produced a list of eight names. After looking over the group, he read the first name.

"Katerina Kokkinou. Come forward."

No one moved except to shift weight from one foot to another while his eyes canvassed their faces. He waited. And waited. Finally he took the nearest woman by her long plaits, which had been growing since birth, and with his knife he flicked off her kerchief and cut one of the plaits clean off at the scalp in three strokes. There was a collective gasp as it fell to the stones. Just as quickly he took her other one and was about to cut it when Maria Christina stepped forward.

"Brother in arms!" she spoke to Zaralis loudly enough for everyone to hear. She had spoken without thinking and suddenly her mind had frozen in panic and she couldn't think of anything else to say. But it was too late. She had to continue or be completely humiliated as Zaralis looked over with squinted eyes at the woman with the horn-rimmed glasses.

"Katerina Kokkinou?"

Maria Christina took a deep breath, "I am Maria Christina Triantafyllou, daughter of Papa Yiorgos Triantafyllos. From the neighborhood of the Prosillian."

"Ah."

"Brother in arms", she repeated, growing more confident with each word. "This list you have with the names of eight women. It is meaningless. It might have been any eight of us. None of us welcomed the Italians into our homes. We were forced to house them. If these eight women are guilty then we are all equally guilty because we would have all done what those eight women did and so you must cut all our braids."

Not a sound could be heard, even the birds stopped singing, as if all of nature were holding it's collective breath while Zaralis looked her up and down. Maria Christina took a step forward and glared at him.

"We always said 'When will our brothers come and save us?' And now that you have come, you treat us worse than the Italians."

Zaralis stared at her with angry eyes, then he looked around at the men and the other women too frightened to nod their heads in assent. After turning back to Maria Christina and thinking a moment, he realized he had no rebuttal. Looking down at his shoes with a sigh, he nodded in agreement and released his grip on the woman's hair and told the others who were assembled they were free to go. When he turned back to look for the woman with the glasses, all he could see was a cluster of head scarves and the backs of the women retreating from the square.

Word quickly spread of Maria Christina's stand against Veloukhiotis' captain, and the men of Metsovo, regardless of politics, now openly treated her with a new respect for her courage. Since old women and girls under ten were exempt from having to gather in the square, Zoitsa heard about the incident from Thimi, who had heard her mother talking about it. Panorea heard it from Lena, while Papa Yiorgos heard it from everybody and he indeed felt a fleeting moment of pride, but he quickly dismissed the notion as his mind began to focus on how he had raised a daughter about whom he knew nothing and who was now completely out of his control.

The weeks that followed were especially sad for the Triantafyllou women. It had been three years to the month when, in the space of six weeks, Pappou and Matoula had died and, as was the custom on this anniversary, their coffins were unearthed and Maria Christina, Panorea, and Lena were obliged to wash their bones in the village ossuary, first with soap and water, then with wine, after which they set them on a table in front of a window to dry. They were then set in a small rectangular box to be stored. Maria Christina, with her uncanny ability to detach herself from whatever unpleasantness confronted her, remained the most composed and unmoved by the sweet smell of Matoula as they opened her coffin lid, or the musk of Pappou as his bones lay covered in his own dust. After the ritual, while her aunts went about their day, Maria Christina walked into the forest where she finally stopped and vomited until she was too tired to stand. Then she sat and slowly laid her head down in the snow and slept until dark.

As the winter passed, it continued snowing in Metsovo. It was another mean season in which the snow would not stop until March. Rumors were rife about the fate of Zervas and his men. Some told of complete annihilation, others spoke of whole groups of survivors. Maria Christina tried but failed to get any information from her contact in Bouboulina. The Triantafyllou household held many special prayer sessions for the safety of Yiannis. Zoitsa and Maria Christina prayed constantly. A collective sigh of relief came to the village when a wounded Metsovite limped home with the news that some of Zervas' men had held out until nightfall and divided into groups of ten to thirty and slipped away, marching until dawn up to the steep cliffs which were beyond the reach of the enemy. Yiannis was with the group of ten with Zervas. Maria Christina's contact also finally left a message at the church that Zervas was well and his plan was to reassemble his forces in ten days in another mountain location south of Ioannina.

Later that afternoon, Maria Christina and Zoitsa, together with Thimi, were in the garden making a snowman of Yiannis, with his mustache and his pipe. At one point Maria Christina stood back to look at their progress and saw Zoitsa step up to the figure and put her arms around it, kiss its frozen ball of a head, and rest her head on its shoulder. It was then that Maria Christina resolved to walk the two days to the camp to see for herself that Yiannis was alive and well. Only to see him. Nothing more.

23

It took three days for Maria Christina to organize a supply mission to Zervas' camp. With seven other women packed like mules, all concerned wives and sisters of men from Metsovo, the group, together with three goats, trekked two days in the snow through the range of the Southern Alps that encircle Ioannina, sleeping in a cave overlooking the city during the day, then continuing silently again by night until they reached the periphery of Zervas' camp just before sunrise, when they were suddenly surrounded by a group of Republican guerrillas. One of the women recognized her brother's voice and a tearful reunion, punctuated with bursts of laughter, quickly followed, as the men relieved the women of their burdens and escorted them to the camp.

Yiannis was standing outside a small, tattered pup tent, shaving with the help of a small piece of broken mirror when Maria Christina saw him and quietly thanked the man who had escorted her. Her first impression was that he appeared much thinner. When he first saw her reflection in the glass, Yiannis froze, then turned to see that it was true. Maria Christina's second impression was that his youth had vanished. His face was gaunt and his cheeks hollow, which made his mustache seem too large for his face. He broke into a wide grin as he wiped the soap from his cheeks and took a step towards her, then suddenly stopped. Besides noticing how altered his face was when he smiled, Maria Christina could see there was clearly something wrong. She held her breath as her eyes darted down to his legs.

"I took a little iron in my hip" he laughed, as he picked up a crutch leaning against the tent and used it as he hobbled towards her, his other arm extended. He was so surprised to see her he didn't notice the sorrow in her eyes at the sight of him so reduced. She took his hand and allowed him to kiss her cheeks and fingers.

"I am so happy to see you, Maria Christina."

She forced herself to smile as she squeezed his hand, "I have come to see that you are actually alive."

His eyes appeared to water "So happy."

She then reached into a woven bag and pulled out two loaves of bread "From Panorea with her love and even her kisses." She smiled as he laughed, then pulled out a bottle of *tsipouro* "From Stahoulis, with many more kisses." She smiled again, then produced a wheel of hard cheese and a pouch of Greek tobacco "From all of us."

"I'm so touched you came to see me" he said, taking her hands again.

But she gently pulled them away and reached back into her cloak and took out a small yellow wool scarf "From Zoitsa, to match your hair. She knit it herself. The work is quite good, don't you agree?"

"Quite" he took the scarf and kissed it, then tied it around his neck.

Finally, Maria Christina reached again inside her cloak and handed him a small amulet with an embroidered cross "From me. Blessed by Patera. To keep you safe."

"I am so happy" he kissed the amulet then shook his head as if to awaken himself as he took the items and, gripping his crutch and bending with difficulty, he set them inside his tent, keeping the amulet in his hand against his cheek.

"As you see, my quarters are much condensed" he smiled, not seeming to mind.

"We had to evacuate in such a hurry I had to leave everything behind. But it was a miracle, I swear it on my life. We disappeared right under their eyes!"

Maria Christina smiled sympathetically as he ushered her towards a low fire in the center of a ring of similarly frayed tents. The two spent the next hour sitting side by side in front of the fire, slowly nursing a breakfast of cracked wheat soup. After inquiring about the men from Metsovo, Maria Christina asked about Haralambos.

Yiannis looked down and shook his head "He was with us in the hills above Ioannina at sunset. At daybreak he was gone. He has friends there so, maybe…"

They were interrupted by the whiskey soaked voice of General Napoleon Zervas who was passing by, followed by his aide.

"Yianni."

"General." Yiannis began to stand.

"Stay as you are!" he barked, his blood shot eyes squinting through smoke from his cigar. He was smaller than Maria Christina had imagined, and much older. His manner was rigid and determined and his jaw was clenched. Maria Christina quickly concluded that he was surely someone she might cross the street to avoid.

"How's your hip?" he was looking Maria Christina up and down.

"Better every day, General."

"Good. And who is this?"

"Miss Triantafyllou, from Metsovo" Yiannis smiled. "My intended bride."

"Indeed!"

"Although she hasn't said 'yes'."

Zervas grinned broadly showing a row of tobacco-stained

teeth, "You'd better say 'yes' and marry him, Miss Triantafyllou, while he's still among the living. You'll no doubt be getting an enviable bargain. Yiannis Petrakis is a prince among men." With that he nodded to Yiannis and touched his heart, then he bowed slightly to Maria Christina, bid them both good night and shuffled drunkenly off for the three hours of sleep he required each day.

The two continued to sit in front of the fire, sipping mountain tea.

"Zoitsa started school. She says it's boring. That she's already learned what the other children are being taught. But she enjoys watching them when they learn something. She says most of the boys are dumb."

Maria Christina had never spoken so openly with a man other than her grandfather. Even though she was devoted to her father, they weren't close. They never sat alone and talked together. She was also more relaxed with Yiannis this time. He was easy to be with, and very smart. Perhaps seeing him so vulnerable made him seem more human in her eyes, more accessible. They talked effortlessly, amusing each other with anecdotes.

"My crazy Aunt Aliki was standing over his coffin when the man's eyes fluttered and opened. So she stared at him a moment then she said 'May I get you something?' And he said 'Water'."

They moved into deeper, more philosophical themes:

"Pericles' closest and most valued advisor was his consort Aspasia. If a woman's opinion was good enough for Pericles…"

"The last thing we need right now is a social revolution."

"What better time? Women are fighting alongside the men."

"You're right. I'll tell Zervas."

And with laughter they moved once again into humor, each intrigued by the other's acuity, until it was time for the women to start back.

Yiannis hobbled back to his small tent, with Maria Christina by his side.

"Zervas says the Germans are arming the countryside. Throwing fuel on the fire of the civil war to splinter and weaken the resistance." He entered the tent only for a moment then emerged with his sidearm, a Browning nine millimetre, and a box of ammunition, "I'll feel better if you take this. Hide it well. Use it if you need to. Remind everyone there are arms in the ceilings in the smaller churches, should it come to that. Zervas thinks it will. Don't be afraid to take to the high cliffs if you have to. I will find you."

As he demonstrated the safety release, Maria Christina nodded, trying to appear cheerful through teary eyes.

"Don't worry. I will take good care of Moumou" she said, as she took the amulet from his hand and pinned it to his undershirt. "And you, please be careful." She was aching to put her arms around him, but took a half step back and hugged herself, "Be careful."

"I will, my dear." He smiled, "And you had better get your dowry up to date."

Maria Christina waved him away.

"Whether you marry me or not is of no consequence, I will always love you" she blurted, then put her hand to her mouth, astonished that she actually said what she had been thinking. But it was the look of shocked disbelief on his face that made her laugh as she hurried away to join the others.

The way home for Maria Christina was with a heart bursting with hope. At first she tried to suppress it. To raise the expectation of marrying only begged the fates to bring it crashing down, but she couldn't help herself. It was as if a cage had been opened and all the rage and guilt had escaped and left in its place the sweet light of love and she felt weightless and free. The intensity of the pleasure was almost painful. Yet she didn't want it to stop, and she had to restrain herself from lagging too far behind the others, since she had decided she would allow herself to dream about him, about them, only until she arrived back in Metsovo.

Zoitsa was waiting at the gate to greet her and couldn't wait to hear every detail: was her father well? Did he send her anything? Having anticipated the question, Maria Christina reached into her cloak.

"Candy! Oh, Babá!"

She wanted to know all about Haralambos: what funny things had he been doing, when was her father coming home? Once in the house, Maria Christina told everyone that Yiannis was well and his spirit was strong and the unit was regrouping and confident. She never mentioned his injury, which he confided to her would always be with him, though less pronounced. As for Haralambos, Maria Christina told Zoitsa he was still backing into things.

"And he told Babá he was in the first grade in school for five years before they put him in the second. And after one week in the second, they put him back in the first."

Tears were forming in Zoitsa's eyes, she was laughing so hard. "Stop! I can't breathe!"

As the autumn of 1944 approached, the Germans were running completely out of provisions and systematically stripping villages of anything edible or useful. Papa Yiorgos gave the last of the gold sacramentals from Agios Demetrius to Maria Christina to sell in Koutsoufliani to help feed the poor. By late October some of the surrounding villages were so devastated that the villagers had to dig trenches in the snow to bury their dead in mass graves. It was then that the German army finally entered Metsovo. Most of the villagers had already taken to the mountains, which so displeased the Germans they began preparing to burn Metsovo to the ground. A small delegation, including Papa Yiorgos and Tatamare, led by Archimandrite Petsalis, met the commander of the Germans in the town square as he sat in the sidecar of his motorcycle and indicated to the driver to turn off the engine.

Maria Christina was on her way home from delivering food and herbal medicine to an Australian flier in the mountains, and had just entered the square when she saw the Archimandrite bow to the commander and speak in German. Papa Yiorgos looked surprised by the Archimandrite's fluency, especially after he recognized the word *willkommen*. The commander was pleased the Archimandrite was speaking German and even laughed once.

"We are a Vlach village" the Archimandrite was saying. "We Vlachs are cousins of Germany. We welcome you as liberators."

"Welcome us? Really!", which was when Papa Yiorgos saw the commander laugh and look around, his eyes settling on Stahoulis' *pantopolio*, which was dark and empty.

"Then where are your men?"

"They have fled to the mountains out of fear. I assure you no one in Metsovo is a partisan. We are Vlach. We welcome you. We have been waiting for you. You are welcome to whatever we have."

Thus the Archimandrite, through cunning and deception, saved the village from complete destruction.

The more the villagers heaped praise on the Archimandrite, the more Papa Yiorgos was convinced that he was a collaborator. Although two weeks later when, in the middle of the night, two German soldiers burst through the door of the Triantafyllou house and started foraging for whatever they could eat, Papa Yiorgos jumped out of bed and repeatedly said the only German word he knew:

"Willkommen! Willkommen!"

In spite of being continually exhausted from overwork, Yiannis found time to send each family member their own letter, explaining that he would be unable to write for some time but they should not worry. His letter to Zoitsa was filled with lessons to live by. He wanted her to always remember that what he was doing was for her and her children, so they could live in a free and independent Greece. His letter of love and longing to Maria Christina touched her deeply. It was as if she was holding his beating heart in her hands, and it was all she could do to keep from staining the paper with her tears.

Zoitsa refused to burn her letter. She had seen so little of her father these last few years, his face was beginning to fade from her memory, and she feared it would disappear altogether like her mother's. She was adamant. Maria Christina understood. She had already decided not to burn hers and sought Lena's advice as how to best hide and protect them.

"Nonsense!" Lena insisted. "My Yiannis never wrote a letter in his life. I'll just put them with my other old letters and no one will know the difference. Just until you're married though" she said with a sly smile.

That afternoon, Zoitsa and Maria Christina watched Lena place the letters in a small box with those of her brother, Pappou, with the promise that any time they wanted they could take them out and read them. Of course, an hour later Zoitsa insisted on going back to Lena's to read her letter, and again once more before going to bed. Maria Christina was too shy to ever ask, but on several occasions when Lena felt her spirits were especially low she would bring out the letter for Maria Christina to read.

In late January of 1945, the Communists went on the offensive once again despite the difficulties of the harsh winter, but they were unable to defeat the Republican forces even with their numerical superiority. Zervas' troops, being mostly ex-army personnel, had more experienced professionally trained leaders than their Communist counterparts, but their enemy's attacks took their toll on both men and supplies. The occasional letter from Yiannis during this time was a mere scribble of a few words indicating he was well and that they were fighting fiercely and with great resolve. Just as Zervas had nearly exhausted his stores and

Yiannis had run out of almost every medical supply, the Allies imposed their will on all the guerrilla groups, insisting they agree to a cease fire and stay within the boundaries they presently controlled. This was especially agreeable to Zervas, who considered it a godsend, and ideal for the Communists, who now controlled most of the country, including most of Athens. The only exceptions were the region around Metsovo and parts of the Peloponnesus, which were controlled by the Republicans. Besides being exhausted, the hiatus would allow them time to recruit, rearm, and reorganize, and for some even take a short furlough.

In early August, as Maria Christina lay in the muggy darkness unable to sleep, repeating the prayer for Yiannis' safety over and over again, she heard a sound from below which could only be the opening of the door. After a moment's silence, she quietly slipped away from Zoitsa, who was curled up next to her, and tiptoed to the door, retrieving Yiannis' Browning hidden behind the chimney apron along the way. She stopped at the door. Listened. More silence. Lighting a lantern, she stepped slowly down the stairs, hammer cocked and ready. When she saw a shadow moving towards her, she aimed the pistol and raised the lantern illuminating Yiannis, with his finger to his mouth:
"Sst!"
Maria Christina became so excited she almost squeezed the trigger of the nine millimetre pointed at his heart. After a guarded greeting, and a quick glance into the other's eyes to see the joy with which they were greeted, they both began speaking at once, and in a moment they were sitting side by side in the hay and whispering:
"Zervas says the Germans will be leaving soon. The Russians have been advancing from the east and the Germans won't risk being cut off on the Greek peninsula."
"Lena's niece, Argiri, married a man from Trikala."

"Still no word from Haralambos."

And so they exchanged the news for the first few minutes, thrilled to hear the other's soothing voice. Then they sat in silence, each with a smile on their face, their shoulders almost touching, listening, smelling, feeling the other's presence. After a long moment, Maria Christina could see that Yiannis was beginning to surrender to fatigue and took his hand and led him up the stairs to the platform where Zoitsa was sleeping. Maria Christina was relieved to see Yiannis' hip had healed well enough that he no longer needed a crutch, and his limp was hardly noticeable, although he still relied heavily on his walking stick.

When he entered the main room, Yiannis stopped to savor the smell of the fire, of the freshly made cheese, the feeling of being home. Papa Yiorgos and Panorea were sleeping on one platform, Zoitsa on the other. Yiannis kissed Maria Christina's hand before he let it go and slipped onto the platform and snuggled next to his daughter. Her mouth, the silken texture of her hair, her sweet smell, together with the weariness of war quickly overwhelmed him, and for the next few moments he silently dampened his pillow with tears of exhaustion. Maria Christina replaced the revolver behind the chimney apron and joined her father and her aunt on the other platform. For the rest of the night she lay awake, too excited to sleep.

Just before dawn, Zoitsa opened her eyes and thought there was a strange man in her bed and screamed, waking everyone. It took her a moment to recognize her father. It was his voice she first identified when he calmly spoke to her.

"Moumou, it's Babá."

As if she was seeing him for the first time, Zoitsa studied his face carefully to make sure she wasn't being deceived before she screamed again and jumped on him, showering him with kisses.

If there was no place like home for Yiannis, there was no event like a homecoming, especially after having spent a cruel winter and a hot summer in his pup tent, having only an occasional meal on the run. In comparison, the winter room was a palace: spacious, colorful, there was always something to eat, and the company was splendid. In a few minutes, Yiannis was sitting in front of the fire with Zoitsa on his lap, listening to one of Papa Yiorgos' diatribes. He had already forgotten the subject he was ranting about, but he was grateful simply to hear the sound of his voice. For most of the visit, Yiannis would remain asleep. There would be no visit to the *pantopolio* this time, not even a walk across the street to visit Lena. No one minded. He looked so tired and thin, and when he was awake, even though the house always seemed to have visitors, he would sit silently with his daughter on his lap in front of the fire, or lie down with her snuggled next to him, his spirit shining through stronger than ever, but only in his eyes.

In the four days he was home, Maria Christina tried very hard never to look at him when others were around, afraid they would notice her adoration. Surprising even herself, the flame in her heart burned ever brighter with each passing day. Just to hear him and enjoy the magic he brought to the house was like kindling. After spending so much time worrying about him, praying for him, it was no small comfort to know he was safe and smiling, and to see Zoitsa so playful instead of anxious and secretive, to know her father was happy again. And then to see Panorea, when it was time once again to say goodbye, with tears in her eyes, taking the liberty of kissing a surprised Yiannis on the cheek. And then the final moment as Maria Christina and Yiannis looked breathlessly at each other before he stepped out of the gate. Even though she carried the pain of knowing he might never return, she couldn't help feeling his hope for them and his love for her in that last glance, and it gave her more happiness than she had ever known.

By October, the Germans were in full retreat through Metsovo to Albania. Zervas and his men waged a continuous war of skirmishes, weakening the fleeing Nazis. In Athens, the national government had returned, and by November Greece was completely free of Axis forces. On December 3rd, the Communists sought permission from the government to conduct a demonstration in Athens. It was denied. The next day, uniformed Communist patrols entered the outlying districts of Athens and targeted police and security personnel. The very next day, they returned in full strength and began attacking government buildings and police stations.

British troops sided with the government, but they were weak. Over the next several days, they were methodically pushed back into smaller and smaller enclaves. The Communists, hoping to gain as much ground as possible before British reinforcements arrived, kept on the offensive, until the government controlled only a little over one square mile of Athens. The area around Metsovo remained free, but Zervas' army was demoralized by the news of the Communist advance in the capital. In the rest of the country the Communists didn't have to fight. No one dared challenge them. But the fighting continued in the center of Athens and in the mountains where Zervas, although considerably weakened, was still master.

In mid December, fifteen thousand of the Communists' best fighters attacked Zervas from the south and east, and from the north through Albania, in a pincer movement designed to deal his forces a final blow. Yiannis was forced to abandon his small field hospital and take up arms. With gun in hand he was now killing instead of healing, which deeply saddened him. With supplies dwindling, casualties mounting, desertions increasing, Zervas tearfully told Yiannis he was giving up the fight. Once the best guerrilla band in the resistance, it was now reduced to two thousand survivors. For ten days Zervas' forces, taking heavy casualties, retreated under the cover of scattered rear guard actions. The British Royal Navy then evacuated them to the island of Corfu, and Zervas' fighting force ceased to exist.

As news of the fate of Zervas and his troops spread, families all over Greece waited to hear from loved ones. The Triantafyllous were no exception. A message pleading for information left at Agios Demetrius for her contact from Bouboulina brought no news. Since October, when the occupation ended, Maria Christina had found only one written message behind the icon:

'To the hand that offers a rose there will
always remain a sweet fragrance.'

It would be the last one she would ever receive. It was a week before names began filtering back by telegraph. This one was fine, that one wounded, the other killed. Zervas was alive, although there were reliable sources that reported he was dead. There was no mention of Yiannis. And there was no way to get to Corfu except by British warship or German submarine. And so Christmas came, and then St. Basil's Day, then a week later the feast of the Epiphany and Zoitsa's eighth birthday, while they waited. And prayed. And waited.

24

"If the Communists had not arrogantly undertaken the operation against Zervas - over three hundred miles away from the main battlefield - they would be masters of the country today without any compromise! It was hubris!" Papa Yiorgos declared while stopping for a glass of tea at Stahoulis'. The same conclusion was on the lips of every Greek in every corner of the world in the winter of 1946, which made Zervas either the hero or the villain, depending on one's political leanings. He had diverted those fifteen thousand Communist troops long enough for English reinforcements to arrive in Athens and successfully turn the tide, gradually pushing Veloukhiotis and his forces from their enclaves and pressing them back street by street. The Communists soon realized that a military victory could not be achieved and they finally agreed to a cease-fire. And so another truce was signed.

While he was pontificating at Stahoulis', Mihalis, the telegraph operator, ran into the Triantafyllou courtyard and breathlessly exclaimed: "Doctor Yiannis is alive! He's alive!"

Only Panorea was at home. She wouldn't dare open a telegram addressed to 'Papa Yiorgos Triantafyllos' but, with a heart ready to burst, she thanked Mihalis and took the telegram and set it on Papa Yiorgos' desk. The next to arrive were Maria

Christina trailed by Zoitsa and Thimi who, when they heard the news, jumped and screamed and danced and offered prayers of gratitude. An hour after Thimi had gone home, Papa Yiorgos came sauntering in and, upon hearing there was a telegram with good news, hurried excitedly into his room where he sat with enforced calm. Grateful for the good news, he closed his eyes and uttered a prayer of thanks, then opened and read the message out loud to himself:

DR PETRAKIS ALIVE
BUT WEAKENED FROM PNEUMONIA STOP
LETTER TO FOLLOW

Papa Yiorgos said a prayer of thanks that the news wasn't worse. When he read it aloud to the others, he paused before he read the salutation:

"With deepest respect, Haralambos Koukoudis."

Shocked by the vagueness of the news, it took a moment before Maria Christina and Zoitsa, who had been holding each other, cried in unison, "Haralambos!"

"He will take good care of Babá," Zoitsa muttered nervously. "I know he will."

"Of course, he will, Moumou," Maria Christina echoed, squeezing her tightly, trying to appear hopeful.

"We are all servants of a higher purpose," Papa Yirgos said as a note of comfort.

The weeks that followed were strained. Everyone wearily went about their lives, waiting for the letter. Little was said in the house that wasn't necessary. In their hearts, both Papa Yiorgos and Panorea feared Yiannis would not survive. Papa Yiorgos suspected he might already be dead and was rehearsing his eulogy honoring Yiannis and his life. Maria Christina and Zoitsa were certain Yiannis would regain his strength and would be home by spring.

In late February, a letter addressed to Papa Yiorgos Triantafyllos was tucked inside a diplomatic pouch among other documents and correspondence from Zervas, and was carried by British warship to the national government in Athens. At the end of March, the letter finally arrived in Metsovo and was delivered to Papa Yiorgos, who sat in his room with the missive on his desk, his hands shaking, mindful that whatever news it contained must be part of God's Divine Plan. He opened the thick envelope and looked at the first of the pages:

'My dear Papa Yiorgos Triantafyllos' it began, and then, in an unschooled hand, praising himself whenever possible, Haralambos took credit for having resurrected Doctor Yiannis from the dead. He began with a short history of himself up to and including leaving the group and retiring to a cave near Ioannina to rest, and then rejoining the company during their retreat. He told in touching detail how Zervas stood at the gangplank and thanked each man personally as they boarded the destroyer.

'At which time he retired to his cabin and collapsed on the floor undiscovered until breakfast. Doctor Yiannis never left his side.'

Minutes later, while reading the letter to the women, Papa Yiorgos paused at that point and commented to no one in particular:

"In spite of knowing all his flaws, Yiannis only sees Zervas' greatness."

He took a moment to file the thought away as a quote for another day before he continued reading aloud: "Doctor Yiannis said it was pneumonia. There was a complete store of medicine on board and he persuaded the chief medical officer to give us what we needed to treat Zervas and the other men who had fallen ill and would be needing medical attention even after we arrived in Corfu."

Papa Yiorgos took a sip of water and continued reading

"Within a few days of Zervas' collapse, Doctor Yiannis came down with the same fever. Both men were so exhausted and weak that the bouts they suffered were extremely serious and demanded my constant vigilance."

Haralambos had not been exaggerating when he claimed to be their savior. For a while, Haralambos' letter propped up the dampening spirits of the household, but then weeks went by and they heard nothing more. It was not until the beginning of June that another letter arrived, also written by Haralambos but dictated by Yiannis. He had suffered a relapse, but had since recovered, though he still wasn't strong enough to sit up and write. In his own voice Yiannis assured everyone he was becoming stronger by the day and would be home as soon as he could make the trip, possibly by June. He closed by thanking and praising Haralambos, without whom he wouldn't have survived, and asked they include him in their prayers.

Although the Second World War had ended and their country was no longer under occupation, for the Greek people the struggle continued unabated, as their own internal difficulties obscured all world events. One quarter of the villages had been burnt, and the ones that survived faced extreme shortages of every description. People were even wearing the clothes of dead German soldiers out of necessity. Packages began arriving from all over the world from friends and relatives. For the Triantafyllous, the first of a series of large boxes came from Yiannis' older brother, Nikos. Papa Yiorgos took it upon himself to open them and distribute the contents among his parishioners, from last year's suits, dresses, and brand new children's clothing, to vitamins and dried and canned food stuffs and even toys. Every few weeks, another box would arrive from Brooklyn, and it would raise their spirits as everyone gathered in the sitting room and Papa Yiorgos would ceremoniously open the box, having first blessed it, and take out the articles one at a time. Everyone would then call out their preference as to whom the article should be given, the grey suit would fit the carpenter's son who was getting married, the child's dress to the tinker's daughter who had just lost her mother. Zoitsa pictured Uncle Nikos from Brooklyn as looking exactly like Saint Nicholas.

It was the middle of July before Yiannis returned to Metsovo, sitting on the back of a mule, smiling with the sun on his face. In spite of the heat, he wore Zoitsa's yellow scarf loosely around his neck. When Panorea first saw him, she held her hand to her mouth. He had grown even thinner. But he was home. Exhausted from his journey, he slept for most of the first few days, eating only small amounts of yogurt and bread. Gradually his strength returned and soon he was sitting up and reading, then sitting by the window and reading, all the while gaining vigor and mass. By the second week he felt well enough to step into the courtyard and watch Maria Christina and Zoitsa tend the vegetables in the garden. Friends refrained from visiting so that he could rest undisturbed. Only Stahoulis stopped by, bringing him some *tsipouro*, and was startled to see his old friend appearing so frail.

Late in the afternoon, at the end of the second week, Maria Christina was sitting on the bench in front of the fireplace, quietly stirring the coals under the day's vegetable pie and watching Yiannis next to her, lying on the platform on his back, sleeping, his arms across his chest, a slight smile on his face. No one was around or expected in the near future so she leaned over and stared at him, studying his face closely for the first time. After another moment she leaned in still closer, until she finally took off her glasses and leaned in to where she could see him best, about three inches from his nose. For a moment she just stared at his nose, his eyelids, his cheeks, then she found his mouth.

She couldn't help herself, she just wanted to feel her lips near his lips, not to touch them, but to feel his breath, so she leaned in ever closer, mouth to mouth, until she could feel his mustache and his breath and almost feel his lips, when Yiannis, dreaming of being wakened at that moment by just such a kiss from those exact lips, could now feel their presence and opened his eyes, startling Maria Christina who yelped, then jumped back and hung her head in her hands.

"What must you think of me!"

For a moment Yiannis was too astonished to speak. He stared up at the ceiling to review the last few moments, then he smiled sleepily.

"I think I should wake to your kiss every morning."

Then he sat up and he looked as serious and as handsome as she had ever seen him.

"Marry me, Maria Christina. Marry me now."

Chills ran down her spine as she turned away and, as if someone else was speaking, she heard herself say "But you haven't been home one full season."

"The winter here is endless. Marry me now."

It was almost a command. As he waited for her response, Maria Christina didn't look at him, but sat on the bench and resumed stirring the coals a moment before she finally looked over at him without speaking. She was thrilled to be the object of his desire, to see it in his eyes. She leaned the poker against the fireplace to disguise the power over him she was feeling, then put her hands on his hand.

"My dear brother-in-law, Yiannis. Perhaps your heart is only aching for something it can believe in. Please, for your sake, just to be sure. Let us finish one season without war. Besides, what would our promise mean to each other if we would break one to make way for another?"

Yiannis closed his eyes before he looked away, embarrassed by his lack of character. He laughed softly to himself as he lay back down. For the last few years he had been having erotic dreams about her. Sometimes, during his darkest moments, he would think of her in her nakedness, her innocence eagerly anticipating him, and it was a reminder that there was a glorious life which awaited him, and he was impatient for it to begin. He also knew the underlying political disagreements in Greece had yet to be resolved, and the peace between the Communists and the Republicans probably wouldn't last the long winter, and who could tell when the next season free from war would occur? It might take the best years of their lives. Zervas believed the next round of the civil war was going to be the longest and bloodiest, and that the Communists had arsenals of the superior weapons left by the Italians and Germans, which were hidden in the mountains and would soon be returning in force. Although most thought the civil war was over and that the Communists had lost, Zervas had always been able to look just beyond the horizon, and there was no reason for Yiannis to think that this time he might be mistaken.

After that first kiss, Maria Christina was so aroused and ashamed she practically hid from Yiannis for an entire week, until the hunger for another kiss became almost too great to resist. As much as she wanted to be with him and feel what it was like to be a married woman, she always assumed that one day soon he would have a change of heart, and she was constantly on her guard for any sign of his inevitable cooling.

Yiannis' health continued to improve and his strength quickly returned. Soon he was giving Zoitsa and Maria Christina English lessons again and eating anything within arm's reach. He was gaining weight so rapidly that Stahoulis, who hadn't seen him in a month, had to look twice when he first saw him enter his *pantopolio*. Yiannis was now strong enough to even relieve old Pandelis. He took the house calls below the main street which divided Metsovo, rich from poor, Anticommunist from Communist. Although everyone knew he was Zervas' personal friend and physician, their history and respect for him transcended politics. Besides, the streets below were nearly deserted, as families of Anti-communists, fearing for their safety, moved in with Anti-communist relatives above main street. The few Communists who were wealthy moved down below to fortify their comrades. Yiannis' old schoolmate, Thomas, who was supporting the Communists, was no longer speaking with any of his old friends and had left Metsovo and was last seen in Thessalonica. Attendance at Agios Demetrius, which was in the Communist district, dropped sharply after the occupation ended and the lines of the civil war were being drawn. Yet the priest still went about his duties with the same enthusiasm. Since his conversation with Tatamare about the sheep and the bell, the priest's whole demeanor had changed so dramatically that he was now known by his parishioners as *Papa Yelastos*, Father Laughter. He was no longer interested in veneration, but in being the servant of God, although he still had his occasional moments of vanity, like when he would complain to Tatamare that he was undervalued or ask him if he didn't think his voice was far superior to the Archimandrite's.

As the weeks turned into the dark months, a courtship was being conducted right before everyone's eyes which no one was aware of but the couple. With a glance here and a smile there, an unexplained and unexplainable burst of laughter, followed by an automatic burst of laughter from Zoitsa, Maria Christina and Yiannis read each other's faces and minds, discreetly communicating with absolute ease. During those rare moments when they found themselves alone, they hardly spoke, fearing that if they engaged each other they might not have the will to stop.

By Christmas Yiannis was looking robust and healthy, like his old self, except his face had matured. He assumed Pandelis' duties completely, while also spending a great deal of time organizing the completion of his house to commence as soon as the snow melted, handing out precious gold sovereigns to insure preferential treatment.

It was already the last day of February 1947, and Yiannis was holding his emotional breath that the peace agreement would hold until April, when the waiting period for their marriage would be over. He left the house in the morning, filled with hope, but he didn't return that night or the next. After everyone had gone to bed, Maria Christina lay awake waiting for him when she heard the door open downstairs. She smiled, then held her breath and listened. Nothing. She waited another moment. Nothing. Gingerly slipping off the platform, she slid the Browning from its hiding place and tiptoed out of the room.

Standing by Afendoula lighting his pipe, Yiannis waited and watched Maria Christina descend the stairs holding a lamp, the gun pointing to the floor. She paused when she smelled the pipe, then hurried down the remaining steps. Having not seen each other for two days, they were excited and began whispering as they sat in the hay, side by side, shoulder to shoulder, knee to knee. Yiannis had delivered a baby and, since there was no veterinarian, he also delivered a foal and put a donkey to sleep. Although it was apparent to her he was excited to see her, she thought he seemed sad, cheerless. Maybe he was just tired. Maybe he had changed his mind. After a moment's silence, he smiled sadly at her and reached into his cloak with a sigh and pulled out a telegram. Realizing the seriousness of the moment, she braced herself as he handed it to her and she opened it. It contained only four words.

THE CURTAIN HAS DROPPED STOP NZ

"Napoleon Zervas?"
"Yes" he nodded. "The peace has ended."
The sudden anguish in her eyes encouraged Yiannis to take

her face in his hands and kiss her on the mouth, hard at first, then softly, tenderly, turning her agony into rapture. Then he looked into her eyes and smiled, and gently moved her head to his breast and they reclined, arms intertwined. Neither moved or said a word for the longest time. Yiannis, eyes closed, listening to her shallow breathing and inhaling the sweet smell of her hair and cheek, Maria Christina listening to his beating heart, exhilarated to be so close to him, yet feeling so deeply sad and foolish for not having married him and not understanding why she hadn't, especially since she knew in her heart how he wanted it so.

Within a week Yiannis had met with Zervas, who had retired from the military and had become a strong political force in Greece in his new position as Minister of Security. Besides insisting he remain his personal physician, Zervas pleaded with Yiannis to help establish the national military medical facilities for the Mountain Brigade, which comprised one third of the Greek army.

Yiannis agreed to join Zervas once again and was commissioned a colonel in the Greek army. He worked doggedly to reorganize what little was available from whatever the British could be persuaded to donate. In the meantime, he kept an eye on Metsovo and once even had a squadron of elite troops sent to the area to chase away a band of guerrillas. Large groups of Communist guerrillas, rechristened 'The Democratic Army of Greece', were now being trained and equipped by their Communist neighbor, Josip Tito of Yugoslavia. With their war cry 'By Fire and Axe', they were attacking police stations at night and killing the personnel. They also executed prominent right wing citizens in their homes and carried scarce food and livestock back to Yugoslavia. But that was only a fraction of the violence in rural Greece. Kidnapping, robbery, and general lawlessness was widespread, and the national army of Ninety-two thousand was very thinly spread. The whole of Greece was a battleground.

The squadron Yiannis sent quickly scattered the guerrillas, but they disappeared only until the troops were withdrawn, then they emerged from hiding and captured the police of a nearby village and paraded them nude down the main street. They then beheaded the chief of police and executed his men.

It was after that incident that Yiannis first wrote to his brother Nikos about the possibility of Zoitsa and Maria Christina coming to Brooklyn until the war was over. After consulting with a lawyer, Nikos was advised that acquiring a visa for a Greek national had become very difficult because of the civil war in Greece and the rising anti-communist sentiment in America. Nikos wired his brother:

NEED LETTER FROM ZERVAS
YOU HIS PHYSICIAN STOP
ZOITSA YOUR DAUGHTER STOP
MARIA CHRISTINA HER AUNT AND
GUARDIAN STOP
LAWYER THINKS IT POSSIBLE
BUT NOT CERTAIN STOP
NICK

As the year passed in rush and confusion, Yiannis was kept busy putting out one fire after another, sometimes literally, as the Democratic Army liked nothing more than to set fire to a Greek Army hospital. In rare moments of rest, Yiannis would recall the last night in Metsovo in the sitting room with Maria Christina. He would recreate it in his mind from the beginning: slipping out of bed and moving quietly to the sitting room. Starting a fire. The wood was damp so it was difficult. Moments later the door opening and Maria Christina entering, looking so intelligent and beautiful under a thin blanket and laying a sheet over the padded bench along the wall. Then holding herself and looking at the floor she spoke very softly.

"I am so deeply sorry not to have married you. It was foolish. I want you to know even though I said 'no' I said 'yes' in my heart. Tonight I want you to believe we had wed, and I want you to say goodbye to me as your wife" at which time she dropped her blanket revealing her nakedness.

Yiannis would remember their lack of shame, the ease with which they joined together, her strength, yet her delicacy. The flow of their love, from romantic to intensely passionate to playful to passionate, and then it was over. Spent. Such ease, such harmony, each anticipating the other as great dancers do. Dazed by it all, they remained joined, bathed in the afterglow, Maria Christina hardly breathing, he more at peace than he ever thought possible.

Maria Christina would also often think about that same night. Nothing she had ever read or imagined had prepared her for it. She would always remember it as the happiest, most profound, even mystical experience of her life.

25

Maria Christina flew through the next few weeks, a whirlwind of infectious energy, laughing easily, sharing gossip with Lena, approaching even the most difficult task as if she were playing. She had lost all sense of guilt and decided Matoula would certainly approve, since it involved Yiannis' happiness. In fact, one might have sworn Matoula's spirit had even entered her body. Before a month had passed, Yiannis arranged to meet Maria Christina at the *kalivi* where they had first treated the English flier. She arrived hours early and built a roaring fire which warmed the small room. She laid out their supper and filled a bucket with snow to melt by the fire for their water supply. The rush of joy when she first heard him kick the snow from his feet, the look on his face when he first saw her, the ease with which they slipped into each other's arms left no doubt one completed the other. There was so much to say and do, so many important things to discuss, and with so little time. For an afternoon and evening in front of a warm fire, they ate and talked and laughed and made passionate love and ate and laughed some more. Of the many things she loved about him, perhaps what she loved most was that he made her feel beautiful.

Later in the night, Yiannis, speaking softly, revealed that Zervas had told him that the Communists were planning to kidnap Greek children during their raids and take them to retraining camps they were building in Yugoslavia. It had been the great fear of their forefathers during the Turkish occupation. After their abduction, the Turks indoctrinated the children and sent them back into their villages as spies and teachers. Allowing the thought to linger a moment, Yiannis then told her he had written his brother, Nikos, in America. Maria Christina grasped the connection right away. At that moment, she was lying in his arms on a platform next to the fire, a light blanket covering them. Even before he was able to ask her to make the sacrifice, she opened her mouth to cry but no sound came. He took her head in his hands and kissed her cheeks and eyes. They both understood how difficult this was going to be. Although she tried to disguise it, the thought of leaving her beloved Greece at a moment when it most needed every one of its able bodied citizens, of leaving her father and aunt and those in the village that relied on her, and of being separated from Yiannis all cast a shadow on the rest of the night and the morning. She told him she understood. Over the last few years, Zoitsa had become increasingly nervous, easily frightened. A sudden noise would make her yelp and even jump off the ground. The once chatty little girl had also become increasingly less so. Maria Christina told him she was convinced it was caused by all the trauma of war and that in America Zoitsa was certain to feel more secure. She spoke of finally being able to see the ocean, and how much fun it would be to live in America, and how easily Zoitsa would adjust since she was already quite fluent in English. They decided to postpone any discussion of marriage until after the war, when they could wed in peace. Maria Christina's heart was breaking and Yiannis knew it, for his was breaking, too. They didn't make love again that night. They were too sad. Nor did they speak much afterwards. There was nothing more to say. Late in the night, Maria Christina boiled some water for tea and the two quietly ate feta cheese and drank tea until just before dawn, when Yiannis put on his cloak, hugged her tightly for a long moment, then kissed her trembling lips, and left without looking back.

26

After several months of reorganizing medical units, Yiannis received permission to reduce his rank from colonel to captain and join the Greek Army's strongest battalion, the 587, where he was most needed as an army field surgeon. Haralambos had followed him, first to army headquarters as his office receptionist, and now to the front as his orderly, reducing his own rank from sergeant to corporal. He was convinced Yiannis could not function properly without him, and without Yiannis functioning properly, Zervas would not be able to perform well. With this convoluted reasoning, Yiannis' wonderfully wily but somewhat mentally limited assistant rushed with him from one village or camp to another to stem the flow of blood in both soldiers and civilians.

As terror increased throughout the country, Zervas decided the way to combat it was by terror. He limited civil liberties, severely punished dissidents, and expanded capital punishment for crimes against the state. Yiannis tried endlessly to persuade him that this strategy would only strengthen the Communists' argument that the government was fascist, which would in turn help them recruit more members and that would only increase terror. But Zervas could not be moved, and Yiannis was becoming increasingly disappointed in his former hero. As he wrote to Papa Yiorgos:

'I do believe Zervas' continued abuse of alcohol and the high fever from pneumonia have muddled his thinking.'

Throughout the year, the pace of attacks by the Communists continued to accelerate, leaving hundreds dead and wounded, including women and children. Many villagers were taken prisoner and forced to join their ranks or be executed. The guerrillas were operating in every corner of Greece with an organized underground network of supplies and intelligence. Nobody was safe.

It wasn't until late August of 1947 that Yiannis could find time to arrange for Maria Christina to bring Zoitsa to the *kalivi*. Zoitsa was so excited she couldn't stop giggling as she and Maria Christina set the blankets on the ground under an old oak tree, in preparation for her father. Zoitsa had made the cheese all by herself and she couldn't wait to see his face when she told him.

After waiting several endless hours, they finally saw him walking up the mountain with his walking stick, smoke puffing from his pipe. Zoitsa ran down to greet him and jumped into his arms, forcing him back a few steps until, regaining his balance, he lifted her high in the air and round and round, all the while hugging her tightly. Then he stopped for quiet, serious hugging. She thought he looked so handsome in his military uniform. When they reached Maria Christina, she was so excited she was unable to speak for fear of embarrassing herself. She kissed Yiannis gently on both cheeks then took his knapsack and showed him his place at the blanket.

News about Haralambos took up the first half hour while they ate and laughed and father held daughter. After dark, sitting around a campfire drinking tea, Yiannis asked Zoitsa what she might think of a visit with her Uncle Nikos in America.

"Really?" Zoitsa seemed excited by the idea.

Maria Christina and Yiannis looked at each other.

"Really" Yiannis confirmed.

"When?" Again she seemed eager.

"As soon as Uncle Nikos arranges for your papers."

There was no more said. Yiannis immediately began teaching them the English words they would be needing for emigration, nouns like visa and stamp. After Zoitsa fell asleep, Yiannis and Maria Christina slipped inside the *kalivi* where slowly and quietly they spent the rest of the night making sweet love with their clothes on.

As the weeks went by and they waited for word from Yiannis' brother, the raids intensified until it seemed the whole country was under siege. In the fall, a force of four hundred guerrillas attacked Grevena, a hill town in Macedonia of twelve thousand, using standard army artillery and heavy machine guns and scorching most of it to the ground. It was an escalation into all out warfare. In response Zervas encouraged the formation of units of self-defence, arming and training those loyal to the national government. The country was awash in arms.

Towards the end of the summer, the Communists controlled over one hundred villages and towns. Guerrilla bands were now executing priests, setting welfare institutions on fire, and kidnapping children. The morale of the government and the Army ebbed to a new low as hundreds of thousands of refugees from towns and villages sought government assistance for housing, food, and medical care. Yiannis was continually overwhelmed. Finally, in late September, he received a telegram from his brother:

PAPERS APPROVED STOP
VISAS TICKETS AND DOLLARS AT
AMERICAN EMBASSY ATHENS STOP
SHIP NEA HELLAS DEPARTS NOVEMBER 5 STOP
WIRE CONFIRMATION STOP
NIKOS

It seemed the letter from Zervas had gotten everyone's attention. The Archbishop of New York, a personal friend of Nikos, had passed it on to the United States Undersecretary of State for Political Affairs, who had it approved almost immediately. Yiannis read the telegram twice before carefully folding it and putting it back into its envelope. His greatest worry would soon be over. He sat on his cot with his head in his hands. Nikos had been to him what Matoula had been to Maria Christina, the one who showed him the way, taught him how to play marbles, educated him about girls. Nikos had indicated - and he wasn't prone to exaggeration - that he had become quite successful. Zoitsa and Maria Christina would be well looked after.

In late September, the couple met again at the *kalivi*. Almost immediately Yiannis showed her the telegram. They hardly spoke the whole night again as they lay on the platform by the fire, holding each other. Before either was ready, they could see the pale light of the sunrise through the small window. Maria Christina now knew the pain of love was equal to its joy. Until now she had only known the latter. Yiannis was always out there somewhere. She might even see him that day. Although the world was in shambles around her, she had been uncharacteristically optimistic and energetic. And now, in one moment, it was gone and what remained was only their veneer.

Just before they parted, Yiannis handed her a small sack of gold sovereigns.

"This will take you to Trikala where you will find the train to Athens. After you buy your train ticket, keep a few sovereigns, and what is left give to your father and tell him I will send more. In Athens you will go to the American Embassy where you will pick up your visas and where my brother has dollars and tickets waiting for your voyage…"

What a week ago was only a possibility had now become an

inescapable reality - America Embassy, dollars, voyage - so that Maria Christina didn't remember until later that Yiannis also warned her to leave Metsovo as soon as possible. He said the Communists were going to try and set up a state within a state in Epirus, and Metsovo would be a necessary lifeline for them. Maybe even their capital. He told her that his battalion was reconnoitring in the mountains above Metsovo together with two others. He then instructed her to alert the citizens and remind them again of the weapons hidden in the churches.

A heavy rain began to fall as they stood in the doorway, forehead to forehead. Then Maria Christina suddenly turned and ran the whole way down the mountain, sobbing, arriving home soaking wet and exhausted. News of the visas landed heavily on Papa Yiorgos and Panorea. Her father just nodded, then turned away while Panorea stoically helped her with her wet clothes and Zoitsa surprisingly chatted away about Uncle Nikos and America. Papa Yiorgos stared into the fire.

"I will take you as far as Trikala where you will board the train to Athens. You will both need western clothes which we can find in Trikala. And your hair will have to be cut."

"No!" Maria Christina exclaimed.

Zoitsa started to cry. She didn't want to cut her hair either just for a visit. But Papa Yiorgos insisted they abide by the customs of their host country. To say the household was upset that night would be to greatly understate the distress in the small room. These were important decisions, life-changing decisions, but these were life-changing times. In any event it would all be done in Trikala, and that was the end of it as far as Papa Yiorgos was concerned, and he bid everyone good night. He was suddenly in charge again.

For the next week, Maria Christina rushed around spreading Yiannis' warning and saying goodbye to friends and relatives. She framed their being uprooted to Zoitsa as being a bright color in the tapestry of their lives. Lena helped them wash and dry, braid then cut the waist length plait at their shoulder, and carefully place them in a box which she handed to her niece. Lena was especially sad to see Maria Christina and Zoitsa leave. She had an eerie feeling she would never see them again, and vowed to keep the letters, which would give them a reason to return. Stahoulis gave Maria Christina the names and addresses of cousins in Brooklyn and Astoria, should she ever need them. Several villagers gave her letters or messages to deliver to friends or relatives who lived in different cities in America, should she happen to run into them.

Two weeks before their departure, just after midnight, Matoula appeared to Maria Christina in a dream, and she reached out to take her hand but it turned to dust and Matoula disappeared at the sound of a burst of artillery fire, followed by the loud whistle of a shell racing somewhere in the distance. Maria Christina was out of bed and had grabbed the Browning before the second burst and suddenly everyone was up and hurrying to the blind room.

Yiannis' battalion had been positioned about twelve hundred feet above Metsovo at the most important pass and road junction, hence the most dangerous. The commander, a Colonel Dovas, a small, square man with wild red hair, had been preparing for an assault for weeks and had requisitioned and received an extra battalion from Larissa. His command now consisted of twenty-three hundred men, which he stationed in the mountains at various strategic points, reinforced with mortars, artillery, and light tanks.

In the silence and darkness of a rainy night, Yiannis' battalion had been suddenly attacked. First came the artillery barrage. Yiannis was awake, lying on his back on his cot, thinking about Maria Christina when he heard the first burst of fire. Before the second, he was up and out of his tent as the shell whistled overhead, overshooting its mark. The next ten hours were spent ankle deep in muck and mud mostly trying to stem the flow of blood, as the battle raged unremittingly. But the three battalions and two companies of communist guerrillas failed to overrun the 587, who fought with fierce determination.

Other Greek garrisons had also suddenly been assaulted. The objective had been to mine, sabotage and control the roads needed by the government reinforcements. Other assaults were undertaken to draw the garrisons away by raiding nearby towns and villages. It was soon evident to Dovas that he was facing a much stronger army than his own. In fact, his twenty-three hundred, many of them untried, were up against nine thousand better equipped, battle tested and trained guerrillas.

Under the cover of fog another battalion of Communists moved unopposed towards the lowest part of Metsovo, where Papa Yiorgos and his family were now huddled in the blind room. Maria Christina was holding Zoitsa with one hand and the Browning inside her cloak in the other, as the sound of small arms fire and grenades could be heard in their very neighborhood. Zoitsa was too terrified to make a sound and was shaking so hard Maria Christina took her hand off the pistol and held her with both hands and rocked her and sang her favorite childhood song in a whisper:

"When I go, my lady, to the fair
I'm going to buy you a rooster.
And the rooster will go Keekeereekeekee
And wake you up every morning."

Just then the door to the blind room could be heard opening. As the sound of gunshots and grenades amplified, Papa Yiorgos leapt to his feet and prepared to use his walking stick as a weapon. A pair of black leather boots appeared on a step, then stopped. Then a hand appeared holding a grenade. Out of the corner of his eye, an astonished Papa Yiorgos saw Maria Christina calmly pull the Browning from her cloak, then quickly aim and squeeze the trigger of the Browning three times fast, two of which shattered the ankle of the soldier, causing him to drop the grenade and fall down the stairs with a groan, landing above the grenade as it exploded, shielding the family but blowing bits of human flesh, blood, and debris in every direction.

Everyone froze for a moment, too frightened to scream or shout or wail when another hand grenade bounced down the steps and landed on what remained of the first soldier. Maria Christina suddenly lunged for the grenade and tossed it up the stairs through the open doorway where it burst in the air, causing a piercing shriek and then a moan of pain. And then nothing. After a moment, Papa Yiorgos put his arms around Panorea and Zoitsa, who was still shaking, and sternly motioned for Maria Christina to give him the gun. She could see the anger in his eyes. How dare she have a gun without his knowledge! Another example of her disrespect! Maria Christina reluctantly obeyed, then cautiously crept up the stairs, suddenly shaking from the fear which had finally caught up to her.

The blind door was covered in the torn flesh of the dead soldier. Maria Christina thought he looked more like a boy than a man as she wondered how they knew the exact location of the door. Could it have been Thomas the veterinarian? It must have been someone carrying out a vendetta against Yiannis or her father for some slight, real or imagined. She felt certain she would never know. The soldier's face was unrecognizable. The gun and mortar rounds continued as she glanced around the stable. Afendoula, together with their other animals had fled through the exterior door which was now unhinged and hanging. With the sound of gunfire and explosions getting closer, Maria Christina closed the blind door, then returned to Zoitsa's side where the child was white with terror.

That night, while the Triantafyllou family remained under ground silently trying to wipe away the horror, the Communists were advancing house to house, street to street. Up in the mountains the attacks against the 587 were repeated with even greater force. For five hours, with morale high, surrounded and badly outnumbered, Yiannis' battalion battled wave after wave of Communists until dawn, when the enemy was forced to retreat. By mid morning all was quiet. Maria Christina cautiously left the secret room with a sack containing the remains of the dead soldier, returning minutes later with two small barrels of water, several towels, a change of clothing for everyone, and Zoitsa's music box.

Over the next few days a series of attacks and counter attacks continued, mostly at night. During the day there was the sporadic exchange of mortar, artillery, and sniper fire. The few citizens who remained in Metsovo remained hidden most of the day and all of the night. On the fourth day, a thick fog enveloped Metsovo until late afternoon. Maria Christina waited for everyone to be asleep before she softly touched Panorea to awaken her. Panorea looked up in amazement as Maria Christina whispered that she would return in a few hours. Then, without explaining herself, she tiptoed up the stairs and slowly opened the blind door.

Maria Christina knew the path well enough to negotiate it undiscovered. Yiannis was not far away and she could not help but try to see him one last time. As she closed the door, she spied the dead Communist's sidearm, a Russian made pistol similar in design to the Browning, lying by his tattered body. She took it out of its case and looked at it a moment, then slipped it under her cloak as she cautiously stepped out the door and into the fog. Twice she was forced to avoid the voices of Communist guerrillas and one time a voice called out from the fog for whoever it was to identify themselves, but she never paused and quietly slipped deeper into the mist until she finally arrived at the outer perimeter of the Greek Army forces. Maria Christina called out in Vlach and almost immediately was answered by a voice she recognized. It was Koureas, a barber from Metsovo, a huge man with a very long and elegantly curled mustache who always wore a cape. Koureas laughed loudly when Maria Christina identified herself and escorted her into the camp and to Yiannis, who was inside a crowded hospital tent of over twenty or more beds, stitching up a young soldier.

In one corner, lifting another soldier from a gurney to a bed, Olimbi, currently a volunteer nurse, was startled when she first saw Maria Christina step into the tent. All of Olimbi's romantic ambitions suddenly evaporated when she saw Yiannis look up from his patient and his face fill with complete joy when he saw Maria Christina. Maria Christina smiled shyly, then bowed her head, turned and exited the tent and waited an eternity, patiently outside, while Yiannis carefully finished the procedure and hurried out to be with her.

Adding insult to injury, Olimbi could see the silhouette of the two coming together, the embrace, the kiss. What she couldn't hear was the whisper of Maria Christina into her lover's ear.

"I love you. With all my heart I love you. That is what I came to say."

That simple phrase pleased him beyond measure. On another occasion he might have leapt and danced with joy, but he simply stood there grinning the widest grin she had ever seen on him. Maria Christina kissed him tenderly on each side of his mouth, then turned and ran back inside the tent and kissed Olimbi sweetly on the cheek and hurried out, kissing Haralambos, who was backing into the tent with a tray of bandages, before she ran back down the mountain through the fog, desperately sad, knowing she might never see any of them again. When she arrived back in the village it was still dark. Unlike the trek up to the camp, the trek down was uneventful until a few steps from her gate when she was suddenly grabbed by her hair from behind and jerked to an excruciatingly painful halt, causing her glasses to fly off her face. With her hand on the nine millimetre pistol, she spun towards her assailant and squeezed twice to his stomach before she even glimpsed his bearded face, then watched as the soldier immediately released his grip and fell backwards.

On hands and knees Maria Christina desperately searched for the glasses, nose nearly to the ground, hoping to retrieve them before other soldiers could arrive. Finally, further away than she ever would have imagined, her hand picked them up. As she started to wipe away the mud, she noticed the left lens was badly cracked. The next day she would sew a piece of black cloth around the cracked lens so that she might at least see clearly through the one good lens. But for that night, after she placed the Russian made pistol into the hand of the dead soldier lying on the ground, she tiptoed down the steps of the little room under the ground and fell into a deep sleep for the first time in four days.

For the next two days the fog prevented planes from dropping supplies. Yiannis' battalion, which was under constant siege, was critically short of food and ammunition. When the weather finally cleared and the battalions were resupplied, the battle resumed for five more days as Greek Army reinforcements were finally converging from both east and west. They had been hampered by fog and the Communist forces that were defending the roads into Metsovo. Finally, on the twelfth day, the last shots were fired in Metsovo and the guerrillas were being chased back into Yugoslavia, with Yiannis and Haralambos following up the rear with their small field hospital strapped to mules.

That morning Lena hurried into the Triantafyllou courtyard and called everyone by name as Maria Christina opened the blind door.

"Is Thimi here?! Is Thimi with you?!"

One glimpse into the tiny room and it was clear that Thimi wasn't there. Lena burst into tears. As the day wore on and the sounds of war receded, more and more of the villagers joined in the search for Thimi. The next day the search widened but no trace of the chubby little girl was ever found, and everyone concluded she had been kidnapped by the Communists and taken to a retraining camp in Yugoslavia or Bulgaria, and sadly returned to the work of clearing rubble and rebuilding roofs and walls.

Afendoula wandered back in the evening, desperate to be milked. The goats were lost but Tatamare gave Papa Yiorgos two from his dwindling herd. The rooster and chickens had never been far away. With the help of Tatamare they rehung the door and the women cleaned and disinfected until once again all seemed normal. And so, in two more days, the few who were left in the village, including Stahoulis, Doctor Pandelis, Tatamare, and her cousin Sophia, came to say good-bye to Maria Christina and Zoitsa. Papa Yiorgos decided that while he was away, Panorea should stay with Lena, who put her arm around her good friend, knowing how lonely she would be without them, and walked behind them up to the square, where Panorea pinned an amulet on each of them and gave them each a tearful kiss. The wagon to Trikala was leaving. With only the clothes on their backs and a few necessities in a small wooden trunk, Maria Christina and Zoitsa climbed onto the back of the wagon and sat among dry goods and barrels while Papa Yiorgos, in his thick black cape and flat-topped hat, sat up front with the muleteer and chatted, during which Maria Christina and Zoitsa watched as the whole village of Metsovo, huddled on the side of the mountain, became smaller and smaller until it finally disappeared behind another peak of the endless Southern Alps.

27

Even though it was the first of November, it still hadn't snowed in the mountains which undulated down from the Katara pass towards the valleys of Trikala. In the fields the rose trees were still in bloom, the great forest of beeches hadn't yet shed their bright russet and bronze leaves, and the occasional burst of bright red from the oak, all against the stark purple and grey of the mountain crests, inspired Papa Yiorgos to comment to the muleteer that there was no artist great enough who could possibly capture the beauty of God's creation. After an hour or so of chatting, he fell silent. As the wagon continued around and down the mountain, he leaned back on the bench and closed his eyes, letting his mind wander, listening to the clip clop of the mules and the squeak of an ornery wheel. He suddenly saw himself as a boy, racing in an open field toward his mother with his older brother, Petros, who had died of cholera the year Matoula was born. He had hardly thought of him these past few years except on his name day. How the time had flown by. So many loved ones come and gone. Nothing had turned out the way he had thought. Petros. His wife, Thimi. The children. The weight of responsibility had imprisoned him early in his life. He opened his eyes to change the subject and quickly engaged the muleteer about the possibility of rain, pointing to the curly edged cloud formations in the eastern sky.

The wagon veered off the road and stopped to allow a small convoy of army trucks to pass. Maria Christina sat leaning against a barrel in the wagon bed, holding Zoitsa to her breast, combing her curly hair with her fingers, silently praying these men and supplies were headed towards Yiannis and his battalion.

For Maria Christina, leaving a dangerous world behind and going into the unknown with her frightened niece was simply exchanging one set of fears for another. She had never been further than Igoumenitsa. The world beyond Epirus was a complete mystery. She had heard about electricity. It could light your way, but would kill you if you touched it. Automobiles were fast and more comfortable but they forced everyone else off the road and they frightened the animals. Robbers were everywhere. You couldn't trust anyone. Maria Christina tenderly kissed the top of Zoitsa's head. Being able to hold Yiannis' and Matoula's child was like holding the two people in the world she loved most. Her niece was already almost nine. Her adult face was beginning to show itself. Although so much had changed for almost everyone in the last seven years, Zoitsa knew only the sameness of war. America would be good for her. To grow properly, a child needed to live in peace. As these thoughts occupied her mind, the convoy passed and the wagon continued on its way.

As soon as Metsovo was out of view, Zoitsa had begun to cry softly. She missed Thimi and worried about her safety. Maria Christina put her arms tightly around her and rocked her, assuring her that Thimi was safe and had been taken to a camp where they would treat her very well.

"And when the war is over, my golden girl, she will return to Metsovo just like we will. And everything will be as it was before the war. When we were all happy."

Having lost her mother and best friend and afraid of losing her father at any moment, Zoitsa's greatest fear became losing Maria Christina, leaving her as helpless as her dear aunt without her glasses. As a result she now clung to Maria Christina like her aunt clung to her glasses, and almost always kept her in her line of vision.

At midday they stopped for their meal and to water the mules. While the muleteer tended the animals, Maria Christina and Zoitsa laid out a wedge of feta cheese, pieces of dried apple, and a loaf of bread. As soon as he sat down, Papa Yiorgos started talking about his wife, Thimi, and how much he missed her. It reminded Zoitsa once again of how much she missed her Thimi and she lay her head onto Maria Christina's lap and silently wept as Papa Yiorgos, oblivious, continued his reverie. It was the first time Maria Christina ever heard her father talk about his life so openly, how he had met and married his Thimi, how she had been his guiding light. How losing her was like taking a cloud and forever covering the sun. Then he sighed and looked down and ate silently for the rest of the meal. He was the first to finish and returned to the wagon, downcast. For the rest of the day he spoke very few words.

By the time they arrived in Trikala it was dark, but there were electric lights hung on poles. Maria Christina and Zoitsa were astonished by the lights, which illuminated the street more than the fullest of moons and were reflected off the wet cobblestones. As the wagon continued through the town, they stared wide-eyed at all the lights in the houses and stores and the many vehicles on the streets that weren't military. Finally they stopped in front of a small hotel. The innkeeper didn't think it was at all odd when the priest checked in with two young women and wanted a single room and one bed was fine. They were from Metsovo.

In the early morning, while the girls slept, Papa Yiorgos crept out of bed and took Maria Christina's glasses from the bedside table and left the room. Walking through the town invigorated his spirit. He bought a small cheese pie and ate it as he canvassed all the windows of all the stores that sold women's clothing, finally choosing one because it seemed to sell everything they would need.

When Maria Christina awoke, she and Zoitsa spent the better part of an hour searching for the precious glasses, while Papa Yiorgos stood outside the optometrist's shop waiting for it to open, making a list of what each of the girls would need: one church outfit, two every day outfits, one coat, one pair of shoes which they should keep shined. After he dropped off the glasses, he hurried back to the hotel to take the two on their first shopping trip for ready-made clothes.

Maria Christina suddenly became the helpless woman she once had been, needing someone to see for her. It was deeply humbling. The whole morning was a blur of colors and shapes. In the store she was being dressed in western clothes by an aggressive saleslady: skirts and blouses, suits and hats. She had always relied on Matoula to decide on her wardrobe and could only hope the saleslady had at least a modicum of taste.

Papa Yiorgos insisted the travellers wear their new everyday western outfits out of the store and asked the saleslady to wrap their old garments for him to take back to Metsovo. Maria Christina insisted on keeping them "For when we return home." With arms full of packages, the two followed Papa Yiorgos out of the store in their new western garb and walked uncomfortably down the street, praying the saleslady was telling the truth that the stiff leather of their new shoes would soon soften and stretch. They felt as if they were wearing costumes, not clothing. The fabrics felt weightless and flimsy. The hats were not very practical. As they sashayed down the street behind Papa Yiorgos, the two became giggly pretending they were vacationing English ladies.

Passing a bookstore, Papa Yiorgos stepped inside and bought

them each a Greek/English pocket dictionary and a newspaper for himself. Continuing down the street, he glanced at the paper's banner headline which was the slogan of the national army 'Freedom or Death'. The priest laughed softly then blessed himself three times as he quickly scanned the other headlines with a smile, 'Communists Lose Battle of Metsovo' and 'Dovas Forces Prove Impregnable'.

When they stopped for a meal at a taverna, Papa Yiorgos ordered pork chops for everyone, a rare treat usually reserved for an extra special occasion. Once again he talked about his Thimi, but this time he confused several facts and dates. And then he suddenly stopped in the middle of a word and vowed that when he went home, he would read the entire encyclopedia starting with the A's. To Maria Christina he seemed too young to be so confused. Perhaps he was just tired. Since Matoula's death, she had been aware he was aging quickly, but only now did she realize the time she would have to make her peace with him was shorter than she had thought. And yet, he also seemed uncharacteristically free and jolly. Maybe being away from the critical eye of the community made him feel more relaxed.

On the way back to their hotel, they stopped at the optometrist. Maria Christina sat while the optometrist adjusted the frames of Pappou's glasses on her face as he tried to sell her a more modern feminine frame. Papa Yiorgos agreed with him, but Maria Christina adamantly rejected the notion, and Papa Yiorgos immediately backed down. Their last stop was to buy a mid-sized steamer trunk. The girls stayed outside the store looking at their reflection in the window. They agreed that even though the saleslady was loud, her taste was quite good. The simplicity of design and color vaguely reminded Maria Christina of the clothes her contact from Bouboulina wore. She concluded they probably didn't look as silly as they felt.

The medium sized steamer trunk was delivered to the hotel later that day. Two bibles, all their new purchases, their old

Metsovo clothes, several sets of undergarments, night wear, Zoitsa's music box, their braids, and the two best hand woven pieces from their house, gifts for Nikos Petrakis and his wife Eleni, not only fit in the one steamer, but there was room to spare. Packing was completed and the trunk closed in less than ten minutes.

Exhausted, Papa Yiorgos laid down for his afternoon nap and didn't awaken until after dark, which meant it was too dangerous to be out on the street, so the three sat in their room in front of a small fire and listened to Papa Yiorgos talk about what a great man Zoitsa's father was and what a goddess the child had for a mother, just like his own wife, Thimi, whom he missed so much, until he caught himself wandering and suddenly stopped, laughed bemused, excused himself, and bid everyone good night.

The old priest lay in bed awake for hours, thinking about Maria Christina. Her independence challenged him. Frightened him. He finally acknowledged her exceptional abilities and his own fault in not recognizing them before now. He even felt guilty that he had deliberately tried to retard her development, although he did think at the time he was doing what was best. And in his mind he had forgiven her, but he could not totally release the anger he felt towards her and he couldn't explain why. He knew Matoula's death was part of God's Divine plan, as it had been that Judas betray Christ. It occurred to him that although one might forgive Judas, if Judas were in the room, one couldn't help but be angry with him. Clearly, then, one could forgive and still be angry. This simple realization satisfied him sufficiently to allow him to finally surrender to his fatigue, and he rolled over and went to sleep.

In the morning, the train station was crowded with soldiers. As he helped Maria Christina carry the trunk to the baggage car, Papa Yiorgos was explaining for the third time how Yiannis had arranged for someone to meet them at the station in Athens who would take them to Zervas' home. Then he ushered them up into the passenger car, which had a single row of seats on either side of a narrow center aisle. When they found theirs, Papa Yiorgos picked Zoitsa up and held her tight.

"I love you, Moumou" he whispered in her ear. "Go with God."

Then he kissed her on both cheeks and on her forehead and held out his arms to Maria Christina, who couldn't quite reach him with Zoitsa in the way. But they did manage to have their arms and hands touching.

"I love you, Patera. And wish you good health."

"I wish you good health as well, daughter. Go with God."

"Thank you, father. I will write."

Though she continued to smile, Maria Christina's heart was sinking. Her father easily might have said he loved her. He would have to Matoula. Even to Panorea he might have been able to utter those words. But not to her. He turned and hurried out of the car as the train started to move. Standing on the platform, he waved goodbye to his daughter, who was waving back, her lips still frozen in that smile. Suddenly his granddaughter appeared in the window beside her aunt and blew him kisses.

The priest watched the train as it became smaller and smaller. Rather than feeling sad, he began to feel weightless. For the first time since he was a boy he was without responsibility. After the train had disappeared, he remained on the platform for a long moment plotting his next move. His original intent was to wait the two days for the wagon to return to Metsovo, but the day was young, the sun was shining, and the fields and mountains were so enticing that he decided to take his time and walk home from Trikala. His first stop was to check out of the hotel and leave the wooden trunk with the owner with instructions to the muleteer that he was already on his way home. He then telegraphed Yiannis that the girls were on the train, then went for a coffee and a *tsipouro* and a quiet read of the morning newspaper.

After two shots of *tsipouro* with his two coffees, the second of which he asked to be brewed with extra sugar, Papa Yiorgos started back to Metsovo, stopping every hour or so to sit and admire God's glorious creation.

Maria Christina stared out at the passing countryside for a long time, thinking about her father. With a sigh she finally concluded that, having to say goodbye in such a hurry amid such confusion, one could never express what the moment deserved, and she decided to remain confident that when the war was over and she was married to Yiannis, she and her father would finally become as close as she had always dreamed. Zoitsa was more interested in reading the newspaper than watching the passing landscape. When her grandfather discarded it in the hotel room, Zoitsa picked it up and started reading and rereading what she thought were the most interesting stories. Maria Christina made a mental note she would buy her niece a newspaper every day.

Small herds of sheep were grazing along the side of the tracks. As she continued to stare out the window, Maria Christina wondered how many generations it would take to rebuild the herds to pre war levels. That thought led to her lamenting the passing of her own childbearing years, which then led her to Yiannis. No matter what momentarily diverted her attention, her thoughts always returned to his sweet face, their sweet simple love.

As morning bled into afternoon, the chatter among the passengers in the smoke-filled car quieted down. Zoitsa moved across the aisle and squeezed in next to Maria Christina on her seat. They shared a piece of feta cheese and bread with several dried prunes. The landscape changed to flat acreage of farmland.

There were several stops where the two stepped out of the car for some air and huddled together on the station platform for a minute or two, then hurried back to their seat long before the conductor called for boarding, afraid the train might leave without them. Sundown came quickly. At the front of the car, a baby started crying and continued for an hour or so until, finally, the clickety clack of the train through the darkness put them all to sleep.

At the first sign of evening, Papa Yiorgos found shelter in a small cave and built a fire while he could still see well enough to gather wood. He opened his small sack and took out the remains of the cheese and the bottle of water. The small fire cast shadows onto the wall of the cave which, after a while, appeared to Papa Yiorgos like the silhouettes of the licking flames of hell. Staring at the wall for a long time, he began to see himself in those flames. He was indeed in hell. He was utterly alone. Of course, there was Panorea always hovering but, still, he was alone. Alone and desperately lonely. He put his hands to his face and began sobbing. Then, suddenly he was raging, only this time it was not disguised as prayer.

"Why did you let this happen to me! Why did you take her from me! And my Matoula! What have I done to you that you should deny me so! That you should punish me! Your servant! Speak to me, Lord! Show yourself …!"

In that moment he realized what he never had the courage to admit to himself. He wasn't angry with Maria Christina. He was angry with Him. The Divine Planner. His vengeful Design that had made him feel so bereft. It was in that moment that he had an epiphany. He realized his own sin. All those years lost. All that time resenting her, even as an infant, blaming her for her mother's death. How could he have been so unforgiving? Even as he watched her live with her handicap, resenting her even more for having it. He was a small, small man. The one person whom he should have held closest had slipped through his life unloved and unacknowledged, and it was for that the Lord was angry and he deserved His wrath.

Papa Yiorgos sat convulsing in sobs which came from the deepest part of his soul. How sad for an old man. Alone and lonely, punished by God. He spent the next hours begging for His forgiveness and vowed that, as soon as he returned home, he would sit down and write Maria Christina a letter and tell her how much he loved her and how proud he was of her and beg her forgiveness.

28

The train finally pulled into the central station in Athens, waking the weary travellers as it jolted to a halt. Maria Christina and Zoitsa exited the train and were walking towards the baggage car, when a young man in a suit walked up to them and introduced himself.

"Miss Petrakis? Miss Triantafyllou? Good evening, ladies. My name is Mihalis. I am an aide to Minister Napoleon Zervas. I am to be your driver and guide while you are in Athens. The Minister sends his compliments and insists you join him for breakfast in the morning."

Mihalis then ushered the dumbstruck travellers into the back seat of a big black sedan, Zervas' personal car, then he retrieved their trunk from the baggage car. The girls had never sat in anything nearly so luxurious as the soft leather seats. The car whisked them across the endless city past dazzling lights and magnificent buildings. As taxis sped by them on the wide boulevards, the two travellers spent the entire ride pointing out things to each other, a shop that only sold shoes, another just furniture.

In a section populated with mansions, Mihalis drove the sedan through large wrought iron gates and came to a stop in front of the largest house they had ever seen. After exiting the sedan, they stood arm in arm looking up and around with eyes wide when the front door opened and an attractive young maid greeted them. With a smile, Mihalis introduced her as his wife, Magdalena. She greeted them, then ushered the travellers inside and up a grand staircase to their room, explaining that the house was being lent to the Minister while he looked for an apartment which better suited his taste and temperament. They would sleep in the master suite. The Minister preferred one of the smaller bedrooms.

The remainder of the night unfolded like a dream. The bedroom was more than half the size of their whole house, grander than either ever imagined a king's might be, with four large windows and two French doors which opened onto a balcony overlooking a walled garden. They declined Magdalena's offer to unpack for them, and followed her as she showed them the toilet and how to flush it, the sink with running water, and the bell to summon her, if they wanted something to eat, then she bid them good evening, and left.

For several moments the two were too overwhelmed to speak. Then Zoitsa ran into the bathroom and flushed the toilet, flicked on the light and turned on the tap to watch the water flow. Maria Christina wasn't quite sure whether the high platform with a canopy and dozens of fluffy white pillows was where they were supposed to sleep or if it was a purely decorative piece. After much stifled giggling, the two decided it must be the bed and carefully took most of the pillows and laid them on a chair, then carefully lay on top of the bedcovers and held hands for the rest of the night. Neither could sleep. Twice during the night Zoitsa climbed out of bed and went to the bathroom to turn on the light and flush the toilet.

By dawn they were washed, combed and dressed in their church clothes. While they waited silently in the opulent dining room for Zervas, Magdalena served them feta cheese, stewed prunes, bread, butter, and mountain tea from Epirus in thin porcelain cups like the ones Pappou had brought home from Bulgaria, which were stored in a cabinet in their sitting room with the family's other treasures. Maria Christina was beginning to understand what everyone was fighting for: some to protect such wealth and beauty, mansions, assistants, and power, while others to escape their poverty, hunger, and despair.

The two wide-eyed travellers sat silently across from one another for a half hour, until Zervas strode into the room and greeted them with his booming voice. Maria Christina remembered him as a much larger, rounder man. He was thinner, his beard was trimmed and his hair slicked back. He was on his way to the Peloponnesus for an inspection of the troops and would be gone for several days, but for now he was entirely focused on the two young ladies and their plight. He told Zoitsa how much he admired her father and what a pleasure it was for him to look after his daughter while she was in Athens. Her father had told him they had never been to a city bigger than Metsovo.

"Don't worry about a thing, Yianni, I told him. You get them to the train station, I'll get them to the boat."

After a half hour, when Zervas had to say goodbye, he held Maria Christina's hands and looked into her pleading eyes a moment, then smiled.

"Don't worry about a thing" he whispered as he kissed her cheek. "You take good care of his daughter. I'll take good care of him."

The thought made Maria Christina smile the rest of the morning. At the American Embassy, Mihalis led her swiftly through the process, photographs, fingerprints. Zoitsa would be listed on Maria Christina's passport as 'Zoitsa Petrakis, niece'.

Magdalena had prepared an excellent lunch for them: lamb

stew with onions and potatoes and baklava for dessert. Every bite was savored by the two, who had never tasted anything quite so delicious, and Maria Christina wanted to know everything involved in its preparation. After lunch, due to Zervas' influence, Maria Christina's visa was waiting and a courteous clerk showed her where to sign and the smiling bursar gave her a fat manila envelope from Nick Petrakis, which contained two hundred American dollars in assorted bills and two tickets for the passenger ship, the *Nea Hellas*, which was sailing for New York the next day. The girls were too excited to nap, so Mihalis took them for a tour of the city. At the Acropolis, when Maria Christina first saw the Parthenon, she had to keep herself from weeping. It was the perfect shrine for the Greek nation: ancient, broken and proud. She shook her head and looked out over the city, and then at Mihalis, who was about the same age as the guerrilla whom she had killed in her father's stable. She wondered which of the two would be the future of Greece.

The weary travellers slept through tea and didn't awaken until 7:30 when Magdalena knocked softly, then entered their room to see if they required anything and to announce that dinner would be served in half an hour. The two sat silently in the dining room while Magdalena and Mihalis served them goat soup, a leek pie, and tea from Epirus, all at Zervas suggestion. Neither was hungry but ate out of politeness. When they were finished, they thanked the young couple, excused themselves, and went to their room where they lay in bed until late in the night, holding hands and talking about all of the things they had seen since they left Metsovo. Just before she fell asleep, Zoitsa curled into Maria Christina and said softly.

"I miss Babá."

At that moment, near the Yugoslavian border, Yiannis was

thinking about his daughter while sitting around a fire with Haralambos and Olimbi. Yiannis was surprised by how truly happy Olimbi had been about his proposed marriage to Maria Christina. Her spirit was as large and generous as her person. Of course she was convinced Zoitsa had greatly influenced her father's decision, but felt it was probably best for everyone. She had a myriad of choices, while poor Maria Christina really had none, other than her widowed brother-in-law. Having volunteered as an army field nurse, she enjoyed the work so much that she eventually enlisted. Haralambos pulled a few strings to have her assigned to their unit. Since the Communists had retreated, there was little for them to do at the front and the three often found themselves sitting around a fire, chatting and sipping *tsipouro*. From their very first meeting Olimbi enjoyed Haralambos immensely, even though he was practically old enough to be her father. She was particularly fond of punching him on the arm whenever he made her laugh.

Yiannis appeared congenial, but beneath the surface there was a growing sadness. He often worried that his life would be cut short. He knew the Communists would not give up easily and that there was still a long war ahead, and he despaired that he might never see his daughter and Maria Christina again. So much of his life seemed wasted in longing, longing to see his daughter grow, the sound of her laugh, longing for Maria Christina's love and comfort, and he mourned the never ending stream of young men, some still boys, broken or choking on dreams now out of reach. This one would never play soccer again, that one would never sing. The accumulation of it all produced a great sorrow Yiannis carried hidden under a still plucky exterior while sitting around a fire, drinking *tsipouro* and waiting for the Communists to mount another attack.

Papa Yiorgos continued grieving as he journeyed back to Metsovo. He was sorely ashamed of his sin and vowed to spend the rest of his days doing penance. He even vowed to refrain from drinking *tsipouro* for the rest of his life, no small sacrifice, since it was his favorite earthly pleasure. In the afternoon, he entered the main chapel of the Roussanou Monastery high atop a jagged mountain peak called Meteora, where he stayed all night and prayed. At daybreak, he continued on his way, anxious now to return to his flock, grateful for God's blessings, with a lightness he hadn't felt since he was a boy.

As he was leaving the village of Kalambaka at the foot of Meteora and was beginning the long climb up the mountain to Metsovo, he began composing the letter to Maria Christina in his head. He had already decided that 'My dearest darling daughter' would be the salutation when he heard the muffled sound of a woman crying for help. Moving quickly towards the voice, Papa Yiorgos first saw two overturned pails spilling milk onto the red earth. He quickened his pace and soon saw a man strike a young woman with one hand, his other covering her mouth. She was pinned against a fallen tree and struggling to resist him.

"You there! Get away from her!" the priest cried, waving his walking stick as he hurried towards them, not realizing when he saw the muzzle flashes and heard the two shots that he would be dead before he hit the ground.

A band was playing as Maria Christina and Zoitsa stood on the pier and looked up at the huge hull of the TSS *Nea Hellas*, once again too overwhelmed to speak. They had never seen anything made by man at such close range that was so enormous. They were travelling second class: one hundred eighty dollars per adult and ninety per child. Maria Christina made a note of the amount. It was her plan to repay her future brother-in-law every last cent he had advanced them.

The *Nea Hellas*, with its twelve hundred passengers and three hundred crew, left the pier with Maria Christina and

Zoitsa leaned against the railing, arm in arm, waving goodbye to Mihalis and Magdalena, who had driven them to the pier in Piraeus. Before they were even out of sight, Zoitsa asked to go to the front of the boat to see where they were going, but Maria Christina insisted on staying for as long as she could still see her beloved Greece. Zoitsa was looking forward to finally seeing her Uncle Nikos and America, and wondering what her new friends would be like, while Maria Christina was praying to the Virgin to keep everyone safe until they returned.

Even after land had finally disappeared in the mist, Maria Christina remained at the railing, thinking about what her father always said about the Lord not closing one door without opening another, when Zoitsa firmly took her aunt's hand and pulled her away from the past and led her to the front of the boat, and towards their future.

29

For two days a light rain washed away any trace of the milk that had been spilled by the hapless young woman from Kalambaka before anyone noticed Papa Yiorgos, lying on his back in the mud, staring startled at the sky. His murder was a mystery. Robbery wasn't the motive. He was found to have a small pouch of gold sovereigns on his person. There was no evidence of a struggle, only the two bullet holes, one in the chest, one in the forehead. There was speculation he was murdered by a godless Communist, or someone with a vendetta. It was still very dangerous to be walking around alone and unarmed. Within two hours of the discovery, Papa Yiorgos' eyes were closed and he was bathed by two local women, wrapped in a sheet and then a blanket, placed under a tarp in the bed of a small wagon, then taken in the rain by two monks to Metsovo.

Upon hearing the news all color except yellow drained from Panorea's face and hands and didn't return. It was as if her whole reason for being had suddenly been stolen from her. The funeral was extremely well attended. Panorea and Tatamare wept throughout the service. People from neighboring villages flocked to pay their last respects to Father Happy. Archimandrite Petsalis led the mass with two priests in assistance. On the way to the cemetery the Archimandrite was overheard telling the other priests what a splendid, humble, thoughtful, and rare man Papa Yiorgos was. How the priest sometimes sought his advice on matters of moral significance when a parishioner was having a problem.

"I'll be praying *to* him, not *for* him" the Archimandrite was saying. "There is no question in my mind he will be a saint in heaven as he was on earth."

30

If it was true that the Lord never closed one door without opening another, for most of the passengers, the *Nea Hellas* was that door. Nicknamed 'The Ship of Dreams', the big steamship was filled with immigrants to America with little in their purse but with hope in their hearts that a new life in a new land would bring them peace and undreamt of prosperity.

Once the ship was in the open sea, Captain Thomas greeted everyone on the loudspeaker. With a warm and welcoming voice he spoke about the size and speed of the vessel, the sailing time, fifteen days, the ports at which they would be stopping, Naples, Gibraltar, Halifax, and finally on to New York. There was a large children's playroom, a ballroom, a movie theatre, and a bar.

Their cabin had two sets of bunk beds. When they first entered, Zoitsa excitedly climbed up to a top bunk and told her aunt how glorious it was, but after a few minutes she climbed back down and never returned. She then opened a door to what she assumed was a closet, but which revealed a flushing toilet and a sink. She immediately flushed the toilet and turned the knobs on the sink and water rushed out. Everyone had lights that shone by flipping a small switch, flushing toilets, and indoor fountains except the people in Metsovo, and she wondered if someone shouldn't tell them about such things. After they unpacked, the first thing Zoitsa did was to write her grandfather and ask him to instruct the mayor he should fix the situation immediately.

As she was writing the letter, their two cabin mates shyly entered, having been lost this half hour: a twenty-five year old widow, Angela, and her seven-year-old daughter, Alexandra, both in mourning clothes. They were on their way to Paramus in the state of New Jersey to live with Angela's brother. Her husband had been executed by the Security Battalion in their village square in the Peloponnesus along with five other men. As they retreated, the Security Battalion set fire to several houses, leaving Angela and Alexandra and the other survivors to watch helplessly as their whole village burned to the ground.

Maria Christina would always remember her days on the boat as being a very happy time: the steward playing the chimes to announce meals three times a day, dining tables covered with crisp white cloths, long buffet tables crammed with foods from America, many of which people from the small villages had never seen before. Everyone was overwhelmed by the abundance. There was bacon and ham and eggs for breakfast, luscious fruits, meats of all kinds and vegetables for lunch and dinner, and unheard of sweets like ice cream, which became banana splits, a big favorite. There was also an endless supply of snacks and treats in the afternoon, like delicious home made rolls with honey or maple syrup. For the passengers fleeing a war-ravaged country, the voyage was one long royal banquet. At dinner, Captain Thomas would walk around the tables of the huge dining room, talking to the guests. Once he even sat next to Alexandra and chatted while cutting her meat.

Zoitsa was happily occupied being the big sister and guardian angel to the younger girl. Seeing how difficult life had been for her and her mother made Zoitsa appreciate how fortunate they had been in Metsovo. Angela hardly ever appeared at the table, but spent most of the voyage in the cabin in the bottom bunk nearest the toilet. Maria Christina was concerned about her apparent frail health and kept a close eye on her during the voyage.

A chart posted near the purser's office showed the ship's progress, and Maria Christina and the two children followed it every day. For those so inclined there was Greek music in the bar and dancing at night to a band which consisted of a zither, an accordion, and a bouzouki. There was also a *cafenion* where the older men would sit drinking coffee and playing backgammon and pinochle. For most of the passengers it was the first time in eight years they weren't under attack or in fear of one. In spite of the dreary weather, the atmosphere was light and happy. Everyone who wasn't seasick was smiling.

In Metsovo, the mood was more solemn. A light rain had turned to snow. The men with their greatly reduced flocks were now in the lower elevations, and those left in the village had settled in for the endless winter. Lena had become concerned about Panorea and tried to convince her to lock up the Triantafyllou house and live with her until the girls returned. But Panorea preferred to remain in her own house, surrounded by the blackened textiles and fabrics that covered the windows, doors, walls and floors. More and more she was beginning to shun the light and lately rarely even lit more than one candle a day.

Lena would stop by twice a day with provisions and news. Panorea had seldom ever spoken about herself, but now she would sometimes ramble on about how she longed for the children to return, and how she let her own life pass without having had any of her own, and the regret that she didn't have the courage to seek her happiness by running away to Athens. Even though she wasn't running to anyone, she might have found a husband in a city with so many men. She admitted she was both envious and proud of Maria Christina for being so brave, and that in retrospect her own life by comparison was all the more tragic because it was of her own making, which made her want to retreat even further into the darkness.

Tatamare also would stop by two or three times a week to see if she wanted anything, if there was anything in need of repair. She would offer him a glass of water and a spoon sweet, and they would sit, sometimes silently, for ten minutes or more, after which Tatamare would stand, bow gracefully, thank Panorea for her hospitality and leave, reminding her he would be back in a couple of days to look in on her.

Obliged to no one but herself, the poor old spinster still obliged herself nothing but regrets, and wasted her days sitting in the dark, watching the snowflakes dance around the tiny fireplace window, waiting for the next anniversary of her brother's death so she could wail with the other women.

Pappou had always told Maria Christina the ocean was the blue of the Greek flag, but all she had ever seen of the sea was various shades of grey and green and white. It had been overcast since they left Piraeus and, other than a walk around the decks, the three spent most of their days indoors in the children's playroom where Zoitsa played with Alexandra, teaching her English words she would need to know like 'visa' and 'candy'. On the second day of the voyage, Maria Christina discovered the ship's library and decided that each day she would read to the children from the book she borrowed, *A Child's History of the United States of America*. It told about the founding fathers, the structure of the government, and the constitution which, she pointed out, was inspired by the government created by Pericles in ancient Greece.

"What kind of government do we have now?" Zoitsa asked in response.

Maria Christina thought for a moment. How could she explain in simple terms that the Greeks were an old people in a young country, in existence only since 1821? That although their ancestors had given birth to the modern idea of democracy, their Danish king was in England with his government and his army, leaving a vacuum which the Communist Party was eagerly filling? And that the Republicans, like Babá, hated them and the monarchy equally, and wanted to return to the democracy of Pericles. "Greece is not sure what kind of government it wants to be" she finally answered with a sigh. "That's what the war is about."

Tuesdays and Fridays were movie nights. They were always well attended. Neither Maria Christina or Zoitsa had ever seen a moving picture before and went to every screening: *The Philadelphia Story*, where Cary Grant was still in love with slim Katherine Hepburn, or Humphrey Bogart and wispy Lauren Bacall in *The Big Sleep*. Handsome, dashing men chasing slender, even petite women, convinced Maria Christina that the world really did view beauty differently than they did in Metsovo, just as Pappou had told her, and that being slender was in fact considered attractive in the rest of the world. But now that she was happily spoken for, she didn't want to be attractive to any other man, and decided she should wear her headscarf again.

The day after the *Nea Hellas* left Naples, the sun rose in a cloudless sky. When Maria Christina went out on deck and first looked out over the sea, the water and the foam were finally the true colors of the Greek flag. She stood in the sun for a long moment, holding the railing and staring out at the endless blue and white striped sea. She began to weep. She was in love. She was so happy just to be standing there, thinking about him. The sea was safe, beautiful, even nurturing. The sway of the big ship as it churned its way towards a whole new world, rekindled her hope that in the end all would turn out well. Looking down she could see dolphins swimming along with them. Letting her mind wander, she recalled Pappou and how everything he had ever said turned out to be true. "I'll go drown myself in the well if it's not true!" she recalled his voice so clearly. He had even predicted both wars before anyone. The thought of his smile made her smile even as she continued to weep. Having been caught up in the present and future, she realized how little thought she had given to the past for some time now. Maybe there was such as a thing as a Divine Plan after all. She thought about Matoula, how much of life she was missing, seeing Zoitsa grow, and how much she herself had grown these past years. She pondered the sad fact that, without their passing, her life would not be what it had become, which brought her back to Yiannis, without any logical connection to the special way he sometimes grinned at her after he kissed her. She had sold the beautiful intricately carved oak and black pine chest that Pappou had fashioned for her dowry along with her other weavings, and now that she needed one, she didn't have one. She was amused by the irony. Maria Christina promised herself she would take this trip with him some day and stroll on the deck arm in arm on their way to America to visit Nikos and Eleni, and with that she meandered off to join Zoitsa, who was now feeling comfortable enough to go to the children's playroom with Alexandra unsupervised.

That same morning it was bitterly cold in Metsovo. For several days a dense fog continued to enshroud the hills above the village, where the 587 had once again been regrouping. Yiannis had already organized his hospital tent and had just finished writing a letter to Maria Christina and Zoitsa. At his feet was a sack filled with canned meats, sugar, flour, and coffee pilfered from the kitchen supply. He was looking forward to taking it to Papa Yiorgos at first light and getting news of the girls when the sound of grenades and machine gun fire exploded all around him.

Surrounded by guerrillas, the entire battalion was suddenly ankle deep in snow and blood. Over five thousand rebel forces from Yugoslavia had slipped back into Greece and had spread across the Pindos range. Reinforced by thirty-five hundred other fighters, they had moved down from the high mountains under the cover of the thick fog. Yiannis' battalion became the defenders of Metsovo. As the battle raged, it moved down into the streets. Most of the men being away, the fight was joined mostly by the women and the older children, using their little stone houses as small forts, until the attack was finally repulsed. Yiannis' hospital was quickly overwhelmed with casualties.

Panorea was awakened early that morning by the sound of grenade and machine gun fire, and quickly took Yiannis' Browning and sought refuge in the blind room where Lena soon joined her. With the sounds of the battle echoing in the streets all around, the old women remained in silence in the dark, praying they would not be discovered. The pistol in Panorea's lap was so much heavier than she had imagined.

"Just point and pull the trigger" Papa Yiorgos had counselled her, although he never showed her how to reload it, and she wondered what she would do when she ran out of bullets. It was then she realized that people she couldn't identify seemed to be moving in the house above.

Around midnight, there was a second attack, fiercer and stronger, and unyielding, which partially succeeded but in the end the Communists withdrew. Then, a little before dawn, another attack which involved savage hand to hand combat with pitchforks, knives, hunting rifles, and bayonets. The Communists were stunned at the strength and ferocity of the women, and at sunrise they withdrew again. For several hours it was quiet.

As soon as she thought Yiannis could spare her, Olimbi asked him for permission to check on the needs of her relatives as well as Papa Yiorgos and Panorea. During the two hours Olimbi was gone, Yiannis and Haralambos continued to work feverishly. When she returned, Olimbi went back to work immediately assisting them, as she reported.

"My family has evidently fled to the forest. The Triantafyllou house is being occupied by our army. They said they had seen no priest nor any old woman. No one else was around. But the house was dressed for mourning which was why they liked it. The lack of light."

There was nothing anyone could say to console Yiannis as he continued to sew a piece of torn flesh to a soldier's thigh, methodically, carefully. Someone in the house obviously had died. He thanked Olimbi and prayed it was not one of his girls, who were supposed to be somewhere safe on the Atlantic. Zervas had assured him he would see to it. Still, Yiannis hadn't heard from anyone and, in spite of the fact that nobody could say when the Communists would attack again and how many days the army would be able to hold out before reinforcements arrived, he could not stop worrying about them nor rest until he knew they were safe in New York. It was probably either Papa Yiorgos or Panorea who had died. Perhaps even both. But he couldn't afford to be diverted any longer. The wound was not yet completely sutured and there were still so many more men to mend.

As the *Nea Hellas* cruised towards Halifax, Maria Christina was awakened by the sound of someone using a key to enter the cabin. As she tensed, a sailor silently stepped over to the porthole window and locked it. The weather, though foggy and drizzly, otherwise seemed calm. A half hour later, Captain Thomas announced over the loudspeaker that there was an impending storm and the guests would be well advised to stay indoors. In twenty minutes the porthole was under green water. The waves were mountainous, and the ship was lurching. Maria Christina was holding a frightened Zoitsa in their lower bunk. The wind was roaring. They had never heard anything so loud. During huge wave troughs, the stern lifted out of the water and the whole ship shook from the vibration of the propeller. The ship was in the control of the sea. It was terrifying. Captain Thomas kept the bow into the storm and kept pressing. Later when they saw the chart at the purser's office, Maria Christina realized the ship had made absolutely no progress for eight hours. For almost that many hours she held Zoitsa and quietly prayed with her. Neither knew how to swim, and Zoitsa was frightened of drowning, as if even an Olympic swimmer could have survived in these waters. Maria Christina was never afraid. Once she would have been petrified, but now her will to live was so strong she felt invincible. She would survive somehow, and bring Zoitsa with her.

Angela, seasick since Piraeus, began to vomit. Her retching made Zoitsa sick, then Alexandra. After several hours Angela became panicked and started snivelling hysterically, and Maria Christina had to leave Zoitsa to comfort her. At that moment Zoitsa, abandoning her own fear, went and held a terrified Alexandra, all the more frightened because her mother was out of control, and rocked her and sang:

"When I go, my lady to the fair
I'm going to buy you a rooster.
And the rooster will go Keekeereekeekee
And wake you up every morning."

Nobody went to breakfast or lunch. Nobody could even think about food. Finally, the sea became calm. At dinner, Maria Christina and Zoitsa were the only passengers at their table. The smell of vomit filtered through the air in the lower deck and even into the dining room.

Maria Christina spent the next few days idly knitting or strolling around the decks, as the big ship slowly rocked back and forth, day and night, never breaking its rhythm. The sea was like a great blue and white meadow they were gliding through. It was what some might have imagined heaven to be. The feeling of being safe and at peace was enveloping and everyone on board radiated a rare happiness.

At each port, the *Nea Hellas* would take on *The Atlantis*, a national daily Greek language newspaper. The Civil War had subsided when they left Gibraltar, but by the time they arrived in Halifax, they were greeted by a stack of newspapers covered in ice that were delivered to the ship with the headline 'Civil War Rages On' and described what it termed 'The Second Battle of Metsovo'. Copies of the newspaper sold out immediately and were passed around and read and reread by all the passengers, including several times by Maria Christina, until it was finally discarded by everyone but Zoitsa, who continued to read and reread it.

For Maria Christina, the time between Halifax and the next newspaper became an eternity of sleepless nights, days worrying, unable to eat, hungry for news of Metsovo. Finally, the ship stopped early in the morning, fifteen miles out of Manhattan, to board a dozen immigration officials. They lined up the tables in the dining room in long rows and examined everyone's travel documents as the ship continued on its way into New York Harbor. At dawn, everyone crowded on the decks to watch the tops of the skyscrapers of Manhattan gradually appear above the horizon. Passing the Statue of Liberty, people were openly crying and holding each other. Maria Christina put her arms around a weeping Angela, while the two children were also hugging each other and weeping because they soon would be saying goodbye. Maria Christina also had tears in her eyes, but for an entirely different reason. She so did not want to be there.

31

Even at home, Nikos Petrakis, or 'Nick', as he preferred to be called, always wore a dark grey or navy pinstriped suit with a maroon silk handkerchief stuffed in the breast pocket, although when he watched television or listened to music he exchanged his jacket in favor of a cashmere cardigan in navy, tan, or grey. His shirts were white, their collars starched, and his tie was either polka dots or stripes. He was tall and thin. His hands were small, with long delicate fingers that obviously had never labored. His nails were manicured weekly. He spoke Athenian Greek like Yiannis but, from the shape of his head to the lankiness of his torso, he was nothing like his younger brother. Yiannis was a blonde, Nick had black hair flecked with grey. Yiannis' eyes were brown, Nick's were blue. Yiannis loved being out of doors, Nick preferred indoor activities. Yiannis would play the clown and laugh full-throated, whereas Nick, with his dry sense of humor, would smile wryly at most, unless it was truly knee-slapping, at which time he might emit one short *ha*.

Eleni Petrakis, or 'Helen', was quite attractive in her mink coat and matching hat which was worn fetchingly at an angle. A brunette with enormous energy, she had a tendency to be slightly overweight, something she monitored closely. A Greek-American who claimed to be descended from an important family who owned the olive press in a village above Sparta, she was actually of more humble origins. Her paternal grandparents were circus performers, and her maternal grandparents worked for the family who owned the press. Her parents emigrated to Queens in 1912, where her father suffered a nervous breakdown shortly after their arrival and never left the house again, forcing Helen's mother to clean houses for their survival. Having grown up in such meager circumstance, Helen took great comfort and pride in her husband's success and dressed and acted her role of the wife of an affluent businessman in the larger Greek community with total dedication.

After the couple kissed Zoitsa and shook Maria Christina's hand, Nick led them to his brand new 1948 dark green Buick sedan.

"The first of the new forty-eights" Nick volunteered as he opened the back door for the two travellers, who had no idea what he was talking about.

He smiled, realizing his stupidity. "The car. It's brand new. It's next year's model. I'm sorry. It's nothing."

He then asked Maria Christina for their luggage receipt. As he waited for her to produce it, he lit a Chesterfield with a silver lighter. With the luggage receipt in one hand and the Chesterfield in the other, Nick went off to claim their baggage, leaving Helen with the girls. Clearly Helen was excited.

"It was Zoitsa's blonde hair I spotted first" she spoke in English in a husky voice.

"Nick said you understand English. Do you? A little?"

"A little" Maria Christina smiled.

Helen looked back at Zoitsa and continued as if Maria Christina had said the two were completely fluent.

"Your Uncle Nick was very upset with your father for not inviting us to his wedding. I was so sorry to hear about your mother. Are either of you hungry? I'm planning a nice dinner. New York steaks. Do you know steak?"

"Beefsteak? Yes." Maria Christina understood the word.

Helen went back to addressing Zoitsa again "I don't know why your father didn't come with you. Your Uncle Nick says he had to stay and be the hero."

And so she continued until Nick returned with a young black porter wheeling the trunk on a dolly, which easily fit into the Buick.

On the highway circling Manhattan, while the girls stared in amazement at the skyline, Helen teetered between being helpful and boasting as she pointed out the important landmarks.

"That's the Empire State Building. One hundred and two stories, isn't it Nick?"

Nick insisted they call him 'Nick' or 'Uncle Nick' and his wife 'Helen' or 'Aunt Helen'. When he spoke to his niece he dropped the diminutive of Zoitsa's name and called her 'Zoe', his mother's name. He considered calling Maria Christina only Maria, or even Mary, but quickly abandoned the idea. She seemed too complicated for such a simple name. She was pleasant enough, and poised and quite elegant for a girl from a mountain village, but he sensed she was hiding something. He couldn't put his finger on it. He was certain that she was much stronger than she looked. Her handshake was that of a man. A working man. But it was more than that. Behind her demure manner, she seemed to him someone who might be defiant by nature.

The two travellers were uncomfortable sharing a car with two strangers with whom they were now destined to share a life. When she couldn't refrain any longer, Maria Christina interrupted Helen to ask about news of the war in Greece. Nick had been too busy with his business to have kept up, but he thought it had been quiet the last few days, but would stop for *The Atlantis* on the way to the apartment. Helen was only vaguely aware of the trouble, understood it less, and what little of it she did know she found depressing.

"Greeks fighting Greeks. It has ever been thus." she laughed derisively. "It's crazy, isn't it Nick?"

Fifteen long minutes later they were driving over the Brooklyn Bridge.

"Twenty-seven people died during its construction, isn't that right, Nick?"

After another fifteen minutes, which felt like an eternity, Nick stopped at a Greek record store which also sold the Greek daily, and Maria Christina, with trembling hands, was reading aloud an account of the last days of the 'Second Great Battle of the Civil War'.

"The Minister of Defence, Napoleon Zervas, announced at a news conference on Friday, that the Greek National Army and Air Force in a coordinated strategy of simultaneous air and ground attacks had successfully defeated the Communist forces, bringing an end to the nine days of ferocious attacks against the 587."

"Thank God!" Zoitsa blurted.

"Oh, good!" Helen injected "Good news?"

Maria Christina smiled and nodded to Helen, although she herself wasn't comforted. There was no reason to think Yiannis had come to harm, or her father, or Panorea, but there was equally no reason to think they hadn't. She glanced at the paper and then summed it up so as not to bore her hosts.

"He added that the Communists had withdrawn back into Yugoslavia."

Nick and Helen's apartment was on the fourth floor of a seven story building facing Prospect Park, Brooklyn's largest public park, five hundred eighty-five acres, which included a ninety acre meadow, a zoo, an Audubon center, a sixty acre lake, and seven baseball fields. At first Zoitsa refused to get out of the car. The city had overwhelmed her. She wanted to go back to the ship and to Metsovo immediately. She simply stared out the window and watched a girl about her own age, with dark tight curly hair, skipping rope by herself across the street. The girl reminded her of Thimi and she began to cry. Nick and Helen understood and quietly stepped out of the car, while Maria Christina held Zoitsa and rocked her.

"This is your father's brother, Moumou. We don't want to insult him. It would make your father very sad. We'll only stay one season if you want, then return to Metsovo."

"He doesn't look like Babá."

"He looks like Babá as much as I looked like your mother."

This seemed to satisfy Zoitsa enough to step out of the car.

The apartment building had a doorman who also operated the elevator, a tall, elderly black man with white hair from the state of Alabama, Henry. He greeted them with a smile and a small salute as he introduced himself and opened the door. Neither girl from Metsovo had ever been so close to a black man before and they couldn't help but stare at him. He understood and simply nodded and smiled meekly as he ushered them into the elevator.

"Rain this afternoon" he said to Nick and Helen as he closed the doors and pushed a lever. Suddenly the little room lurched upwards. Zoitsa yelped and jumped several inches off the floor. Maria Christina put her hands on her niece's shoulders and laughed softly in her ear. This was meant to be fun. It immediately calmed Zoitsa enough to realize she was in no real danger. But when the room stopped and Henry flung the doors open, Zoitsa was the first one out.

The view from the apartment's spacious living room was of the park's extensive meadow with a forest beyond. Upon entering, Zoitsa clung very closely to Maria Christina who was following Helen, who in turn went directly to the kitchen to turn on the oven for the baked potatoes. Maria Christina was amazed by the stove. Helen turned on a burner and tried to explain how it worked with gas coming through a pipe in the wall which, when lit by a spark, made a fire, but what Maria

Christina understood most was that there were no coals which needed tending. She also marvelled that with a turn of the knob you could raise or lower the flame.

While the oven was warming, Helen showed them their bedroom and insisted on helping them unpack. Among other things, she noticed the appalling meagreness and lack of style of their wardrobe. Their old fashioned coats were completely out of the question. In the meantime Zoitsa had been exploring the bathroom, turning on the faucets, flushing the toilet, eyeing the tub. After the second or third flush Helen stepped into the bathroom and turned off the faucets.

"We must not waste water, dear. Would you like a bath before dinner? I think that would be a very good idea, don't you Maria?"

As Helen was adjusting the water for the tub, Nick walked in.

"Taking a bath? Try some of this."

He took a bottle of purple liquid from the side of the tub, opened it, and poured a capful into the tub under the faucet. Immediately bubbles sprung up which made Zoitsa laugh and Maria Christina's eyes widen in wonder as the bubbles continued to multiply and billow. America was a wonderland with bubble baths, rooms that flew up to the sky, fire you could turn on and off.

Minutes later in the kitchen, Nick was pouring himself a Jack Daniels on the rocks, while Helen was washing the potatoes and speaking in hushed tones.

"What have you done to us, Nick? Who are these people? They're like Greek hillbillies. I even had to show them how to use the bathtub. Don't they bathe in those villages?"

"Nonsense" Nick almost snapped back.

"I thought Metsovo was a good sized town."

"I never said that."

"You were always talking about it."

"Because Yiannis lived there." He was adding exactly three

drops of bitters to his drink. "They may be a little backward, but they both seem intelligent enough and very well mannered."

"How do we even know they are who they say they are? Did you see their papers? Georgia Pepas says a lot of Greeks are coming here pretending to be someone's relative so they can sponge off them."

Reaching for a Chesterfield, Nick shook his head, exasperated, "As a matter of fact, Zoe looks exactly like my mother but with Yiannis' hair."

At one o'clock Helen served hors d'oeuvres in the living room: stuffed grape leaves she had made, olives, a commercial feta cheese, and Nick's favorite, a tin of beluga caviar, nestled in a bowl of crushed ice, surrounded by thin toast, chopped egg, onion, lemon and sour cream. Zoitsa fell in love with it at first bite and had to be told by Helen not to eat the caviar with its little spoon like it was cereal. But Nick found it amusing and hushed Helen.

Maria Christina presented them with the two precious wall hangings from Metsovo, one of geometric design and one which depicted the village. Nick seemed pleased, but Helen was so effusive, bordering on the dramatic, in her appreciation of these gifts that Maria Christina couldn't tell if she actually liked them or not.

"I know just where I'll put them" Helen kissed Maria Christina and Zoitsa and set the tapestry of Metsovo under the glass coffee table.

"For everyone to see" she beamed.

She then took the geometric tapestry and set it delicately over the back of Nick's easy chair.

"Tell her you're supposed to hang them on the wall" Zoitsa protested in Vlach in a whisper to Maria Christina.

"Ssst" was Maria Christina's almost silent response as she looked around for Nick who, at that moment, was lighting a Chesterfield and pouring himself another Jack Daniels and bitters.

Maria Christina and Zoitsa were more comfortable speaking Greek, and Nick would translate the occasional word or phrase for Helen, who understood a certain amount of Greek but wasn't confident enough to speak it. When Helen called them to the table, Nick put on a recording of *La Traviata*.

"My favorite opera" Nick smiled as he sat to eat. "You know, Zoe, it was composed by an Italian named Giuseppe Verdi."

He then told Zoitsa the very sad tale about the tragic young woman, Violetta, with tuberculosis. The story was wonderful, the music beautiful, and the meat was the most tender and juicy Maria Christina and Zoitsa had ever tasted. They were reluctant to try it at first, because they thought it hadn't been cooked enough, which amused Nick, who was taking great pleasure in all their new delights. After dinner, Helen took Zoitsa across the hall to meet Anne, the girl Zoitsa had seen earlier jumping rope.

When Zoitsa left the apartment, Nick escorted Maria Christina back into the living room. After she was seated, he handed her a telegram addressed to him but meant for her, which he said had arrived ten days ago and had come from Metsovo. As she opened the telegram, silently praying it was not bad news, her heart sank as she heard

Nick say "I am deeply, deeply sorry, Maria Christina."

The telegram contained seven words.

YOUR PATERA PASSED 5 NOVEMBER STOP
LETTER FOLLOWING STOP
LENA

After a moment of silence, Nick put his hand on her shoulder "Are you alright, Maria Christina? Is there something I can do?"

Stunned, Maria Christina didn't respond for a moment, then looked up at him and spoke softly "We will need mourning clothes."

32

"Maria, you'll be needing a nice black coat."
"No, Helen. After this morning we won't be leaving the apartment." Maria Christina smiled sadly and rested her hand on Zoitsa's shoulder, as the elevator in Martin's Department Store continued up to the floor devoted to children. When the doors opened, they were greeted by display after display of toys and stuffed animals of all sizes, including one big giraffe that almost touched the ceiling. On their way to the children's clothes, Helen noticed Zoitsa stop and quickly pet a life-sized stuffed lamb before continuing.

A few days after their shopping trip, Helen stepped into the guest bedroom to retrieve Christmas ornaments from the top shelf of the closet. When she turned on the light, she was aghast at the sight. The bed, the chair, the window, the paintings, all her careful color coordination had been draped in black. Later in bed with Nick she couldn't stop talking about it.

"It's bizarre. Now I know why she needed all that black fabric. Can it be good for Zoe? It's like living in a Halloween tableau."

"I told you, it's their custom."

"I don't care. It's mentally unhealthy. No wonder the child is so nervous. You haven't seen the room."

Early every morning Nick drove to his business in Manhattan.

Helen very often went with him. She then would go by taxi to the bank to make a deposit or to make a delivery to a special client, and always she would shop. But every afternoon, without fail, while Maria Christina and Zoitsa napped, Helen was home to watch her favorite soap opera on television, *Stella Dallas*. It was her time to be alone with young and beautiful Laurel Dallas, who had married socially prominent Dick Grosvenor, while her down to earth mother, Stella, a rather low class woman, watched from afar. Nick and Helen loved watching television in the evenings.

At first, Zoitsa was uncomfortable in a strange house with people she didn't know, but before long she was sitting on the arm of her uncle's large club chair, watching *The Small Fry Club* at 7:00 each night, for which he would make a special effort to be home. It was when Maria Christina and Helen would be preparing dinner in the kitchen and he would relish the time alone with his niece. It was hosted by Buffalo Bob and, although it was meant for children, Nick once in a while would emit a 'ha'. Nick had convinced Maria Christina that Zoitsa should be allowed to watch television even during the mourning period, because it would help improve her English.

Without children of their own, Nick and Helen soon started thinking of Zoitsa as their own daughter. Nick thought she was very smart. Her nose was always in *The Atlantis*, which he now brought home every day. And he wanted her to have piano lessons. He would buy a piano and put it in the living room. He also wanted to put her into school right away, but Maria Christina insisted she not leave the house or play music until after the mourning period. Nick thought he knew what was best for the child and began to contemplate having more control. He could see an eventual confrontation with Maria Christina. In a showdown, he was sure Yiannis would side with him. But what if something happened to his brother? Maria Christina was not the least bit intimidated by him, and he knew that taking Zoitsa away from her would not be easy. Helen disagreed.

"Don't be silly. It's single aunt with no visible means of support in a mountain village in the middle of a civil war in Greece, versus well-heeled uncle with wife in New York, isn't it, Nick? She can't even pay a lawyer, for god's sake. Isn't that true?"

From the moment she arrived, Maria Christina was not happy in Brooklyn. Everyone seemed to be skating on the surface of life. Style with no substance. As she wrote Lena:

'There are many marvels in Babylon,
but it is a narcissistic culture.
And nothing has taste.
There is no tomato in the
tomato, no onion in the onion.
And a black dust is in the air which settles on everything,
and when you wipe a table
it needs to be dusted again in less than an hour.'

Maria Christina and Zoitsa did most of the housework, leaving the maid, Maggie, a squat black woman in her forties, who came twice a week, without much to do to earn her wage. Maggie was aware they were only temporarily in the United States, so she never worried about losing her job. She just took advantage of the free time to bake some of Nick's favorite cookies, or polish the silver, or make southern fried chicken which Helen adored.

That year, Thanksgiving coincided with the twentieth day since Papa Yiorgos' death. Nick and Helen had just left to go to Helen's sister's in Queens for the holiday meal when at ten o'clock Maria Christina shut the door to her bedroom, sat on the chair and, as was the custom, began rocking back and forth. But all she succeeded in emitting was the sound of air. She simply had no feelings about her father's death. She didn't miss him. Her relationship with him was always bound to the future. The only thing she mourned was that now her dream that some day he would grow to love her, respect her, even be proud of her had died with him. He would never see her married or hold her children. He was gone and had left her with few if any happy memories of him.

Spending so much time in her bedroom during the mourning period enabled Maria Christina to reflect on what had happened in the last weeks and all that was new in her life. She needed to be quiet, to think, to remember, to dream. For those weeks, Nick and Helen, who were in the habit of hosting Sunday dinner after church for up to twenty people, refrained from their normal entertaining except on his name day, December 6, when Nick had his annual large party. Maria Christina stayed in her room, but Zoitsa charmed the guests, singing a song she knew for a silver dollar promised by her uncle.

In a camp near Konitsa, Yiannis' boots made sucking sounds as he lifted them out of the mud on the way to his tent, while reading the pages he had just received from his daughter.

> 'Athens has buildings as high as mountains. Streets wider than the village square. Sidewalks wider than main street.'

The descriptions of their adventure made Zoitsa and Maria Christina seem even further away.

Maria Christina finally received a letter from Yiannis.

> 'In spite of all the recent troubles, the builders have pledged to begin working on the house shortly. By summer they promise the roof will be done, and the fireplace, and the windows and doors will be complete. There will be some delay due to the amount of damage suffered during recent battles, but as soon as that work is finished they will return to our house. Unfortunately still no news of Thimi.'

Maria Christina noticed that, although he tried to make his letters positive, Yiannis' handwriting had started to tilt slightly backwards. It had been moving in that direction and it concerned her. As Yiannis once helped strengthen her spirit through humor, she would use it for the same purpose.

'Americans walk faster, talk faster, gesture faster, everything they do is at a much faster pace and a less calculated manner, such that if they had to do one or two things over again because of their haste, they would still finish at the same time as one more cautious, and with any luck at all might even come in first. But then they all have digestive problems.'

She began to focus on Helen as her Haralambos.

'She speaks so fast neither Zoitsa nor I can understand her. Her life is devoted to her skin care. Her favorite thing to do is to have her hair washed and curled at a shop. Or have lunch out with a client and then go shopping. Every season the style of clothes changes and her wardrobe with it.'

She wrote that Nick was an angel and he loved his younger brother very much and both Nick and Helen were very dear to her and Zoitsa. She also wrote that the couple generally seemed to like each other a great deal, were fun to be around, and often did a dance in the sitting room called *the tango*.

But it was of little help in raising Yiannis' spirit. The civil war had already lasted years. The army was becoming stronger all the time but the situation was worsening. Morale in general was extremely low. Guerrilla raids in Greece were at their height and were now carried out with more cruelty. Not a day passed without three or four such attacks. The brutality of the Communists severely damaged any possibility that their party might emerge a popular organization in Greece. Hundreds of children were being abducted. Tragic scenes were taking place in countless villages. Mothers clutching onto their sons and daughters were brutally beaten. Villages were totally empty, their inhabitants having fled to towns, seeking refuge in makeshift shanties and living on food rations that were distributed by a government with extremely limited financial means. Far from home, deprived of every comfort, both the soldiers and the people were becoming dispirited. To make matters worse, the Communists began mining all the roads, which made travelling impossible, unless one was led by a military escort with mine sweeping equipment.

Nick began to read *The Atlantis* once again after putting it down a few years ago, with the thought that Greece was committing suicide in a disinterested world. He still felt the same, but the girls rekindled his link to his homeland, and it made him ache for it. More specifically, he ached for word of his mother and father, who had disowned their eldest son when he went for a short visit to an uncle in the United States and never returned, but instead remained in New York and foolishly married Helen. It was the unfinished business of his life. Helen only saw *The Atlantis* as something in which to wrap fish heads. She was much more interested in the end of the mourning period, because then she would take the girls shopping to "ha ha" improve their wardrobe. Besides two skirts and two more sweaters for each, Maria Christina would need a cocktail dress, and Zoe should have at least one party dress. Helen was now dedicated to pushing Maria Christina out socially as soon as possible, with the hope that in very short order a match would be arranged with someone.

"She could just as easily fall in love with a ship owner as a sheep owner."

"Helen, I suspect she's engaged to someone in Metsovo."

"What, she's going back to marry some Greek who doesn't know how to flush a toilet? Don't be silly. Here she could marry a professional or a business man and have a life. She's got good bones and a good body, doesn't she, Nick? As soon as I fix her up she'll be very attractive, you'll see."

Nick almost laughed. He did find his wife amusing, and her logic irrefutable as she continued.

"First thing we do is to eighty-six the kerchief, don't you think, Nick? Men here are not as horny as those men in those mountains where sometimes even a sheep looks good."

So Nick made a reservation for twelve at the Copa Cabana night club in Manhattan for the night immediately following the mourning period. Among the guests would be two eligible bachelors he thought might be interested in Maria Christina. He was also looking forward to seeing his favorite entertainer, Desi Arnaz, and dancing the rumba with Helen.

Zoitsa was also looking forward to the end of the mourning period. She could finally go out and explore the park with Anne. Twice during that three-week period, Anne knocked on the door to see if Zoe could come out and play. An only child, slightly overweight and cheery, she was shorter that Zoitsa and almost as smart. Anne's father, a doctor, and her mother, Marcia, had fled Germany before Hitler took power. Zoitsa invited her to come in and play, but Anne declined because it was her designated time to be out of doors in the fresh air.

Her Uncle Nick said he would enrol her in school, which would be fun. He would also buy her a bicycle like the one she had seen Anne ride up and down the sidewalk every afternoon after school. There were no bicycles in Metsovo, and Zoitsa couldn't wait to learn to ride one.

Maria Christina was looking forward to the day only with dread. She didn't want Zoitsa to go to school here in America, but Nick was right. Of course she should go to school. But wasn't the child challenged enough already? Wouldn't it stress her even more? Maria Christina also agonized about the unknown temptations that might lay out there, from which Zoitsa needed to be protected. How Maria Christina longed for the quiet of the endless Southern Alps. The first thing she would do at the end of this period would be to go to the park and find a place where no one could see or hear her and just sit and look at the clouds for a few hours.

On the fortieth day anniversary of Papa Yiorgos' death there was a huge snowfall during the night which covered Prospect Park like a blanket. In the early morning the street was completely quiet. There were no cars. No people. Maria Christina opened her bedroom window and looked out at the pristine winter scene. She was imagining the letter she had received the day before from Yiannis, his handwriting tilting back even more. And then some of his thoughts mixed with some of her own.

'I saw Panorea. She seemed strange. She said I shouldn't worry. That she had my gun and she wasn't afraid to die.'

It had been only forty days since she had left Greece, and yet the war now seemed so far away.

'Olimbi and Haralambos send many kisses.
If you ask me they have become more than just friends.
Or maybe it's just the war.'

The world was so huge and complex and Greece was so small and complex.

'In any event, every day brings us one more day
closer to the end.'

Maria Christina closed the window and dressed for a walk in the park.

33

Although Maria Christina had planned to spend most of the day alone, Helen had insisted her morning be spent at the beauty parlor, washing, shaping, setting, manicuring, and pedicuring, during which the young woman from Metsovo sat rigidly as she was being made over, astonished at the very idea, while Helen chatted with whomever. The rest of the day was spent shopping for a cocktail dress for her debut.

After several hours of trying on dresses in three different fitting rooms, Helen finally chose a Dior copy, one of black lace over pink satin, with a sweetheart neckline that revealed a hint of cleavage. With just a touch of make-up Helen had expertly applied, and a strand of her pearls around her protégé's long swan neck with its smooth porcelain skin, Maria Christina was totally transformed and ready to be presented to society.

That night at the Copa Cabana, Nick introduced Maria Christina to the assorted group of well-heeled friends he had invited, as they arrived at the large table he had reserved next to the dance floor. Among the guests were the two bachelors in their early thirties. Helen directed the seating. Next to Maria Christina she placed tall, dark, refined, Chris, who owned a thriving candy business in Brooklyn. Directly across from her, she seated a ruggedly handsome Alex, who owned a company that manufactured party favors. Nick had chosen well. The two attractive and eligible young men were opposites, and Nick and Helen were hopeful one or the other would find Maria Christina appealing, and they couldn't wait to see which of the two Maria Christina would prefer. Match making was exciting.

Nick ordered Maria Christina a Manhattan. Since she had arrived, she had revealed very little of herself beyond a somber exterior, and Nick thought liquor made the real 'you' emerge, and he was determined to sound the depths of this mysterious creature before the evening was over. Maria Christina didn't know what a Manhattan was, but didn't want to appear rude, so she accepted it and drank it as if it was wine. After only a few sips she felt a little lightheaded. Desi Arnaz stopped by the table to say hello to Nick and Helen and to bum a Chesterfield. Nick introduced Maria Christina as a member of his extended family visiting from Greece. Desi welcomed her to America then kissed her hand, which made her blush.

The two unattached Greek-Americans had only a limited interest in Greece, and seemed somewhat indifferent to the young single lady from Metsovo with the horn rimmed glasses. Nick had ordered for the table and, as the shrimp cocktail was served, Maria Christina drained the Manhattan and ate the cherry, which she found to be delicious. A bus boy took her glass as soon as it reached the table and a waiter poured her a glass of dry white wine, while the Desi Arnaz orchestra began playing a rumba. Nick and Helen and several other couples stepped to the dance floor, while the two young men left the table for a quick conference in the men's room.

For Maria Christina the evening was magical. The room was enchanting, the people looked so elegant and beautiful, the orchestra was thrilling. The Latin beat was infectious. She only wished Yiannis had been there. After their voyage, they would come to the Copa to watch Nick and Helen move so freely yet so controlled. Maria Christina loved to dance. Since she was a little girl, she and Matoula would dance, even if it was just to their own singing, but it was always best at festivals when there were musicians, and they would dance as long as the music played. After several turns around the floor with Helen, Nick took Maria Christina's hand and led her to the floor for a quick rumba lesson.

Having never shown her arms or exposed so much of herself below her collar bone in public, Maria Christina felt as though she was dressed in an undergarment, and it made her self conscious and restrained while dancing. Yet she moved extremely well and learned quickly, and with her tiny waist she looked wonderfully lithe to those watching, even to a few of the women. Then the orchestra took a break and Lobster Thermidor was served. It was then Maria Christina realized that whenever she took a sip of wine, it seemed the waiter would immediately refill her glass so she was unable to calculate how much she actually had consumed. She took off her glasses and pretended to look at someone telling a story across the table, but for that moment she wasn't listening but simply didn't want to be distracted while trying to determine how many glasses she had emptied. It was during this brief moment that everyone was able to see her sapphire eyes and their long lashes, which were set off perfectly by her chestnut hair and her skin, the color of a ripe white peach. They were able to appreciate how uncommonly beautiful she was, as if by taking off her glasses it had somehow removed a veil. Even Helen later admitted to Nick that she couldn't take her eyes off her protégé.

The two bachelors suddenly seemed interested in Maria Christina. Although she appeared shyly submissive, neither of them felt their interest in her was reciprocated.

In order to keep her engaged, they asked her about the war. Alex seemed genuinely interested, but it was obvious to her that

Chris was only pretending. Maria Christina was gracious but answered her two suitors' questions with as few words as possible so as not to encourage them. She was not the least bit interested in cultivating their friendship. In fact, she thought they were both rather ill-mannered. They had just met, yet they acted overly familiar, as if they had been members of her family or close friends from childhood. Of course she kept looking to Nick, sitting at her elbow, for guidance. But Nick said nothing. He simply insisted Maria Christina have a lemon liqueur with her desert, and encouraged, even insisted she dance once with each of the men at the table and join the conga line that began snaking through the large room.

As the evening progressed, the two bachelors became increasingly competitive for Maria Christina's attention, each trying to out talk, out dance, out charm the other. Having never consumed so much alcohol, Maria Christina was now dancing with Alex without inhibition, but in her mind she was dancing with Yiannis who was at that moment somewhere high in the snow-covered mountains between Greece and Albania, thinking of her while sitting around a little stove in his tent with Olimbi and Haralambos, nursing *tsipouro* in the afternoon, enjoying the silence, knowing that probably sooner rather than later the hospital cots would once again begin to fill with broken men and boys.

Through the drinking and the laughter, Nick sat in a haze of Chesterfield smoke and watched Maria Christina dance. She was graceful, tasteful, elegant, but above all she was very sexy. It was like watching a beautiful animal. He could clearly see there was a purity about her. An authenticity. The way she moved when she danced reflected different facets of her, the shy maiden, the temptress. But what he found most interesting were the moments when she seemed to possess a strength he could only compare to a steely and determined warrior. It was during one of those moments when Nick noticed Chris watching her while discreetly chewing on his napkin. In fact, looking around the table it seemed all the men were either stealing glances or blatantly staring.

Nick suddenly felt guilty. He had taken advantage of her innocence. His brother had entrusted his sister-in-law to him and he should have been her protector, not caused her to be on display like a barn animal. He could tell the men were imagining having her in every position. Feeling ashamed, he went to the dance floor and gently put his hands on her shoulders and spoke softly in her ear.

"Come, Maria Christina Triantafyllou. Time to go home."

"Thank God Zoitsa was sleeping over at Anne's" Maria Christina said, just before she passed out in the car.

In her bathroom, Maria Christina knelt in front of the toilet and vomited while Helen stood by with a glass of water and a towel.

"Really, Maria, you must try and control your drinking."

Later, in the Petrakis bedroom as the couple was undressing, Helen was in a self-congratulatory mood.

"You have to admit I did a wonderful job, didn't I, Nick? Say it. I want to hear you say it."

"Yes, you did, dear. A great job."

"Getting her married will be easier than I thought. And not just married. But married well. In fact, very well, don't you agree?"

"I'm not sure you're right. Alex asked if he could show her the sights, to which she smiled sweetly, and then in English so there would be no mistake about it, she said 'No, thank you, Alex.'"

"I don't know why you can't just ask her if she has a boyfriend."

"It's not something you ask directly, like you don't ask someone how much money they have. You ask someone who knows them to tell you. Like a relative. I'll write to Yiannis."

"Well, I asked Zoitsa, but she didn't know if she had one or not, but she said she didn't think so. Although she said there was this guy named Stahoulis, who came around from time to time to see if they needed anything. But he has a wooden leg, so I doubt it."

On Monday, Nick took Maria Christina and Zoitsa to meet the principal of Public School 107, who sent them to see a student counsellor, who took Zoitsa into her office and gave her a simple reading, writing, and arithmetic test, and determined that, rather than start her in first grade, she was pleased to announce that Zoitsa was smart enough and had learned enough arithmetic and English to start her only two grades below her normal fifth grade. She would be in the third grade for two weeks as a trial period, then they would re-evaluate and determine what grade would be most appropriate to her abilities. It was difficult for Nick to hide his disappointment. After the meeting, he decided there would be no more Greek spoken in the house. Only English.

Zoitsa's third grade desk was small for her and her two knees protruded from either side, but her English improved very quickly, and she was constantly explaining to Maria Christina the meaning of certain words. When they were alone, either in their room or walking in the park, the two often broke the 'No Greek' rule and spoke Vlach to each other. It was important for Maria Christina to keep the language alive for her niece. Nick had heard them several times, but didn't intervene. It wouldn't have been smart. The Vlach language was a bond between them it would be futile to try and break. Besides, he was not without his own arsenal of weapons to lure his young niece. Not having had a father for so many years, Zoitsa was hungry to feel the essence of a man and loved nothing more than to sit on the arm of his chair and feel his face with her cheek when he needed a shave. She also grew to love opera and played Nick's records over and over, until she could even sing along and act out the parts, which delighted him no end. He was able to nourish her natural thirst for knowledge and exposed her to so many new things, from trains that went under ground to hot dogs with mustard and relish at Coney Island, to the museums, the planetarium, the ballet, the best restaurants, the Oak Room at the Plaza Hotel, or the Café de la Paix at the St. Moritz, both of which his company supplied. And, of course, there was shopping. On all of these outings Nick insisted they be alone. He used this time to subtly indoctrinate Zoitsa into being a true Petrakis.

Zoitsa was taking great delight in every aspect of her new life. Even though she was ordered to use the elevator only when necessary, that it wasn't a toy, she outsmarted the authorities several times a day by inventing excuses for going up and down with Henry.

"I need to go down to check the position of the sun, Aunt Helen. For my homework." Or "Henry, I need to go up and get a glass of water. I'm very thirsty."

It was her favorite thing to do whenever Anne had an after-school lesson and couldn't play with her. Most of the time, though, she and Anne were together. They would walk to school, sometimes skipping the whole way, then they would meet in the schoolyard at recess. In the park, they would spend hours swinging on the jungle bars or playing one or the other's game of hopscotch. Zoitsa had taught Anne the Greek version of the game. Jumping rope presented a problem, so Zoitsa cajoled Henry into holding one end of the rope so they could take turns jumping. One day, Henry introduced the idea of tying one end of the rope to the pole which held up the awning, so the two girls could jump together.

As for Maria Christina, her first walk in the snow-covered park was disappointing. There were footprints everywhere. Walking until she could no longer see a building, she continued until she finally couldn't see a footprint, then she climbed to the top of a knoll and lay down in the snow. She remained still, just listening and looking at the puffs of clouds in the sky. There were still distant sounds of voices and car horns. She closed her eyes. The snow felt warm, comforting. She lay her hands on it and imagined lying in the forest above Metsovo. After a long moment she heard a man's voice:

"Hey! You!"

She opened her eyes. An old man walking his bulldog was calling and waving up to her.

"You okay?"

She sat up and waved down to him. As he walked away, she stood, brushed the snow off herself, then walked slowly back to the apartment deeply saddened. It seemed in Brooklyn there were too many people in too small a space to ever be alone.

34

After the first two weeks of school, some of the boys in the yard began to make fun of Zoitsa's heightened sensitivity and foreign accent and would devise ways to scare her. At first it was done at a distance with firecrackers and banging garbage cans, and now one tiptoed behind her and yelled loudly. When she screamed and jumped, her arms flailing, there was a chorus of laughter.

"Sorry I make you djump" he smiled, mimicking her foreign accent.

As Anne watched helplessly, the boy continued.

"I was calling to my friend Dzimi who have trouble to hear."

Zoitsa glared at him a moment then grabbed him by his ears and threw him angrily to the ground. The two wrestled on the concrete, Zoitsa getting the best of him.

"Stop it!" an older dark-haired boy pulled Zoitsa off the humiliated and slightly bloody bully.

"What's the problem, Grease ball?" someone called out to him.

The boy addressed the group which had quickly gathered, "Don't you know? She was in the war."

It was the first time Zoitsa ever heard the term "grease ball". That was when she first realized what a big world it was and how being Greek wasn't necessarily celebrated. That night, as she was falling asleep, Zoitsa promised herself that she would never again let anyone see she was afraid, and she would lose her accent even if it took forever.

After that incident, no one ever teased her again. The war had touched almost everyone. An uncle, an aunt, a brother or cousin, everyone either had or knew a family that had lost someone in the war. This piece of information spread throughout the school and suddenly Zoitsa was singled out for both admiration and pity. Of course it didn't hurt that she was striking to look at, a natural athlete, and very smart, amazing her teachers and classmates with her understanding of arithmetic, but especially her knowledge of the United States government and its history. At the end of the month, she was promoted to the fourth grade.

For Christmas, Helen took great pains decorating the apartment: red candles replaced white, red bows tied around vases and lamp bases, pine branches around the door frames in the living room, and Santa Clauses everywhere. Most startling to the two from Metsovo was the day a man delivered a recently cut pine tree and helped Helen set it on a stand in one corner of the living room. That evening they helped decorate it with balls and lights and little toy like objects. Each day until Christmas morning, presents wrapped in shiny paper with beautiful ribbons and bows kept accumulating around its base.

It had just begun to snow on Christmas morning when they all gathered around the tree to exchange gifts. Because of the occasion, Nick had opened a four-ounce tin of beluga caviar, which was being passed around with its accoutrements as presents were being opened. Three cashmere cardigans for Nick from Helen, one in red, to wear on Christmas Day, one in pale yellow to wear on Easter, and one in white.

"For when you want to appear younger to the ladies" she smiled from behind his chair, then leaned down and kissed him.

Nick gave Helen a diamond and onyx bracelet, which delighted the girls, who had never seen such a fine piece of jewellery. Maria Christina's gift was a beautiful black wool coat with a beaver collar. Zoitsa received the life-sized lamb she had petted at Martin's department Store and a brand new shiny red Schwin bicycle with training wheels. At school, Zoitsa had made Aunt Helen a quilted potholder with an embroidered 'H', and for Uncle Nick a remarkably accurate pastel portrait of her father, smiling, holding his pipe near his mouth. Her art teacher was so charmed by the sketch, she had asked the shop teacher to make a nice frame for it. Nick was deeply touched, and kissed Zoitsa with tears in his eyes. Maria Christina had knit them each a scarf which she had started on the *Nea Hellas*. It felt strange to exchange gifts on Christmas day. In Metsovo they would be exchanged on St. Basil's Day, January 1st. But what was truly unsettling was that here in America it seemed gifts were valued in monetary terms. Several times Helen held one up and estimated its price.

"I'll bet this cost more than thirty dollars!"

After all the boxes had been unwrapped and their contents admired, Nick insisted on showing Zoitsa how to ride her new Schwin. Maria Christina and Helen watched from the window as Nick, holding the bike with Zoitsa on it, began running down the sidewalk, then running faster, finally letting go with a push and Zoitsa riding for twenty feet into Henry's waiting arms. Nick was laughing like a schoolboy. Maria Christina was touched by the scene. Her thoughts immediately wandered to Yiannis and Nick playing together as boys.

Yiannis so loved his brother and was ever so grateful to him. He said as much in his letters to him. He also wrote he had found the woman he wanted to marry when the war was over, and this time he would invite him and Eleni to the wedding, but he couldn't disclose his intended's name just yet. He thought it only proper he tell Zoitsa first and be in the room when he told her. In any case, during the course of a war, anything could happen, feelings could change. Yiannis was more honest with his brother about the course of the war than he was with Maria Christina or his daughter.

'More than ever the guerrillas are looting the pharmacies and hospitals. There are many wounded and sick while medicine is insufficient. Except for a few islands Greece is burning from one end to the other.'

In his letters to Maria Christina, Yiannis' tone was much different.

'Winter is almost over. Is time moving more quickly?'

In spite of his attempt to sound cheerful, when Maria Christina examined the writing, not only were the letters slanting backwards, but some of his words dragged on as if he had to struggle for the strength to lift the pen off the paper. It worried her deeply.

On January 8th, Zoitsa's tenth birthday, Nick invited her friend, Anne, and her parents and they all went to Radio City Music Hall to see a movie and the famous Rockettes, and then to the Plaza Hotel for dinner. The waiters brought a cake with candles and everyone sang 'Happy Birthday'. When they returned to the apartment there was a brand new upright piano with a large red bow in the living room next to the sideboard. Zoitsa was beside herself. She said it was the best birthday ever. Her lessons began the next day and she soon memorized several pieces she would play for everyone after Sunday dinner which, of course, delighted Nick.

For Maria Christina and Zoitsa life continued quietly through the rest of winter and into the early spring. Every day they would read *The Atlantis*, fearful of finding news of escalating violence, but the reports remained eerily quiet. One day, Maria Christina realized Zoitsa seemed to be less sensitive to sudden noises and movements. She seemed to be calming down. Just before her Easter vacation Nick was notified that Zoitsa would be promoted once again and would begin the last quarter in her own age group in the fifth grade. Nick was overjoyed, and told everyone how extremely proud he was of his little niece.

On Sundays, after church, the regular group of relatives and friends once again congregated at Nick's for dinner. Either Alex or Chris and sometimes both would be there. There was also another young man, Paul, a rather tall, slight man with a van dyke, who was studying for his doctorate in Physics at Princeton University. Of the three Maria Christina preferred Alex. His sense of fun reminded her of Yiannis. But she never showed or accepted any interest from any of them other than as family friends.

One night at dinner, Nick was complaining to Helen that one of his employees, Gracie, who answered the phone and took customers' orders, was suddenly leaving at the end of the week to be married without having the courtesy to give him proper notice.

"After ten goddamn years! Total lack of consideration!"

"Calm down, Nick. I'll call the employment agency first thing in the morning. They'll find someone right away, don't they always?"

Everyone but Maria Christina continued to eat. After a moment's silence, she sat up straight; "Nick." She waited for him to look at her. "You see I speak a little English. I know basic mathematics. Maybe while we remain here you will help me repay your kindness."

Zoitsa stopped eating and looked at her uncle. Maria Christina was suddenly on trial. Nick looked at Zoitsa who was waiting for his answer. A glance at his wife alerted him of her disapproval. On the other hand, a refusal would most certainly be seriously frowned upon by his niece.

"Thank you, Maria Christina" Nick responded after no more than the second's reflection. "Thank you, yes. It is very kind of you to offer."

Later that night, when Nick and Helen were undressing:
"You can't be serious about her replacing Gracie."

"It's not rocket science. You answer the phone. You take an order."

"And you make nice with the customer. And she's never even picked up a telephone much less talked on one, Nick. Ever! Even in Greek!"

"She'll learn."

Nick's company, *Prospect Farms*, was a three-story warehouse on Greenwich Street in lower Manhattan. Nick insisted on paying Maria Christina fifty dollars a week, which she gratefully accepted. She quickly became quite efficient in her new job and the customers were all charmed by her accent. Nick was reassured he hadn't made a mistake, and even Helen had to admit he was right and she was wrong. Maria Christina gave Helen twenty dollars from her salary each week to help run the household, a sum which somehow never found its way back into the household but was applied to the purchase of a new miracle skin cream or diet supplement. Maria Christina also sent twelve dollars to Panorea along with a letter detailing their adventures. The remaining eighteen dollars were for her and her niece's expenses. Since Nick saw to it that Maria Christina almost never had to put her hand in her purse, each week she was able to deposit at least ten dollars in the savings account Nick had opened for her.

Helen started to suspect that Nick might even be developing a crush on Maria Christina, so whenever she would see them in conversation she would sit herself in his lap or massage his neck and interject her own thoughts into whatever they were talking about. For Maria Christina, Nick had quickly become the brother she never had. He was her guide, her protector, her guarantor that she and Zoitsa would never be left alone in this strange world. She understood and shared Yiannis' reverence for him. Nick was gentle but strong, honest and generous, his judgement not always perfect, but mostly sound, and he treated his help fairly and with great dignity.

"The way a man takes care of his employees is a window into his soul" Lily, his widowed secretary, concluded one day with tears in her eyes as she sat at her desk stirring her coffee with a thin wooden stick. She had just told Maria Christina that Nick had bought her daughter a beautiful gown so she could go to her high school senior prom properly dressed.

By spring vacation Zoitsa didn't need the training wheels on her bicycle and she and Anne would cycle to the zoo or botanical garden or to one of the fields to watch a Little League baseball game. Marcia Landis was overjoyed her Anne had made such a fine friend and was giving her daughter more freedom of movement, so long as they were together and were home by five.

Spring came to Brooklyn with more flowers than Maria Christina had ever imagined, on the trees, in the fields of the park, even in the church. Whenever she could, she would go on long walks just to traipse through the forest or lie down in the meadow. The war in Greece seemed to have come to a standstill, but the uncertainty remained. It was as if everyone was holding their collective breath. Then three letters arrived from Yiannis. One to Nick and Helen, thanking them profusely once again for their generosity. A second and a third were to his daughter and Maria Christina. All three contained different sentiments appropriate to their relationship, but all three contained the news that his tour of duty would be up at the end of the year, and he had decided the war was going to be over for him. He had given his all and the National Army had reached its greatest strength ever, about one hundred and thirty five thousand men, and their equipment and organization had improved significantly. He had long ago grown tired of seeing the suffering and death and feeling the longing. It was time to return home to Metsovo and continue his life.

Maria Christina wept at the news. Zoitsa screamed. Nick was reserved in his reaction, as was Helen when he told her. Nick desperately wanted Yiannis to quit the army, and his first reaction was joyous but, because he had no one from his own family in America with whom he could celebrate and share his success, he had always hoped Yiannis would eventually make his home in Brooklyn. Zoitsa felt the same. Helen didn't know Yiannis, but would be saddened by the loss of Zoitsa, should Yiannis decide to remain in Greece. Maria Christina, of course, couldn't wait to return to Metsovo. She had all but begun to despair that their exile would never end. She immediately wrote to Panorea and Lena that they would probably be returning sometime in late autumn to prepare for Yiannis' return in January. For days Maria Christina quietly walked on a cloud. Nick wrote Yiannis, reiterating his proposal that he relocate to Brooklyn and become a partner in *Prospect Farms*, but in his heart he knew Yiannis would never be happy in any city, especially one in America.

In mid June of 1948, the lead story in *The Atlantis* heralded an offensive by the National Army against the guerrillas' main bases which linked Greece to Albania and which were grouped in a series of ridges at an altitude of five to eight thousand feet, with steep slopes that were either rocky or covered with dense forests. The Communists referred to these fortifications as 'the impregnable fort'. The guerrillas had prepared two lines of fortifications, an outer defence, which blocked the passes that led to the bases, and an inner, a series of machine gun emplacements, perfectly camouflaged and reinforced with a covering of logs and earth and protected by minefields. The two lines of defence were manned by over twelve thousand fighters.

The National Army had deployed forty thousand men, supported by air force and artillery. Maria Christina and Zoitsa read the news every day with great trepidation. The war had all but disappeared from their lives for weeks, and now the newspaper was saying the battles were murderous, and that the Army was unable to breach the Communists' outer defence. For ten days, the paper reported mounting casualties. Finally, on July 8th, the paper claimed the National Army had managed to breach the outer defence, but there had been heavy losses on both sides. Reinforced by the 587, the battles took place for the next two weeks. To Maria Christina, Yiannis always seemed to be in the eye of the storm. She was almost afraid to ask the Holy Virgin to keep him safe again, yet she had to plead. Once more, to beg. And she did. Whenever she wasn't actually speaking to someone else, she was speaking to the Virgin.

"Blessed Mother of God, please keep him safe. Please, please, keep him safe. Blessed Mother of God, please keep him safe. Please, please, keep him safe."

Towards the end of August the Communists began retreating back into Albania. The paper reported that the National Army did not pursue them this time. Yiannis' most recent letter revealed that the guerrillas, who used to wear clean grey uniforms, were now wearing rags.

> 'Their hair and beards look like nests. Many are without shoes. It has been the largest, longest and most difficult battle of the war. Zervas wrote me he thought the result would be decisive. That this time the rumors of peace were likely to be fact.'

Most of the letter, however, was not about the war but about their new life and had an optimism Maria Christina thought he had lost. She was now more hopeful than ever. She almost didn't care about the status of the war as long as Yiannis was safe and they could return home. Living for the future in the present is most difficult, because you're living in neither. And so it continued for Maria Christina as the days slowly passed and the summer appeared suddenly and the heat and humidity seemed to be slowly strangling her. Fall came, but the intense heat continued in Brooklyn and didn't abate until mid October. Zoitsa started the sixth grade as Maria Christina began making plans for their return to the high Southern Alps and her beloved Metsovo. She reminded Zoitsa in Vlach each night as her niece climbed into bed and inched herself closer against her aunt:

"It has been a wonderful adventure, Moumou. But soon it will be over and it will be time to return home."

35

The sniper knew it was a hospital tent, but that didn't mean it shouldn't be a target. Whoever it was would be patching up some soldier so he could return to the fight and kill the sniper's comrades. The sniper was a quarter mile away, high in an oak. Soon it would be light and he would be easily spotted sitting on the bare branch. His back was aching from sitting motionless in the same position for two hours and he was debating whether to adjust his position, when he noticed the shadow which suddenly appeared and was moving through the tent. This would be his third target of the day, and he wasn't sure if he could register a kill. The first was a miss. It stepped away at the last second. The next was that afternoon, the last member of a squad on a routine patrol. He was in the hospital now and the sniper wasn't certain if he was still alive or if he had died.

Through the scope he traced the shadow as it moved across the side of the tent then stopped, bent over for a moment, then once again stood erect. He would be pulling the trigger for the poor and downtrodden, the overtaxed and under nourished. He would pull it for the liberation of the women of Greece, who were suffocating under the heavy yoke of their fathers and brothers. The country had to join the 20th century "By fire and Axe" if necessary. There was going to be a new Greece.

His older brother had indoctrinated him. Three years ago his brother, Achilleas, had been arrested for violations of the 'penal law', a convenient charge against Communist guerrillas. He had been taken to jail and then disappeared. There were inquiries made by their mother, but the authorities told her there was no record of his ever having been in prison. The sniper assumed he had been executed like so many others. His brother's smiling face was the image he held in his mind, while he strained to see as clearly as possible. Then, he slowly exhaled as he slowly squeezed the trigger. The familiar kick. The sniper laughed quietly to himself when he saw the silhouette spin, then hit the ground.

"Sniper! Yiannis! Stay still!" Haralambos lay on the ground clutching a bottle of *tsipouro*. Yiannis had been giving special attention to a young man from Metsovo, the baker's son, who was in critical condition. He had been shot through the neck by a sniper while out on patrol. His father had written Yiannis, knowing he was in the 587 as well, and asked him to keep an eye on his only son. Yiannis knew the family well and in fact had delivered the boy's two younger sisters.

That night, Haralambos had asked Olimbi to marry him, and to his great surprise she said yes. Haralambos immediately went and told Yiannis and insisted he be his best man and that the two immediately share a *tsipouro*. Yiannis was delighted their friendship would continue in Metsovo after the war and was looking forward to having that drink, but wanted to check on the baker's son one more time before he retired for the night.

"SNIPER!!!" Haralambos screamed. "SNIPER!!!"

The camp suddenly erupted in gunfire as the soldiers began shooting in every direction, hoping one bullet would somehow find its mark. Flares lit up the night sky. Haralambos lay in the mud, watching the look of bewilderment in Yiannis' eyes.

"Yiannis! Don't move! Do you understand me?"

Yiannis didn't understand. He just lay with his head in the

mud in a pool of his warm blood and wandered to his childhood. His father was overseeing a footrace between Nikos and him. The winner would get a fig. Before the race was finished, his mother's face appeared with tears streaming down her cheeks. His last clear image was of Matoula, as he first saw her dancing during the summer festival of the Prophet Elias. She looked so young and beautiful, it once again took his breath away. Only now did he realize and recognize the young girl she was dancing with was Maria Christina. That was his last clear image. After that, there was only the feeling of warmth, then all sound became silent, then nothing. Doctor Yiannis Petrakis ceased to exist.

The sniper silently crept down from the tree. Achilleas would have been very proud.

36

It was a hazy grey Saturday afternoon in Brooklyn. The ground was crusted with ice, but the air had warmed, so it was melting into a thin layer of slush. Zoitsa was sitting with Anne on the stone wall that surrounded the park. Anne had been explaining to Zoitsa the meaning of the word *holocaust*. Zoitsa was reminded of the Chaimaki brothers. She remembered that they always had a piece of candy in their pocket for her. She hadn't seen them since she was about six or seven. The village was occupied by the Germans then and everyone was terrified of them. One day, when she was in the village with her aunt, she noticed their store had been shuttered. It opened again sometime later, but the owner now was a Vlach, a son of a shepherd. After her story, the two continued sitting silently on the wall for a long time, sad and frightened by the cruelty of men. It was then Zoitsa saw Maria Christina walking towards her. As if forewarned, Anne excused herself and, after checking both ways for traffic, began skipping across the street in the slush towards their apartment building.

As she stood before her niece, Maria Christina's head was tilted and she smiled sadly. Zoitsa could see something was wrong. Speaking very softly while holding Zoitsa's face in her hands, Maria Christina told the child how her Babá had joined her mother in heaven. After staring at her aunt for a long unblinking moment, the deepest part of Zoitsa's heart burst. Maria Christina had never heard anyone cry so deeply or so sorrowfully as she gently scooped up the limp and trembling child, now blinded by tears and, holding her close, carried her home.

In the apartment, Maria Christina took Zoitsa into their bedroom and set her down on the bed. Then she took Zoitsa's little music box, wound it, and placed it in Zoitsa's hand. Zoitsa held the box next to her cheek as the tears continued to flow. Maria Christina was too stunned and distraught herself to weep. She lay next to her niece and held her while the chimes rang out, until they slowed and finally stopped, and the two lay silently for the longest time.

When the telegram arrived, Nick was in the living room with Helen, watching the weather forecast on television. As soon as Nick heard the knock and the words "Western Union" he froze. Still, it might be nothing. While Helen answered the door, Nick sat staring blankly at the television, waiting. Helen could sense Nick's anxiety level increasing, so she carefully opened the envelope for him. As she was handing him the telegram, she happened to glance over the first few words which included *Ministry of Defence* and *regret*.

"Dear God, Nick. It's dreadful. I'm so sorry."

Nick sat stunned. Even though Yiannis was younger, Nick had always looked up to him. Yiannis was the athlete, the excellent student, the mediator between Nick and his parents, and sometimes even between the two adults. He was Nick's only best friend for as long as he could remember. He consulted him on every important decision in his life and now, suddenly, he was gone. For a moment he couldn't catch his breath. Flustered, Helen rushed to pour him a Jack Daniels with three drops of bitters, but her hand was shaking and she poured more than a capful. She picked up a fresh glass, poured the bourbon again and added about five drops of bitters and rushed it back to him.

"Who will tell Zoe?" he said hoarsely as Helen put the drink into his hand.

Maria Christina was in her bedroom, sitting by the window, watching Zoitsa and Anne sitting on the wall and wondering what they were talking about so seriously. She was knitting Helen a sweater, blue and white, the colors of the Greek flag, when she heard the doorbell ring. Her mind then wandered to Panorea. Over the year, Maria Christina had come to miss her more than she had anticipated and wrote her frequently. In her last letter, Panorea wrote about herself for the first time, her aches and pains, her garden. Until recently, Panorea had viewed herself only as her brother's insignificant servant. He was able to summon her with just a lift of his eyebrows. With his passing, after a long period of deep sadness, unwilling even to eat for days, a new Panorea had emerged. Lena had written several letters heralding the various stages of this transformation. Her aunt was now stronger. She stood taller. A Panorea capable of joy and able to express grief. After being coaxed and prodded, she even joined the circle of dancers for a few steps at the Liberation of Metsovo festival in the square. Papa Yiorgos' death seemed to have freed her from her life's obligation, one she had come to believe was divinely directed, her spinsterhood somehow being meant to serve his widowhood.

Maria Christina was wondering how different her aunt's life might have been had she been liberated from her brother earlier in her life, when she heard what she assumed to be laughter from the living room. Setting down her knitting with a smile, she walked to the door and opened it slightly. As she listened more closely, she was unable to tell if it was laughter or in fact choking sobs.

Nick was openly sobbing when Maria Christina entered the room. Helen was standing over him, wiping his face with his handkerchief. Clearly, Helen needed help.

"We just got a telegram. Nick's brother Yiannis was killed.

He's very upset. Maybe you should be the one to tell Zoitsa. Nick's too upset, aren't you, Nick."

Nick sat holding the drink and the telegram, his chin on his chest. Maria Christina stood frozen. She was stunned by the news but, after only a moment, she put her hand on his shoulder.

"I'm so very sorry, Nick. Of course I'll tell Zoitsa."

The doorbell rang. Maria Christina answered it. Two more telegrams. One for Maria Christina Triantafyllou and Zoitsa Petrakis, the other for Nikos Petrakis. Maria Christina handed Helen the one for Nick and quickly left, reading along the way how broken-hearted Zervas was, and how sorry he was to have let them down. The one to Nick expressed the same sentiment, albeit more briefly, then said he had arranged to have the body shipped to Metsovo and into the care of Archimandrite Petsalis, who would handle the funeral arrangements.

After spending the rest of the day trying to console Nick and Zoitsa and to calm Helen, by the time Maria Christina went to bed that night she felt as though, like Yiannis, she no longer existed. Only in the morning she would awaken and Yiannis would not. She was neither able to weep nor wail. The well of sorrow was now too deep to express with tears. She only wished she could vomit. Perhaps it would help relieve the grief lodged in the deepest part of her stomach.

37

In Metsovo, on the ninth, the twentieth, and the fortieth day of a death, family and friends gathered at the deceased's home to share their grief and celebrate life. Grieving was an organized ritual which took place at designated times, allowing the bereaved to release the sorrow which had been building since the death, each memorial being further from the last, until the shock and loss was absorbed into the normal passing of life.

Because they were in America, Zoitsa invoked Papa Yiorgos' argument that one had to respect the ways of one's host country, and the old ways of mourning need not be observed. In no mood for a confrontation and mindful of her obligations towards Nick's business, Maria Christina reluctantly agreed and only kept a candle lit on her dresser, in front of her icons, to mark the period. Otherwise, she sat dutifully at her desk at *Prospect Farms* and cheerfully, mindlessly chatted with customers. Zoitsa continued in school. Although just ten, Zoitsa felt she had already seen too much, lived too long. She was deeply angry, and it wouldn't pass easily. Papa Yiorgos' gift to her. But even more troubling was that she was now frightened in a way that resembled being chilled to the bone, where no amount of heat seems to relieve the cold. A sudden loud noise now terrified her more than ever. If she heard a fire engine on her way to school, she would run back to the apartment building to make sure it wasn't on fire, making her late for class. A car backfiring would send her running into the nearest doorway. Helen thought she should see a psychiatrist, but Nick thought they were only for crazy people.

"Zoe isn't crazy, she's just upset. She just lost her father for God's sake."

Zoitsa naturally clung more than ever to the strongest for protection, her uncle, and even climbed into his and Helen's bed the night she learned of her father's death and every night since, leaving Maria Christina to sleep and grieve alone.

Having kept silent for a whole week, Helen could no longer hold her tongue. While Nick was taking a bath and she was creaming her face, she shut the bathroom door.

"Nick, you must immediately retain two lawyers. One for custody and one for immigration."

Nick waved her away "There's no need. Maria Christina's reasonable. She'll want what's best for the child."

"Just to be safe, Nick, don't you think?"

"We must not ask Zoe to choose between us, my dear. She already has. There'd be nothing served by fighting Maria Christina for custody. Zoe will be eleven in a few weeks and any judge would ask her who she would prefer and who knows what guilt she may feel? We could be the losers. Let Zoe finish her education. Then, if she wishes, she can go back to Metsovo. And she'll have something to offer the community. That's how I will approach Maria Christina and I'm quite sure reason will prevail."

"Well, I hope you're right, Nick. You always are. I guess it could get ugly. But you should still get into the immigration thing. In any event, after the forty days, no more black armband. Alright, Nick? It's depressing. And no more Zoitsa sleeping in our bed. She should move into your den. Everyone should have their own room. I'll make her a nice girl's room and there'll be plenty of space for your desk in one corner, you'll see."

Zoitsa hadn't seen her father in over a year, and then for only a single day and night in the little *kalivi* in the mountains, when she had been so excited about going to America. Had she known she would never see him again, she never would have left. Unlike the image of her mother, which had become lost to her, Zoitsa desperately wanted to keep her father's face fresh in her mind. She also wanted to know anything and everything about him and she thought the one person in the world who knew him best was her Uncle Nick. As a result, she pestered him to a degree which approached annoying.

"Tell me another story about my father."

She would then take the photographs of her father in the living room and her portrait of him, which was now resting on a small easel on the piano, and sit on the couch and look at them and imagine her father and his face during the excellent story her uncle would tell. Nick employed every childhood memory, every fable and book he had ever heard and read to keep the supply of stories endless. The unconditional love he received from his niece made him feel as though at last he did indeed have a child, a beautiful daughter. And Zoitsa was very careful to be his perfect daughter.

Nick took over the responsibility of Zoitsa's education, including her home work. The two spent more and more time alone together. Zoitsa learned quickly, and Maria Christina was taken aback one Sunday morning when she walked into the dining room before church and saw Nick and Zoitsa having breakfast and reading the *Dialogues of Plato* aloud in English, Nick reading Socrates of course. She smiled sadly. Pappou had always insisted on being Socrates with her.

Lena and Panorea had both written about the solemnity of Yiannis' funeral, conducted by Archimandrite Paschalis at Agia Paraskevi, and described the overflowing crowd. Most of the men from the village were away in the army or with their meagre flocks, although there was a sizeable contingent of war veterans, some from surrounding villages, to whom Yiannis had ministered during his years as a field surgeon, some missing arms or legs, many weeping openly like women. Stahoulis sat with the other veterans and was openly sobbing. There were many tearful maidens as well, their best hopes dashed. After the ceremony, Stahoulis held an open house at his *pantopolio* for coffee, and *tsipouro*. There were fresh baked cakes and cookies, courtesy of the baker, grateful for his son's life.

By the end of November 1948, *The Atlantis* reported that the Greek General Staff had ordered a general attack on all remaining key guerrilla mountain positions and that many of these positions were taken, lost, then recaptured, sometimes changing hands three times. The casualties on both sides were already in the hundreds. But Zoitsa had stopped reading *The Atlantis*. She now wanted nothing more to do with Greece or Greeks. She no longer had any interest in Metsovo, nor in speaking Vlach. She would speak it reluctantly, to humor her aunt. But never in public, and only a few sentences at a time. The more she learned of the glory of the ancients and their ideals, the more she grew to despise modern Greece and it's people.

"How could a group who started so gloriously become such barbarians and fools."

She was actually paraphrasing an op ed piece in the *New York Times*. Her sixth grade teacher, Mrs. Haverkamp, a tall, thin, sparkling elderly woman from the old school, had instructed the class on how to read the paper. First, how to fold it so it could be read on a crowded subway. Then she taught them to read the front page and continue inside to finish each article in its entirety. Then the editorials, then the obituaries, which Zoitsa found fascinating, even comforting when she realized most people lived to be quite old. A whole life summed up in a few paragraphs. And such important people. It was inspiring to the young girl from Metsovo, who had already decided she wanted to be remembered on that page when she died.

Nick and Maria Christina continued to read *The Atlantis* for a few more weeks, then Nick put it down one day, disgusted, and never picked it up again. There seemed to be no interest among any of them in the fate of Greece and its bloody senseless war. During Sunday dinners, some of the older people would chat about the war in passing. The younger people referred to Greece as "the old country" but knew almost nothing about it.

At the end of forty days, Nick arranged a memorial service for Yiannis at the Greek Orthodox cathedral in Manhattan with Archbishop Athenagoras officiating. After the choir had finished singing the hymn *Eternal Be His Memory*, the Archbishop announced he would be reading a eulogy he had received written by General Napoleon Zervas. Slowly and with great reverence he began reading Zervas' words.

"A good man died forty days ago. As good a man as I've ever known."

Zoitsa listened with tears streaming down her cheeks, aching for her father. Nick hated Zervas. He knew the pompous ass was responsible for recruiting and retaining Yiannis in the army, exploiting his patriotism. Maria Christina sat stoically in the front pew of the church with Nick, Helen, and Zoitsa, and stopped listening after a moment. The eulogy ended with a plea for the Greeks in the Diaspora to remain steadfast in their support of the mother country, and in this way honor the life of Yiannis Petrakis and all the other brave men and women who had given their lives so that Greece would endure in freedom. Helen, having been moved to tears, thought the General's eulogy second only to *The Gettysburg Address*.

After the service, there was a buffet in the basement and more expressions of sympathy for Nick and Zoitsa from friends and family. Maggie the maid was there. Maria Christina hadn't seen her since she had started working at *Prospect farms*. By the time Maggie arrived at the apartment, Maria Christina had left, and by the time Maria Christina returned, Maggie was gone. When Maggie went to express her sympathy to the family, she immediately sensed the depth of Maria Christina's loss. When she first took her hand and looked into her eyes, she couldn't help but notice they were vacant, lifeless. She bent and kissed Maria Christina's hand then leaned in to whisper in her ear.

"You ever feel like talking, Maria, you call me, hear?"

Later, a few of their closest friends returned to Nick and Helen's where they swapped stories of their respective childhoods. After everyone departed and the leftover food stored and the dishes done, the carpet swept and Zoitsa was sleeping for the last time in Nick and Helen's room, Helen was standing by the door which was open a crack, straining to hear the conversation in the living room that Nick had been planning to have with Maria Christina. Nick was holding his suit coat and taking off the black armband when she entered the room. His voice was tired.

"I'm afraid we must discuss your future, Maria Christina. Yours and Zoitsa's."

"Yes, of course" she sat on the end of the couch, furthest from his chair. "You know we are expected in Metsovo for Christmas."

Nick looked at her, then took a breath, laid his coat neatly over the back of his chair and spoke softly "I know you want what is best for the child. Her safety is paramount. In that regard nothing has changed. Greece is still the same dangerous place it was when Yiannis sent you here. Besides, Zoe wishes to remain here. She feels safe here. She is flowering. And she so enjoys her school and is excelling. She wants to continue. We should allow her to continue. She can always go back to Metsovo. When she is finished with her education she will be able to contribute something to the community besides babies."

While Maria Christina was examining his argument, he continued.

"Of course you know we want you to stay here as long as you wish. You are family to us and Zoe would be heartbroken to see you leave. And Helen. And I would hate to lose you at *Prospect Farms.*"

Nick made a great deal of sense to Maria Christina. Besides, she had no doubt Zoitsa would finally return to Metsovo. She felt certain that for Zoitsa, much of the magic of America, like any novelty, would eventually fade, and she hoped her niece would begin to see the country in a more realistic light.

Christmas wasn't as amusing for everyone this year. Especially for Zoitsa. The tree seemed silly, exchanging gifts even more so. She had been home with tonsillitis when they were making Christmas presents in school and refused to make even a drawing for anyone. Nick had also begun to become irritable, sometimes even downright ornery. One day he even yelled at Helen for buying juice oranges instead of naval. The atmosphere was becoming tense. Maria Christina remained quietly inconspicuous, spending most of her time at work or alone in her room. Her duties regarding Zoitsa had become reduced to insisting that her niece fulfil certain obligations, such as writing to her great aunt, Panorea, or cleaning the bath tub after using it. The child was becoming increasingly belligerent, but would finally condescend to do whatever.

"Just to get you off my back."

On Saturday afternoons, Maria Christina would take Zoitsa to a movie either at the *Carlton*, which showed Hollywood movies, or the *Plaza*, which showed only foreign and classic films. Maria Christina preferred comedies. Love stories made her too sad and war movies were depressing. Zoitsa preferred mysteries. She loved predicting the end. Maria Christina always packed a snack, pistachios, fruit and cheese, but Zoitsa declined them and insisted on popcorn. Going to the movies seemed to be the only fun the two had together any more.

After a winter of hardly any snow, spring came early to Brooklyn. By the end of March, there were small leaves on tree branches, the smell of fresh green, the very beginning of life. But the more things burst into flower, the less Maria Christina felt like being in the park, and the more Zoitsa wanted to be outdoors. There were a few concerns expressed by her teachers that Zoitsa seemed distracted and didn't volunteer as much as she used to. She was always prepared, but less engaged. By the end of the term, she rallied and came home with a glorious report card for Nick to sign.

Nick always rented a house in Oyster Bay on Long Island for the month of August. He and Zoitsa spent most of their time in the water, while Maria Christina and Helen sat on the porch or on the beach under an umbrella. The sea was a constant reminder to Maria Christina of how quickly and constantly things change. She could hardly bear to look at it, and so spent the most of the month with her back to it, knitting an afghan.

By the fall of 1949, the National Army had emerged victorious. The Communists had surrendered. The guerrilla war was essentially over. It was painful for Maria Christina to think of all the blood that had been shed. The loss of her sister, father and beloved in so short a time made her question whether God was not a just and good God, but a cruel and sadistic One who enjoyed watching his creatures starve or kill each other. Sometimes, she would sit in her chair by the window late at night while everyone slept, knitting and thinking. What God would allow such suffering as she had seen and endured? Was the soldier that tried to rape her part of His Divine Plan? Then she remembered Pappou once telling her that an old monk he had met in his travels said he had a revelation that it was through the fusion of spirit, or the God-part of man, and man the animal, that God was actually able to experience his own creation. And that He didn't interfere because he was actually suffering along with the rest of us. She realized she could have allowed the soldier to have his way and then have been on her way, but the truth was she chose to kill him. She wished to kill him. Men make these decisions. Not God. God had given man the free will to choose. How sad and painful His creation must be for Him. How disappointing, especially when evil is being done in His name.

Maria Christina would sit for hours, contemplating ideas like these, some more outrageous than others, until by the time she returned to her bed she was drained completely of thought and ready to meet the world again in the morning, a somber, sober, thoughtful, aging, unmarried woman, continuing dutifully on her way, stumbling through life, no longer living in the future, which held no more hope than the present, which held no hope at all, and all the while desperately holding on to the past, the memories.

38

A week after Yiannis' forty-day memorial service, a tall stranger in a long tweed overcoat and hat, smoking a pipe, stood in the middle of the square in Metsovo wondering where to begin. Deciding to start at Stahoulis' *pantopolio*, he stepped inside, ordered coffee, and struck up a conversation with Stahoulis who, after he delivered the coffee, returned to shredding cabbage behind the counter. The man had been studying Greek just for this occasion and, between what he had prepared and Stahoulis' meager English, he was able to tell his story. His name was Malcolm Ryder and he was an architect from Windsor, England, and he was looking for a woman in about her mid twenties, who was a member of the underground resistance and had nursed him back to life during the war and with whom he had fallen in love. He hadn't stopped thinking about her and had come to ask her to marry him if she was still available. She would never tell him her name, but he described her as wearing round horn-rimmed glasses. He told a startled Stahoulis how his friends thought he was probably delirious, but no other woman measured up to her.

Stahoulis concluded the flier's friends were probably not mistaken and that he must be talking about Maria Christina Triantafyllou. In order to keep this crazy man from rushing to

America and being a burden to poor Maria Christina, Stahoulis told him he knew who he was talking about, but that she was living somewhere in America, married to an important man in government, like a mayor. After a second cup of coffee, Malcolm Ryder, deeply disappointed, left his card with Stahoulis and began his journey back to Britain.

Stahoulis recounted the incident to Lena who passed it on to Maria Christina. Lena also wrote that the whole village was buzzing with the news that in Athens a list of the one hundred and fifty names of the secret resistance group, Bouboulina, had surfaced and her name was on it. Maria Christina smiled and became immediately teary at the thought of Bouboulina and the flier Lena wrote about. He had been the one who had called her "My Angel" and kissed her hand and told her that her lips reminded him of the English rose, "Scarborough Fair".

39

Years sometimes come and go in which nothing much occurs to mark the time. No births, deaths, no Acts of God which would make one note the date. Just the same routine with small, subtle changes. These insignificant years gradually recede in one's memory until they are lost, leaving only the important events to connect the dots of one's life. But time doesn't stand still. Change occurs. One is constantly being shaped by minor events, slowly, slowly, like water dripping on a piece of stone. That was the hope of both Nick and Helen, as they tried to fashion Zoitsa into their American ideal. Maria Christina, on the other hand, was determined to instil in her niece the traditional Vlach values, some quite at odds with those of Nick and Helen.

For the next few years nothing noteworthy occurred in the Petrakis household. One event Maria Christina might have marked fifteen years ago, before she saw the world through her grandfather's glasses, was now quickly forgotten. Alex had been relentless in his pursuit of her. The fact that she seemingly couldn't be possessed made her all the more alluring. As her English improved, he realized she was also quite the wit, in fact more than almost anyone he knew. His first approach was through Zoitsa. Befriending her would certainly bring him closer to her aunt, but it didn't help. When she saw him jumping rope with Zoitsa and Anne, Maria Christina thought it was sweet but remained unimpressed. He then became more direct, trying to engage her, flirt with her. She was even less interested. She was, however, always pleasant and courteous towards him, which Alex misinterpreted as warmth.

After one Sunday dinner, when everyone else had gone home, Alex stayed behind to talk to Nick. He confessed that he liked Maria Christina very much and would like to ask her to marry him, but he didn't know the protocol for Vlachs, and since her mother and father were both dead, he was wondering whether he should just ask the question directly, as he would normally do in America. Nick thought for a moment. There was no mention of a dowry. That would be another plus for a helpless waif.

"Alex, let me think about it. Maybe I'll even talk to her. I'll get back to you."

"Bingo!" Helen boasted, later in their bedroom. "He's a good egg, that Alex, but I think maybe we could do better, don't you, Nick?"

"Nonsense" Nick shot back. "He's a very good egg. And she wears glasses."

"Georgia Pepas liked those glasses so much she bought herself a pair just like them. I think they look very smart."

Nick waited until the following Sunday morning to discuss the proposal with Maria Christina. He asked her to join him in the living room. Pouring himself a bitters and soda, he bid Maria Christina sit and went directly to the subject.

"Alex has asked me to approach you about the possibility of marriage."

Maria Christina didn't respond.

"Well, Maria Christina, what do you say? He's a very good man. I will vouch for him. He would be a good husband for you. A good father to your children. And he asks for nothing but your devotion."

Maria Christina nodded and spoke quietly "I believe he is a very good man. And it is a very kind and generous offer." She took a breath and looked down at her hands, folded in her lap. "I was promised to someone. Someone I loved very much. He was killed in the war. I will mourn him every day for the rest of my life."

Nick understood immediately. It was pure old country. They had probably slept together, and Maria Christina considered herself his widow, and would continue to dress in deep sombre colors until the day she died, and never give herself to another man. After he told Helen, neither she nor Nick ever spoke of it again.

But Alex was resolute. The following Sunday he asked to speak to her for a moment. When they were alone, he asked her if she would honor him by being his wife. He had even purchased an antique diamond ring which he held up to her with pleading eyes. She smiled sympathetically and touched his sleeve with her hand.

"Dear Alex. I am honored you would ask me. But you would never be happy with a woman whose heart you could never possess."

For everyone but Zoitsa, life continued as before. For her, these years were punctuated with occasions she was certain she would remember forever. The day the piano appeared in the living room and the one when she started taking lessons. The day she moved into her very own room with her own record player.

Early in her eighth grade year, P.S. 107's vice-principal, Mrs. Brown, arranged a conference with Nick. Zoitsa had scored in the ninety-ninth percentile, the highest possible, in an aptitude test which measured her ability to reason logically. She urged him to consider having Zoitsa apply to Hunter College High School for Intellectually Gifted Young Ladies, which was located at Hunter College in Manhattan. She explained that in order to be considered, an eighth grader had to take an intelligence test, after which only those whose quotient was at least one hundred and fifty, or genius, need apply. She was confident Zoitsa fell into that category. She also recommended that, if she were to apply, she should become involved in some organized extracurricular activity, like the Girl Scouts or perhaps the children's choir at their church, because she thought Hunter was not only looking for students with gifted intelligence, but those whose interests extended beyond academics.

Nick had always been convinced that if Zoitsa had the best education, her future in America would be assured and she would never think of returning to Metsovo. He had already made an application on her behalf to the Berkley School for Girls, a prestigious private school within walking distance of the apartment. To be admitted, the student needed good grades and money. Connections were also important, but one had to convince the board that the student's parents would be generous alumni contributors. This was all fine with Nick, since he was essentially guaranteed that if Zoitsa maintained good grades while at Berkley, she would be admitted into one of the top tier of colleges. And yet there were any number of private prep schools in the New York area to which Zoitsa would probably be admitted, but there was only one Hunter College High School for Intellectually Gifted Young Ladies. For Nick, that would be glorious. His brother's daughter. It would be evidence of the superior intelligence of the Petrakis' family.

Zoitsa thought the Girl Scouts was for simpletons and her church didn't have a children's choir. She turned her eye to something she thought was far more impressive: P.S.107 Student Government President. She was arguably one of the most popular in her school. Locking any doubts or fears tightly away, she immediately began strategizing her campaign. She was determined to win, not because she was competitive by nature, but because she knew it would please her uncle. His approval meant everything to her. It was the fuel of her ambition. She deliberated for a long time on her choice of a running mate, then it came to her. She had been noticing stories of racism and poverty in the newspaper and on television, the segregation in the south, the negative reaction of certain white professional baseball players to a black man, Jackie Robinson, playing against them. Although there was a minimal African-American presence in her school, the number was large enough to effect the outcome of any close election. She decided to go with the current of history and chose Dennis Parks, someone she hardly knew, a light-skinned, well-liked boy with blonde frizzy hair. The boy never suspected Zoitsa's motives weren't pure and laudable. Neither did Anne, who was her campaign manager. She was proud of her friend for making this brave political statement. On the day of the election, the students put their trust in the war refugee with the African-American vice-president in a landslide victory. Nick couldn't stop bragging about his niece.

Even as Zoitsa thought all these events would be forever etched in her memory, they would eventually be eclipsed by more important, life-changing ones. In early April, Anne told Zoitsa that she and her parents were moving to Israel to help build a homeland. It was sudden, like death. The decision had been made the night before. Zoitsa was crushed.

One week later, as she sat on the park's stone wall and watched the movers carry the last of the Landis' furniture out of the building, Zoitsa decided she would never have another best friend. Not ever. It would only result in breaking her heart. She had already lost two best friends, and she was only thirteen years old. First Thimi and now Anne, sitting in the back seat of the taxi, looking through the window at her. As the moving men were closing the doors of the van, Zoitsa began to cry. She started kicking the wall with her heels hard, kicking harder and harder. She was angry. As the taxi moved down the block, she could see Anne was crying, too.

Less than an hour later, Zoitsa received two acceptance letters in the mail. One was from The Berkley School for Girls, the other from Hunter.

Nick thought no one would believe she had been accepted by the elite Hunter College High School, so he insisted she go there at least for one year, even though it meant she would have to take the subway for an hour each way and change trains twice during rush hour.

As Zoitsa numbly wandered through the bitter sweetness of the day, she gained an insight into one of the questions that had bewildered her since she started school in America. Although she was popular in her class, with Anne gone she now had no actual friends. She had always been pleasant to the others, but she maintained her distance. She had no interest in cultivating their friendship, and now she knew why: she was exceptional. Superior. Her new school song even told her so.

'I'm Sarah Maria Jones,
I have Hunter in my bones,
My name is written in my umbrella.
Jane goes to another school,
Isn't she a little fool,
And when I meet her on the street I tell her.'

Zoitsa sang with great gusto along with the other girls during Hunter College High School assemblies, and because she was beginning to realize that her budding breasts and angelic face and blonde ringlets were quite attractive, she began to develop a self-confidence that bordered on smug. Having to negotiate the subway alone every day at rush hour, being shoved and groped while reading the *New York Times* with her arm around a pole to keep from being pushed out of the car by the swarm exiting at Wall Street, made her feel more and more independent. One afternoon, crossing the platform to change trains on her return trip from school as she waited for the local to arrive, a man in a grey topcoat exposed himself. The first time Zoitsa was shocked. A week later he was there again exposing himself. But this time she was prepared.

"It looks just like a penis but smaller" she smiled as her train pulled into the station.

The flasher seemed embarrassed and quickly covered himself as he backed into the shadows and disappeared from view. Zoitsa was growing up fast in the city.

There were no other girls from Brooklyn at Hunter. Other than having lunch with the same group of girls in the college cafeteria, Zoitsa almost never socialized with any of them. Most of the girls lived in Manhattan, and her apartment in Brooklyn was too difficult a trip. Twice she accepted invitations to play bridge at one of the girl's homes on Riverside Drive, together with some of her other lunch mates, but she turned down their third and fourth invitations. Although the girls were exceptionally smart, some of them much smarter than she was, she concluded none of them was even a little funny, and not one had any sense of style. As a result, she made no new friends at Hunter. But she didn't mind. Her best friend was her uncle and he was more than enough.

Long after Yiannis' death, a general sadness continued to linger in the Petrakis household. Even a celebration, like the one in honor of Zoitsa being accepted at Hunter, reminded everyone of those who would never be present for any of her triumphs. Nick and Helen now only ventured out twice a month, unless it was someone's birthday or their anniversary. Maria Christina always opted to stay home, excusing herself with a headache or a bit of indigestion. After a number of refusals, Nick stopped asking unless it was a special celebration.

Beginning with teaching Maria Christina English vocabulary when she was in the third grade, Zoitsa had slowly taken over the role of her aunt's tutor and over the years turned into her critic in every subject from philosophy to cooking.

"You have to live as though there is no heaven or hell."

"The beans are overcooked again."

In general Zoitsa was kind enough to her aunt, but she had stopped listening to her opinion about anything, as if her old ways and life experience counted for nothing. But Maria Christina patiently persisted, repeating the same proverbs evolved over a thousand years of Vlach history. To each one, Zoitsa would have a ready response.

"One hand can't clap alone" Maria Christina would say.

"But it can snap it's fingers" would be the reply.

"Even if the apple rolls from the tree it will remain in its shade."

"Since only half my shade is Vlach, I must have rolled into the Athenian shade."

Undeterred by Zoitsa's sass, she continued to slip them into their conversation believing that repetition would forever lodge them in her niece's mind. She understood that her role in her niece's life had been greatly diminished, being reduced now to simply standing by, ready to reprimand her if she crossed the line. To Nick, Zoitsa could do no wrong, so discipline was left entirely to Maria Christina. Even though Zoitsa often tested the boundaries, she rarely crossed over. Only very occasionally did Maria Christina have to put her foot down.

"No, Nick. It's late enough and she has school tomorrow."

"I'm sorry, Helen, but she must stay in her room until she apologizes."

Sometimes Zoitsa would snap at Maria Christina with "Why don't you just go back to Metsovo and leave me alone! You're not my mother!"

To which Maria Christina would calmly reply "I will one day, my angel, when you're ready."

"Oh, really? When will that be? When I get married? I may never get married."

"I'll keep that in mind, Moumou."

"I've asked you to please not call me that."

Maria Christina sometimes wondered if she was just wasting her life away. There was so much to rebuild in Greece. But as Nick's business continued to grow and he hired more help, he made Maria Christina his Office Manager. She refused to accept any salary increase. She was just grateful that Nick allowed her to continue to be part of Zoitsa's life. Nick had not taken Zoitsa away from Maria Christina. The child wanted to be an American. Needed to be. The truth was that Maria Christina had lost Zoitsa to America.

40

During the next eight years, Maria Christina spent her free time sitting by the window in her bedroom, knitting, crocheting, embroidering, her hands always busy, determined to leave something of herself behind. Sometimes her thoughts wandered back to Metsovo, to Yiannis' unfinished house, his vineyard, having a meal at the makeshift table under the sycamore, happy thoughts. She longed for the Southern Alps. She would close her eyes and imagine she was standing in the sun, high in the mountains in November, looking down at the mist which often blanketed the valley in the mornings. Trees glistening with ice, being unable to tell the snow-capped mountain from the clouds. She missed sitting in their old kitchen, snapping the ends off string beans, the smell of yeast filling the room from kneading yellow dough in the bread trough for corn bread.

"How I wish tonight I could sit with Panorea and Lena around a fire" she would sometimes say to herself. They would be gone soon. And soon Zoitsa would be off on her own. What then? The girl already didn't want her old aunt around. What joy could there be in life with no one to share it. Maria Christina was beginning to face the fact that soon she would be alone in the world. On nights like this she would sometimes sit for hours by her window, a half glass of wine from Matoula's Vineyard on the table next to her.

To honor the memory of Yiannis, Costas Stahoulis maintained the vineyard for Zoitsa, and had even been making wine these past two years. Most of it he sold in his *pantopolio*. He sent the proceeds to Zoitsa along with a case of the year's vintage. Nick refused to drink it, declaring the color too pale and the bouquet too fruity to be potable. Zoitsa, taking her cue from her uncle, also rejected it. Helen tried it once, thought it very light but quite tasty. But whenever Maria Christina felt especially low, she would pour herself a glass, then savor every drop, sipping it ever so slowly through the night, as if she was drinking small drops of Yiannis' soul.

It made Zoitsa sad to think that Maria Christina had sacrificed her own life years ago so she could care for her dead sister's child, and now she seemed content simply to exist without purpose, measuring her life only through her niece's milestones. She was still so young and not unattractive.

"If she'd just get rid of those glasses. And the kerchief."

Although she was still only in her early thirties, Maria Christina seemed middle aged. Her hair, which she now wore in a bun, was turning grey, and her complexion had grown gradually paler. Yet it wasn't that she looked so much older, it was that she acted older. There was a stoop in her posture, and she was losing weight ever so slowly, almost imperceptibly. Only someone who hadn't seen her in a year would have noticed and think she might have been ill. She still hadn't shed one tear over Yiannis' death, even though there were reminders of him everywhere in the apartment: family photographs of Nick and Yiannis as children, Yiannis and Nick in college, Yiannis standing in front of the Eiffel Tower. For Maria Christina, Zoitsa now reminded her more and more of both her parents. Yet none of the photographs had nearly the same effect as looking at Zoitsa. More than a glance became an invitation for little pin pricks to her heart: when she cocked her head like her mother or smiled in her crooked way exactly like her father. She sometimes even reminded her of her own father, the way she bit her lower lip while listening intently to something. She occasionally wondered about her own mother and which of her mannerisms she had inherited, and she would close her eyes and try to imagine what her angelic face must have looked like.

Zoitsa started to also see the old man emerging in her uncle, and it worried her. His hair was rapidly thinning and becoming greyer. Helen wanted to dye it but he wouldn't hear of it. Since his brother's death he had become less jovial. Forays to the Copa Cabana had become rare, even when Desi was performing. Once there, Nick danced only a few dances and with much less enthusiasm. He was past wanting to be on the floor, and was content to sit back and watch the others. He was satisfied with his life. He loved his wife, enjoyed his business. He was beguiled by his niece. He prayed to God that nothing unexpected would destroy the calm. Everyone was happy and healthy, what more could any man ask for but nothing?

To Zoitsa all her relatives now seemed to be in various stages of dying. It made her even more determined to live her life to the fullest. Like her mother, she became the family's eyes and ears to the outside world. Her interest in newspaper items now developed into a desire to be at the center of any newsworthy event as an unbiased reporter. Always more interested in the action than the cause, she would take the subway here or there, this time to march against the burning of books in public libraries, then to a political rally for presidential candidate Adlai Stevenson. Her fears were still locked tightly away, a battle she was continually fighting and winning.

Friendless by choice, Zoitsa still tried to fit in at Hunter. Pleated plaid skirts, sweater sets, knee socks and penny loafers.

She took classes with names like Print and Broadcast Journalism and College Level Literature, and worked studiously to rid herself of any trace of her Greek accent, which she replaced with what is referred to as 'Broadway English', used by classically trained actors. It was an attitude as well. Her favorite actress was Bette Davis, and she would imitate her at every opportunity. The package became more and more refined so that, by the time she graduated Hunter, she was accepted by all three Ivy League colleges she had applied to, including Barnard College for Women, which was part of Columbia University. Columbia was Nick's preference because she wouldn't have to leave New York and could still live under his roof.

Zoitsa was now the star of the Greek community in Brooklyn, the bar by which all other young Greek girls were being measured. At weddings and other celebrations when Zoitsa danced, all eyes would be on her, her strong, perfect body, her style and grace. Insisting on selecting her own clothes, Nick would give her his credit card and she would take a taxi to Martin's Department Store where she would pick out whatever she wanted, whatever she fancied.

The girls at Barnard wore what they had worn at Hunter, only now they preferred button down shirts under their sweaters and saddle shoes instead of loafers. Zoitsa, however, had moved on and had adopted a non-conformist look inspired by Sophia Loren in *Bitter Rice*. She had taken to wearing black eyeliner, black turtle neck sweaters, black tights and black ballet slippers. She wore pale make-up and refused to wear any lipstick. It amused her that the look made everyone so uncomfortable, even her uncle Nick.

At Barnard, Zoitsa immediately joined the staff of *The Bulletin*, their bi-weekly newspaper. Throwing herself into the work with great enthusiasm, she quickly became one of their favorite reporters. For her sophomore year she was given the responsibility of the paper's New York City Living Editor. As a junior she was selected to be the Politics and Opinion Editor, and in her senior year she was Co-Editor in Chief. She so excelled at Barnard she was offered and accepted a Sidney Hillman Scholarship to the prestigious Columbia School of Journalism, arguably the best in its field in the nation. That year she also gained her U.S. citizenship.

Maria Christina kept postponing her return to Metsovo. She was concerned about her niece and wondered why Zoitsa was so driven, what demons were chasing her. After grade school, high school, and then when she graduated college, she had the same serious talk with her niece.

"Moumou, are you ready to go home yet?"

Even though she knew electricity had come to Metsovo, and with it, indoor plumbing and now even four telephones had been installed in the village, she would reply "Go back to what? Cheese pies and mountain tea for dinner at noon, cooked in a fireplace? Candlelight? Nine months of winter with no indoor toilet? You must be joking. And please, how many thousands of times do I have to ask you, beg you. There is no Moumou. There is only Zoe."

For her uncle Nick, Zoitsa's life was unfolding splendidly. With each milestone he would have a celebration at a club or restaurant and invite those of the original Copa Cabana list with whom he was still friendly, in addition to several newer friends he had acquired along the way. Alex, of course was always invited, and continued to pursue Maria Christina with the hope she might still change her mind one day. He was even convinced he could be happy with her, even if he could never possess her totally.

Zoitsa never invited a guest, that is, until recently. She now had a boyfriend, Brad Walker, a tall young man with sandy hair, four years her senior, who smoked a pipe just like her father's. She had met him at a Columbia mixer, and he had become her mentor. She had been dating him on and off for a year. Now a news producer at CBS, he thought Zoitsa was attractive, articulate, poised, and a perfect candidate for the network, which was looking for female on-camera investigative reporters, a job which Zoitsa was convinced would thrill her uncle Nick.

The young man was always kind to Maria Christina, though rather disinterested in her. Maria Christina thought he was a nice enough fellow, but a time-is-money kind of man, always in a hurry, wanting to give the impression his plate was overly full and that he was in great demand. He made Maria Christina uncomfortable. Zoitsa was aware of it, though her aunt tried to hide her feelings. Zoitsa herself was not entirely at ease with his need to feel important, but she would suppress the thought and dwell instead on the things she admired about him.

Having decided to become a journalist for almost as many years as she had been in America, Zoitsa had also wondered whether she should change her name to make it sound more American. Maria Christina feared it was the real reason, as shallow as it was, that she might decide to marry this young producer.

"Reporting live from Washington, Zoe Walker" Maria Christina heard Zoitsa say aloud one day while lying on the couch, watching the news on television. Then Zoitsa laughed and slapped her thigh.

Zoitsa was now planning to move to Manhattan. She would be living in the Columbia graduate dormitory. She seemed happy. Still nervous underneath, but basically happy. But nervous. There no longer seemed to be any reason for Maria Christina to remain in Brooklyn. She had done what she could. The child was forever formed. She was now well-educated and savvy enough to survive on her own in the world, and she would have the protection and legacy of her well-heeled uncle.

Over the last two years, Panorea wrote only occasionally. Lena's letters had been hinting that Panorea was slowly losing her memory. Lena, too, started complaining about aches and pains for the first time. No one ever referred to Zoitsa's friend, Thimi. During one Sunday dinner, Maria Christina heard the older men talking about the fact that some of the kidnapped children had escaped their abductors' camps and had made their way back to Greece. Many more, however, had disappeared altogether or had been completely indoctrinated into Communism and wanted nothing more to do with their capitalist family. She hoped Thimi was at least one of the latter. Zoitsa had ceased to think about her former best friend. To her it all seemed like a hundred years ago in a land very far away.

It was during another Sunday dinner when Nick mentioned that Napoleon Zervas had died. Peacefully. In his apartment in Athens. No one but Maria Christina and Zoitsa seemed to care. The other younger people at the table thought he was talking about some distant cousin.

A few weeks after Zoitsa moved into the Columbia dormitory, Maria Christina asked Nick if she could speak to him in his office.

"Nick, I have decided to return to Metsovo."

Nick was not surprised. He had been expecting this, now that Maria Christina had become completely irrelevant in Zoitsa's life. He rose from his desk and hugged her.

"I will miss you, my dear" he said. Then he patted her shoulder and said he would arrange for her passage and give her a handsome cash severance. After she left the office, Nick immediately phoned Helen who, upon hearing the news, danced around the kitchen. Zoitsa wasn't displeased either. Her aunt had become burdensome, someone to tolerate, someone she would no doubt some day have to care for and support.

By the next day Nick had already found Maria Christina's replacement, and as soon as Maria Christina had trained the new woman, Nick booked her on a flight to Athens. It seemed they couldn't get her on a plane fast enough. There were only a few goodbyes for Maria Christina, the folks at work, the usual

Sunday crowd, and the priest at their church, who gave her communion. Even though she had hardly seen her since she started working for Nick, Maggie was the only person who was actually sad to see her go. Henry had retired two months before and had been replaced by a self-service elevator.

The night before her flight, Nick hosted a farewell party at the Copa Cabana, for old times' sake. Tito Puente and his orchestra were playing. Zoitsa and Brad delayed their weekend in the mountains of Vermont with Brad's parents in order to attend. That night Maria Christina looked and acted like a teenager. Nick couldn't believe his eyes. He had never seen Maria Christina so ebullient, dancing and eating and drinking. How she laughed when she told the story of Zoitsa's father first milking their cow, Afendoula, when he squirted himself in the eye. Only now the story continued where, blinded by the milk, he stepped into the milk bucket and fell into a cow pie.

It brought tears to Zoitsa's eyes to see her aunt having so much fun. Maria Christina was having such a good time it lifted Nick's spirits immeasurably and he, too, was suddenly his old self again, dancing every dance. He danced twice with Maria Christina. At the end of the second one, he hugged her so hard, it seemed to Zoitsa he would break her into pieces. This was truly the most fun the family could ever remember having.

Later that night, after everyone had a great deal to drink and the band was on a break, Alex sat next to Maria Christina and made one last quiet plea for her hand. With the sensitivity of someone who had suffered great disappointments of her own, she gently turned him down again. Deeply disappointed, he bid her a good voyage, said good night to his hosts, and left the party. Zoitsa then sat next to Maria Christina and took her hand.

"I will miss you, dear aunt" she lied in Vlach. "And when I can, I'll come visit, I promise."

Maria Christina smiled and kissed her niece's hand. She saw through the lie but said nothing.

That night, after Zoitsa and Brad had driven off to Vermont for their weekend, Nick and Helen were in their room getting ready for bed when they heard the water for the tub turn on in the guest bathroom.

"Taking a bath? At this hour?" Nick was climbing into bed.

"Maybe she's trying to sober up before her trip" Helen laughed as she climbed on top of him.

"Maybe it's her one last bath in a tub" he chuckled as he pulled her to him.

After a long, peaceful soak in warm bubbles, Maria Christina rinsed herself off, then washed her hair. She towel dried it, then sat in her chair by the window and continued combing it until it was totally dry. She braided it. Then she took her long braid which had been cut by Lena out of its box and pinned it to her own and coiled it around her head. The alarm was usually set for 6:30, when she would rise and make everyone's breakfast and then be off to work. She didn't bother to set it this night but, rather, she put on her cotton bodice from Metsovo, her sleeveless wool dress embroidered with geometric designs, her satin apron embroidered with flowers, and her embroidered wool slippers. She took Zoitsa's dress from the closet and held it tenderly, as if the child were still inside.

"How things have turned out" she thought to herself. "Where did the little girl go? So much fun to be with, so sweet and loving, things that can't be taught, but that can so easily be lost."

She hung the dress back in the closet then lit the candle on her dresser and said her prayers. She then went to the kitchen where she took an apple and put it in her pocket as she returned to her room. Carefully moving the position of her bed so that it would be facing east, Maria Christina then lay on her back, her glasses in their case in her hands, which were cupped in the traditional manner for supplicants' coins. She closed her eyes and fell into a deep sleep.

Just before dawn, Maria Christina opened her eyes and saw her father standing before her in his thick black cape and flat-topped hat. He looked beatific. He took off his hat with a sad smile and held it against his heart. There were tears in his eyes as he told her how ashamed he was of his behavior towards her. Maria Christina's eyes also filled with tears.

"Oh, Patera. No. It is I who am ashamed for provoking you to anger."

Papa Yiorgos said he had many important things to say to her, and he would tell her on their way.

"But we must hurry, my angel. Everyone is waiting" he spoke excitedly. "So many who know you only through the stories we have told about you. And your mother, she has been waiting these many years to hold you again."

Whether she was imagining it or not, Maria Christina couldn't be certain, but it made no difference. She was ready to follow him. To cross over. To finally see her mother's face. To be with ones she deeply loved and missed.

Maria Christina Triantafyllou closed her eyes and inhaled one long breath. Then she exhaled slowly, easily, until it was entirely expended. She never breathed again. She was thirty-six years old.

41

In Metsovo, November was known as the lost month, the useless month. Most of the men had left with their flocks to the lowlands. The women and young children, having planted their winter vegetables and gathered and stacked their wood for the winter, were now waiting for the vegetables to grow. November had been Maria Christina's favorite month. It was when Matoula would spend most of her day around the hearth or at her loom, and Zoitsa would be sitting on the floor drawing or painting. It was deeply comforting for Maria Christina to be with her sister for so much of the day, not to mention the unparalleled delight she took in making her laugh. Zoitsa was too young to remember that whenever she saw her mother laugh, it made her laugh, too. But then Zoitsa had almost no memory of their life together apart from war. Yet these were happy days, and they still lived somewhere inside her mind's dusty attic as she slept uneasily in her future in-laws' farmhouse in Vermont.

It was Helen who first discovered Maria Christina. Noticing their breakfast hadn't been prepared, she thought Maria Christina had overslept and went to wake her. Her scream woke Nick, who quickly arranged everything with a travel agent and *Litras and Sons Funeral Home*. Zoitsa would have to return from Vermont early. Nick scheduled a four day trip: one day for Maria

Christina's wake and funeral, one for the business of putting any property up for sale, and two for travel.

"Thank God two of the days fell on the weekend" both thought, but never uttered, as they sat silently next to each other on the plane approaching Greece. Zoitsa hated to miss school as much as Nick hated to miss work, but this was their obligation. This was family.

In the cargo bin, Maria Christina lay in a simple pine casket in her Metsovo costume, her hands still cupped.

As the plane approached the Athens Airport Zoitsa realized that, having been someone who always kept her eye on the future, her future was now in Metsovo where she would have to confront the past. She seldom if ever looked back. Whenever she did, it was to something basic, her father's land, the house he was building. Matoula's Vineyard. Once upon a time these were her dreams. Occasionally she felt a tinge of guilt she had never tasted the wine, his wine, named for her mother. But these thoughts made her too sad, so she would quickly return to the present or look to the future for comfort.

Flying over Athens was a minor revelation to Zoitsa. In contrast to how vast it seemed when she drove through it as a child, the city now looked more like one large village with the Parthenon majestically sitting atop the Acropolis. At the airport, while walking towards the baggage area, Nick paused as he passed a phone booth and almost reflexively looked back at it. His parents had no telephone when he left. He stopped abruptly, went back, impulsively picked up the directory and flipped through the pages quickly, frantically, wetting his finger with his tongue, until he peeled back one last page and moved his finger down the line of names. Then he stopped.

"My God" he whispered aloud to himself. "The same address." He fumbled through the money he had just exchanged, found the right coin, dropped it in the slot and dialled.

Zoitsa had never seen Nick so flustered. His hands were shaking. He closed his eyes and licked his lips and waited while the phone rang. It seemed like an eternity before he finally rested it back on the cradle. Zoitsa thought it was just as well. Nick was so unnerved he probably wouldn't have been able to speak. He jotted down the number and they continued toward the baggage claim area.

It was another hour before Nick and Zoitsa had recovered their luggage. Maria Christina's coffin was being loaded into a hearse by its driver and three porters, and Nick and Zoitsa were sitting in the back of a town car, while its driver loaded their luggage in the trunk. It felt strange to both of them to be back in Greece, inside a modern airport, the language, the signs.

It was a sunny afternoon and the drive was pleasant. The travellers rode silently for an hour then stopped for lunch at a taverna. The sun was already behind the mountain when they approached Meteora. Zoitsa remembered that this was where her grandfather was murdered. Her memory of him was of a happy, quiet man. Then she recalled how he spoke about missing his wife. He must have been lonely. The truth was, she never really knew him.

When she first saw Metsovo cascading down the mountain in the distance, Zoitsa was slightly taken aback. She had remembered it differently, though she couldn't explain how. She suddenly became excited as they entered the village. Nick seemed annoyed by its charm. Zoitsa began looking for a familiar face, a familiar store. So much had changed. She chuckled to herself when she saw the utility poles and wires strung along the street, the electric lights in the shops and houses. As they approached the town square, Zoitsa saw the huge plane trees in the courtyard of Agia Paraskevi. They seemed like old friends. She could see St. George's park with its grand old chestnuts. She suppressed a sudden urge to jump out of the car and walk among the leaves and pick chestnuts off the ground. She made a mental note to do that with her uncle. He might find it amusing. Her old life was now returning in a flood.

The hearse stopped in front of Stahoulis' *pantopolio*, where four men were waiting to carry the coffin down to Panorea's, the street being too narrow for the vehicle. Zoitsa smiled when she saw Stahoulis. His wooden leg had been replaced by the latest prosthetic, and his hair was now completely grey. As he stepped out to greet them, he laughed when he first saw her. He hadn't seen her since she was a little girl. With tears in his eyes he hugged her hard and shook Nick's hand. Nick dismissed the hearse and told his driver to return before noon in three days.

Stahoulis led the group down to Panorea's, pointing out the changes that had taken place in the village since Zoitsa had left. Zoitsa held Nick's arm and petted it, something she always did to calm him. She understood he viewed Metsovo as the enemy. She had sensed his discomfort the moment the village came into view. It was strange walking with him here. As Stahoulis continued talking, she pretended to listen but became distracted by a sudden sadness which washed over her. She had an image of her father, carrying his black doctor's bag, walking up the street. His face. Trying to erase it, she concentrated on the old stones under her feet. They seemed to soothe her. They continued on the road until they arrived at the long series of stone steps. The view from here had not changed, the same gardens, the same rooftops. It was as though she had never left.

Lena would have sworn it was Matoula with blonde hair coming towards her. She even had the same gait, the way she swung her arms and cocked her head. Zoitsa was surprised when she nearly burst into tears as she first saw her great aunt. She looked so much older and smaller. Her hair was white and she had a widow's hump. Zoitsa quickly stifled her emotions in order to introduce Lena to Nick. As Lena opened the gate to Papa Yiorgos' house, Zoitsa was struck by how small the garden was and wondered how they could have fed themselves with what little it could have provided.

Lena had the house cleaned and prepared for them. Stahoulis directed the pallbearers to the sitting room, where they set the coffin on the coffee table and placed it facing east. Then the men quietly left the house. Nick followed and offered to pay them, but they refused. Stahoulis was the last to leave, inviting Nick and Zoitsa to show them Yiannis' vineyard and to have a meal at his *pantopolio*.

Lena ushered Nick and Zoitsa into the winter room where the only surviving Triantafyllou was sitting on a bench in front of the hearth, staring out the fireplace window. An older, smaller, paler version of herself, Panorea appeared to be deep in thought and didn't notice anyone enter. Lena quietly bade everyone sit by the low table in front of the fire and share the leek pie she had made for them. After greeting and hugging her great aunt and introducing Nick, Panorea sat at the table and Zoitsa sat next to her. Looking around the room, Zoitsa realized she had always remembered it as much larger. And not nearly so hot. And her aunts were wearing the usual heavy wool shawls, as if chilled and struggling to feel warm again. There was a wire strung along the ceiling from which a single bare bulb was hanging. Among a number of weavings on the walls and covering the windows was one which fascinated and amused Zoitsa: that of a woman, standing in a field of green next to a three legged cow, presenting a little baby with blonde hair to a blonde man with a mustache. Lena noticed.

"That was started by your mother and finished by your aunt when you were about two years old."

Zoitsa smiled, having already decided she would take the treasure back to her dorm.

Panorea looked at her "And you are…"

"Zoitsa." she replied.

"Ah, Zoitsa. And your father is…?"

"Doctor Yiannis Petrakis" Zoitsa was slightly taken aback.

"Oh, Doctor Yiannis! And how is your father?"

"He died, Aunt Panorea" she said with a glance at Lena. "In 1948."

"Oh. That's too bad" Panorea shook her head.

Zoitsa bit into the wild green pie while she digested the last few moments. Then she turned to her aunt with a penetrating stare and smiled "It's nice that it hasn't snowed yet, isn't it?"

"Yes" Panorea smiled and continued eating. After a moment, she looked at Zoitsa as if she were studying her, then spoke again.

"And you are...?"

"Zoitsa Petrakis."

"Ah, Zoitsa Petrakis."

"And your father is...?"

Zoitsa spent the entire meal trying to penetrate the wall blocking Panorea's memory to no avail. Yet without any memory, it seemed that Panorea was happily unburdened, better able to enjoy herself. While Lena cleared the table and laid out the dessert, Nick and Zoitsa went into the sitting room. Nick opened the lid of the coffin. It seemed as if Maria Christina was about to smile. *Litras & Sons* had done a fine job. The touch of color made her look almost alive. Looking at her in repose without her glasses, Zoitsa suddenly realized just how delicate and beautiful her aunt's face was.

Lena joined them for a moment. When she saw Maria Christina, her eyes filled with fat tears which rolled down her cheeks. She couldn't speak for a moment. As she showed them the rest of the house, Panorea followed obediently behind. Lena confessed in a whisper she hadn't written to Maria Christina about how Panorea had deteriorated because she didn't want to worry her.

"And she wasn't this bad until very recently. Now she even forgets to eat if I'm not around" Lena smiled as she opened Papa Yiorgos' room. The door hadn't been opened since his funeral until that morning when Lena unlocked it to clean. Lena showed them the rest of the house. Downstairs there were no longer any animals. Panorea couldn't care for them.

Back in the winter room they ate walnut cake and sipped tea. Lena told Nick how much she loved and admired his brother.

"I think he was a hero."

The conversation remained light, how electricity had changed Metsovo, how air travel was a marvel. It was still early when Lena suggested they retire for the night. The next day would start early and be very tiring, especially for them who had come so far. The weary travellers slept on separate platforms on either side of the fireplace, Zoitsa with her great aunt, and Nick by himself, not at all amused by the Vlach custom of all sleeping together in one room.

The next morning, Nick awoke to find Zoitsa sitting by the hearth having coffee and walnut cake with Panorea, once again trying to penetrate her great aunt's memory. Before he could say 'good morning' he heard wailing coming from downstairs. Lena had opened the door and hung a black cloth over it, signalling someone had died in the house. As the first wave of old ladies passed through the door and up the stairs to the sitting room, Lena laid out sweets and coffee.

Among the first to arrive were Haralambos and Olimbi. They now owned a fine taverna in the village which they had purchased with a portion of her dowry. Zoitsa almost squealed when he introduced himself to her, and again when she heard him call Olimbi 'kitten'. Kitten also had a litter of eight-year-old twins, Yiannis and Napoleon, who looked exactly like their mother. Panorea couldn't remember who died, but she was delighted to be meeting all these new people.

Zoitsa sat with Lena and Panorea. The stream of mourners seemed endless. Maria Christina looked unbearably thin, especially to those who knew her well. Coins were dropped into her cupped hands until they overflowed onto the satin sheet which lined the coffin. Zoitsa felt a reverence toward Maria Christina coming from everyone.

"And what of her husband, the mayor?" Zoitsa was asked several times. It seems the flier from Windsor had stopped for drinks in several other *pantopolia* on his way home.

The stream continued all morning without interruption as

more sweets arrived and other women also took on the responsibility of replenishing the coffee. There were a number of friends and family that sat on the benches around the room, some of whom Zoitsa vaguely remembered. There was one tall woman in western dress who offered her sympathy whom she did recognize. It was her cousin Sophia. She had graduated from Oxford with a degree in languages and chose to return to Metsovo and now taught at the University of Ioannina three days a week and was working as a freelance translator.

She told Zoitsa "No, I'm not married. I don't feel the need to be."

Times had indeed changed.

Nick sat in Papa Yiorgos' office chair with a half dozen bottles of *tsipouro* and a case of Matoula's Vineyard, courtesy of Stahoulis, and two bottles of Scotch from Haralambos, who poured it freely for the men, while Nick listened to stories about Yiannis. He wanted to know everything anyone could tell him. There were veterans with stories, and patients who had stories, and owners of livestock who relied on his brother, though he knew almost nothing about animals. Yet no matter how Nick tried to keep the conversation on Yiannis, it somehow always returned to Maria Christina. It seemed almost everyone also had a Maria Christina story. Nick obviously hadn't realized that she had been an agent for Bouboulina and, once she had been identified, had become a kind of legend in the area. Stories about her had become abundant: standing up to one of Veloukhiotis' captains in the square when even the men were afraid to speak, butchering an Italian soldier with a kitchen knife when he tried to rape her, killing communist guerrillas with their own grenades, and then there was the flier from England. And as imagination puts meat on the bones of a story and one story becomes another, Maria Christina's legend grew, making her greater than in life. And yet it wasn't so much that Maria Christina had become a legend, but that she had become the new face of the women of Metsovo, their fierceness, their selflessness, and now in lore, even their beauty, finally putting to rest generations of them being a source of amusement among the surrounding villagers.

The funeral mass for Maria Christina was scheduled for noon. A wall of people greeted the procession from the house, along the narrow street and the steps to Agios Demetrius, which was already filled to overflowing. Archimandrite Petsalis, his boyish face looking almost unchanged except it was now framed by greying temples, was presiding. He was assisted by two younger priests, one of whom, a rather short, thin man with a long black beard, Papa Pandelis, had replaced Papa Yiorgos. The service vaguely reminded Zoitsa of the service for her mother. The only thing she vividly remembered of that day was how angry Panorea had been with her, but she couldn't remember why. Now Panorea was sitting next to her, and Zoitsa was holding her hand, amazed at the whole spectacle.

After the service, Nick went to the cemetery with the men, while Zoitsa returned to the house with the women to prepare the food. So many of them spoke about Maria Christina Triantafyllou, using all three names, referring to her strength, her courage, and her patriotism.

"My aunt never mentioned Bouboulina or the flier from England" Zoitsa couldn't wait to get the story late that night, after everyone had left.

"I'm sorry. I still can't seem to say her name without weeping" Lena confessed as she finished sweeping the floor. She leaned on the broom a moment, then put it down and sat wearily on the bench by the fire and poured herself a glass of wine.

"Life to us" she toasted and took a gulp. "Maria Christina seldom talked about her life." Lena became choked up again and had to wait a moment. "She always thought that whenever you were talking about your life you weren't living it, only talking about living it." Then she took Zoitsa's hand. "Your aunt lived her life not only for you, golden girl. But first for your mother, whose death she mistakenly blamed herself. Then for your father, whom she loved with all her heart."

These last words stunned Zoitsa.

Lena stood "I'll be back in a minute." She left the room, leaving Zoitsa and Nick looking at each other. When she returned moments later, she held two letters in her hand "Maybe you don't remember, but I was hiding these for you from the Germans. This one is from your father to you, and this one is from your father to your aunt. I think you should have them." She handed the letters to Zoitsa.

Zoitsa read the first few words of the letter from her father to her when she was six,

'My precious Moumou'.

Her eyes immediately filled with bitter tears, so she put the letter back inside the envelope to read later when she was alone. She then took the letter from her father to Maria Christina out of its envelope. She almost gasped when she read the first few words.

'My Darling Maria Christina,
You have given me wings...'

She stopped breathing. She looked at Nick, then looked down to the end of the letter.

'I love you with all my heart,
Yiannis.'

"So much had been hidden from you because as a child you had already experienced far too much. But after your mother died, your father nearly worked himself to death, too wounded to dare think about his loss." Lena spoke softly. "Your aunt became his guardian angel. His reason to live beyond caring for you. Your father fell deeply in love with her. You've had two mothers, my Moumou. They shared your father and you, in many ways, equally."

Zoitsa was dumbfounded by the news, as was Nick, although it made sense to him. In fact he now felt stupid he hadn't guessed. He had noticed that each time she said his name, she would bow her head, almost imperceptibly, but reverentially. But Lena was talking freely and he was deeply curious.

"…and she loved deeply and was loved deeply in return. And she raised a child. Now, what more is there to do in life, golden girl? What did she miss? You can't judge a life by its length as you can't judge the value of a tapestry by its size. Your aunt lived a full rich life. One most people would envy."

Tears were running down her cheeks as she continued. "She once wrote me that sometimes her heart felt as heavy as stone. She couldn't grieve any more. I don't care that your doctors in America say she died of heart failure, I'm telling you she died as a result of slowly choking to death on her grief. Like when you have a bone caught in your throat that won't allow you to breathe. When your eyes can't cry, your heart does. I've seen it before."

After a moment, Nick spoke up "But no one lives happily ever after. Sooner or later each of us has to pick up the pieces and move on with our life."

Lena smiled sadly "Sometimes there are just too many pieces and not enough life."

Zoitsa couldn't listen any more. She was already too tired to stay awake, so she bid them good night and readied herself for bed. As she reflected on the day's events, she realized that if she had known these things about Maria Christina, she probably would have treated her very differently. It was true that her aunt behaved as if she were her mother, she did everything a mother would do, could do. Yet because she didn't have the title *mother* Zoitsa never recognized her as anything but an interfering aunt. Until now. She had lost her mother twice. As she went back to the hearth and kissed Lena and Nick good night, she was thinking about her aunt living in Brooklyn all these years when she could have been adored here, the depth of her sacrifice and commitment to her mother and father. 'It is one thing to be smart', she used to say, 'another to be wise, but most important is to be principled.' But Zoitsa would think no more tonight. While Nick stayed up and talked with Lena about his brother, Zoitsa fell into a deep sleep a minute after she lay down and put her arm around her lightly snoring great aunt.

42

Nick awoke the next morning from a disturbing sleep, wondering where he was, until he saw Zoitsa sipping tea with Panorea. They were sitting silently, Zoitsa having finally given up on penetrating her great aunt's memory bank. The plan for the day was for Nick and Zoitsa to visit the cemetery, then take a walk with Stahoulis to the vineyard and assess the condition of the house.

At the cemetery, the two stood in front of Maria Christina's grave, laden with flowers, still not able to fully comprehend that the Maria Christina Triantafyllou they had lived with was the same one whom everyone had been mourning and praising. Inside the ossuary, Nick showed Zoitsa where her father's bones were stored on a lower shelf among a dozen other shelves in rows, like stacks in a library. It was a simple pine box with no carving and no photograph. On its face, in black paint, was the inscription, Doctor Yiannis Petrakis 1910-1948 Age 38.

Nick continued down the aisle for a moment to let her quietly grieve. It was a profound moment for Zoitsa. Her mother and father were both just bones in a box. She remembered how she and her father used to come and pray over her mother's grave when a voice broke the silence.

"Zoitsa."

Zoitsa and Nick turned to the sound.

"I don't know if you--"

"Tatamare! Of course, Tatamare. How are you? You look very well."

He looked exactly the same, she thought, but shorter, or perhaps it was that she was taller. She kissed the old candle lighter and introduced him to her Uncle Nick. Tatamare vigorously shook Nick's hand "I stopped by the house but there were so many people." He continued to hold his hand. "I met your father not long ago."

Nick was stunned.

"His wife had just died. I don't know if that was your mother – although it must have been, because I believe he said her name was Zoe. But he had come looking for Doctor Yiannis and was told he had been killed in the war. I found him weeping here. I took him home for a cup of tea. He said he had wanted to reconcile with his son. Told me he'd foolishly disowned both his sons when they wouldn't submit to his will. I thought you'd want to know. Anyway, nice to see you both. I suppose you'll be leaving soon. Good voyage, and God be with you."

Then he shook Nick's hand again and kissed Zoitsa on the cheek and left the ossuary. Nick stood frozen. Finally he spoke, explaining to Zoitsa he couldn't go to the vineyard with her. He needed to find the nearest telephone. He remembered noticing one at the telegraph office when he wired Helen that they had arrived. Zoitsa thought it best he be left alone for now. Besides, she was anxious to see the house and vineyard, so they decided to meet back at Panorea's later in the day and went their separate ways.

At his *pantopolio*, Stahoulis insisted he feed her and made the most delicious baby lamb chops with fried potatoes, a slaw, and a garlic dip. He offered her some wine from Matoula's Vineyard. Zoitsa sipped politely and discovered that she quite liked it. Even though it was thin it had a delightful fruity bouquet.

"It gets better every year, don't you think?" he grinned.

After lunch, they walked down the mountain, then slowly through the vineyard. As she touched the tips of the vines, she was reminded of the joy in her father's eyes when he walked with her through his vineyard.

The house now had a slate roof, a door and windows. The wood was stained and the door had black iron hardware. It looked absolutely charming. The interior was still unfinished but for the hearth. Stahoulis had turned it into his winery and stored the wine in large amphora. Zoitsa stood in the middle of the room and looked around while Stahoulis made a small fire, then went outside and drew a kettle of water from the well for tea. Zoitsa sat at the old pine table. While the tea was brewing Stahoulis told her stories about her father, her mother, her aunt. Then, while Zoitsa remained at the table, he took another walk through the vineyard to make notes about certain problems which needed his attention. A half hour later, when Stahoulis returned, she was thinking that, although there was no electricity in the house, she could see the last telephone pole by Agios Demetrius, so it wouldn't be a problem to bring power to the house if someone wanted to live in it. Stahoulis suggested they return to the village.

Zoitsa kissed his cheek "You go on ahead, Costa. I know my way home." She squeezed his hand "And thank you. For everything." Her eyes filled with tears "The wine is beautiful and I know Babá is smiling down on you." She walked him to the door "I'll stop in to say goodbye before I leave. I simply want to stay here a little longer. It's so quiet. Peaceful."

After he left, she took the letters out of her purse and looked at them. She knew this was going to be difficult. She decided to read the one from her father to Maria Christina first. She hadn't read ten lines when she burst into tears. Her father's need for Maria Christina, his deep loneliness without her, his anguish made Zoitsa suddenly realize how empty and hollow her relationship with Brad Walker was, and what real love must feel like. The sun was setting behind the mountain top and she felt suddenly chilled. After foraging for wood, she built herself a larger fire, then she moved the chair closer to the hearth and opened the letter written to her. How difficult it was to read through the tears. In his letter he explained how much he loved her and that it broke his heart to be away from her, but he had to do what he was doing in order that she and her children could live in a free and independent Greece. These words hung in the air. They wouldn't leave. She finished the letter and set it in her lap, then hung her head in shame.

Maybe it was because of what Lena had said about choking on grief, but almost involuntarily she began to cry, how she deeply missed her father, how she would never get to tell her aunt how heroic everyone thought she was. She cried louder, more freely, how she was nowhere in the world, a rudderless orphan holding on to her uncle as if he were a lifeline, living the dream he had for her. How pitiful!

Nick had been drinking scotch, and his eyes were red and swollen from weeping when Zoitsa returned. He had called his father, who was thrilled to hear from him, and he couldn't wait to meet his granddaughter and they made a date to meet for dinner the next evening in Athens. Panorea was with Lena in her house, making a leek pie which she would bring over for their dinner. Nick was amused.

"I told her we were going to Haralambos' taverna for dinner and invited them to join us, but she insisted on having something freshly cooked in the house just in case we wanted to have a snack before or after."

Haralambos' taverna was tastefully decorated and slightly upscale for Metsovo. It even had tablecloths. There were people waiting to be seated. Haralambos was the chef and his goat soap was considered unparalleled. Olimbi was the hostess and greeted them with her gale of laughter in two octaves and ushered the foursome to the table she had reserved in case they decided to come. They drank bottled wine, and Nick and Zoitsa thought the food was exceptional. Whenever he could, Haralambos would step out from the kitchen and tell another story about Yiannis. Zoitsa found Haralambos and Olimbi truly amusing. Haralambos told Nick that Yiannis always talked about his older brother, Nikos. How he was strong and honourable and so smart he could catch flies in the air. How he looked up to him. Nick was in the best of moods. Between the stories and the knowledge of his affair with Maria Christina, Nick was now able to put together the pieces of Yiannis' tragic life. He would tell it all to his father tomorrow night.

During the course of the meal, diners stopped by the table and introduced themselves to Zoitsa and told her how much they admired her aunt. All of a sudden Nick realized that Zoitsa was prattling on to Lena and Panorea about how special and wonderful Metsovo was, and how she hadn't been this relaxed since she could remember, and how much easier life was in the village, and it occurred to Nick that, even though she was speaking to them, perhaps she was really speaking to him. His suspicion was confirmed when she announced that she had decided not to sell the house and vineyard, at least for now. She spoke of Stahoulis' love for the property and the fact that it did allow her a small income. But Nick could feel her slipping away, as if the entire foundation he had laid for her was made of sand and it was being washed away by the incoming tide. He should have discouraged her from coming. He knew there was always a chance that once returning to Metsovo she would want to stay, but he knew the right thing, the correct thing, was to accompany her aunt's body. He had always thought the pull he had felt to Greece was to his parents, their home. But it was more than that. It was Greece itself. The land. The inhospitable soil. The people. The glorious five thousand-year-old civilization to which you belonged. As the evening continued, Nick sat back and began to measure what he had given up by living in America against what he had gained. He could easily pick up the tab for twenty at the Copa Cabana but he couldn't have dinner with his father. He could eat in the best restaurants in New York and yet the simplicity of the food of his childhood, of this taverna, the freshness and purity of the ingredients was much more satisfying than the best of New York. He looked over at Zoitsa. If she wasn't in the car at noon tomorrow, she would be lost to him.

Neither could sleep that night. Nick held his breath when he heard Zoitsa get out of her bed in the middle of the night, take an oil lamp from the table by the door, and exit the room. In the hallway, Zoitsa lit the lamp, took a shepherd's cloak off the rack and proceeded to Papa Yiorgos' room. A fire was ready to be lit in the hearth, so she started the kindling, then sat at her grandfather's desk and took out the two letters. She had decided never to finish reading the one from her father to her aunt. It was too personal and intimate. The one to her, on the other hand, was between them. It was her most precious legacy. She had all but memorized it in the first reading, but she needed to read it again. His words to her, written in his hand.

'Perform every act in life as though it were a prayer.
Don't ever be angry with your parents or your children.'

But again, when she came upon the phrase 'living in a free and independent Greece' she was stung so deeply she had to put the letter down.

Decisions of great consequence are often made in the lesser part of a second. The following moments are spent building a case in favor of the decision. In that instant Zoitsa decided she would remain in Metsovo. She would serve a cause greater than herself. Her mother and father both had died so that she could live in a free Greece. Didn't she owe it to them to at least try and live here? To try and contribute? To try to make their deaths meaningful? And there was her great aunt who needed someone. Family. Wasn't that what family was for? How many meals had Panorea cooked for her? She had no idea, but she knew that she had. And what sacrifices she might have made for her that she would never know, except she knew she must have.

As Zoitsa unscrewed the cap of the ink bottle and took the pen from its holder, she began looking for paper. She would only be postponing her uncle's dream. Or perhaps not. Since childhood, her only dream had always been to feel safe, and old dreams die hard. Lying on the floor in her father's house under the table, while her father was hand-hewing wooden beams with a hatchet, was perhaps her most comforting memory. This afternoon, in her father's house, she had felt a deep serenity. Always trying to fit in meant she never really had fit in. Here she felt a true sense of belonging. She would become part of the new Metsovo. It was where she wanted to be, where she was needed. Maybe she would even start a small newspaper. She would work in the vineyard. Her aunt always told her there was a curative value in physical labor. It had actually been joyous to walk through the vineyard today. And the wine had a nice taste. It made you want another glass. Perhaps she really was her father's daughter.

'Everyone in New York will think I've gone insane, but I can't imagine spending the rest of my life in New York pushing a stone uphill. Nobody here ever heard of NBC.' Zoitsa began cataloguing these thoughts and more in preparation for her conversation with her uncle as she began writing a letter to Brad Walker, begging him to understand, but she would not be returning to the United States, at least for now. She then wrote a letter of resignation to Columbia and one declining the Sidney Hillman Scholarship with deep regret.

Nick had fallen asleep before she returned to bed. When he awoke in the morning, Zoitsa was already dressed and had made the fire and been to the bakery and returned with cream pies for everyone. Nick thought she seemed awfully chipper for a girl who hadn't slept much. It would be an eternity until they were safely in the car and on their way. Until then, he and Zoitsa were planning to go to St. George's park and pick chestnuts for Lena. Although in good spirits, Zoitsa was being unusually quiet, as if she had something on her mind.

It was a dark grey morning as the two sloshed through the red and yellow leaves, picking chestnuts off the ground. After they had filled a small bag and were on their way towards the street, Zoitsa put her arm through Nick's, kissed his cheek and said the words Nick was hoping he would never hear.

"Uncle Nick, I've decided to stay in Metsovo."

The two continued in silence a moment.

"For now" she added.

The modifier made no difference to Nick.

"It won't be forever. Or maybe it will, I don't know. All I know is…"

Nick only heard snatches of her argument.

"I will always be your daughter. Just as I had two mothers…"

Nick had anticipated this moment since he fell in love with her as a little girl and would hurry home to watch *The Small Fry Club* with her. In some sense it was a relief. He knew that sooner or later she would need to get this out of her system, a part of growing up. If you don't make your peace with your parents, with your past, you carry a cross through life. She would be back. Once you live in New York, you couldn't possibly live in Metsovo. Not full time. It was as if Maria Christina had died only when she was confident Zoitsa was ready to return to her homeland. But Zoitsa would be back, before long.

"It's a new world, Uncle Nick. Travelling is so much faster and easier."

When the car arrived, Nick and Zoitsa were waiting at Stahoulis' with Lena, Panorea, Haralambos and Olimbi, and Sophia, who were all very excited Zoitsa was staying, each assuring Nick they would look after her.

Nick had given her the return plane ticket "Use it whenever you're ready. There's also some cash in there. I'll send some more. Wire me if you need anything."

This was one of those years both would always remember vividly.

"You understand, don't you, Uncle Nick?"

"Sure. I understand." And indeed he did. He had his own unfinished business awaiting him in Athens. He was already thinking of buying a place on the water in Glyfada, where he and Helen could live part of the year instead of going to Oyster Bay. He had even wondered how Helen would react to such a notion. Probably not well. But she'd be a good sport and indulge him. She always did. Perhaps with a foot in two worlds he would have the best of both. He hugged Zoitsa hard and for a long moment.

"Kiss my grandfather for me and tell him I'll call."

A sharp clap of thunder echoed throughout the mountains. Haralambos stepped over to the car and opened the door.

"Thunder in the winter means a big snow coming" Nick heard Haralambos say to the driver. "You'd better get started."

Nick put on a brave face as he climbed into the car. He casually saluted the group, then lit a chesterfield for the drive as the car moved away.

As the well-wishers waved and watched the car disappear up the road, snow began to fall. Large flakes were floating through the air. Zoitsa caught one with her tongue as she took Panorea's arm and Sophia took hers and Lena's and they started back to the house. Zoitsa was looking forward to the winter. It would give her plenty of time to look at herself and try and understand, maybe even put to rest some of the demons that had been chasing her. Perhaps it was even time for another best friend.

ABOUT THE AUTHOR

Born in Vermont and raised in Vermont and Connecticut, Richard Romanus (1943) attended Xavier University and received a BS in Philosophy. He then attended the University of Connecticut Law School for a year, after which he left school to pursue a career as an actor. He studied at the famous Actor's Studio with Lee Strassberg and his first major role came as the character "Michael" in Martin Scorcese's classic film *Mean Streets*. In the years that followed Richard Romanus performed in numerous stage productions, films and television shows. In addition to his acting, Richard Romanus is credited as the composer on several films. Together with his wife, Anthea Sylbert, he also wrote and produced *Giving Up the Ghost* in 1998 and *If You Believe* in 1999, for which they were nominated for a Writers Guild of America award for Best Original Screenplay. Since the end of 2001 Richard and Anthea have been living in Skiathos, Greece.

ALSO BY RICHARD ROMANUS

ACT III - A Small Island in the Aegean